THE PERFECT GENERATION

C. P. JAMES

THE PERFECT GENERATION

This is a work of fiction. Any similarity between the characters and situations within its pages and places or persons, living or dead, is unintentional and coincidental.

ALSO BY C. P. JAMES

Clockwatchers: Coming of Age in the Perfect Generation

The Perfect Generation

The Technician: A Cytocorp Story

The Cytocorp Saga (coming Fall 2019)

For Amy

PART I

2019 – 2050: THE MERRIWEATHER PRIZE

1

The girl adjusted her scarf against the cold and hurried off into the darkness, as though Geller intended to follow her. She carried a tray of four coffees but didn't even pause to set them down and properly re-button her coat, so her free hand held it together in front like a bathrobe while he held the door open. Perhaps he'd looked at her in the way Baz cautioned him against—like a snake trying to work out whether it could unhinge its jaws far enough to swallow its prey. He doubted it would've eased her mind to know that his appraisal of her features was purely academic.

Her narrow hips suggested an Eastern European ancestry, though her skin tone and hair may have indicated Greek or Italian. Her slight frame had to lean into the wind to push through it, and judging from the thickness of her clothes to the speed of her gait, he guessed she had little tolerance for cold. He settled on an Eastern Mediterranean descent, perhaps Turkish, Syrian, or even Israeli. 60/40 on the Asian.

He played this little game a lot with people and it never occurred to him it might be creepy on the other end. But Christ, to even *feign* interest in most people, his mind needed something else to chew on. Often, one part of his brain would conduct its analysis while another would deliver the nods and uh-huh's that reassured them he was hanging on every word.

People weren't any more mysterious than a computer. Everything that mattered was hard-coded—reproduction, survival, maybe nonverbal communication. Though the code itself had taken nearly a century to unravel, getting in there and fucking with it was the secret fantasy of any geneticist. Technical considerations aside, what stood in their way was a phony and misguided morality. Mention genetic engineering in passing, and off they'd go to human-animal hybrids and designer children. These were the same people who ate genetically modified grains and drank milk from genetically modified cows on a daily basis. The same people whose hearts bled for people with Alzheimer's or sickle cell anemia but only supported the *idea* of a cure, not the actual mechanics.

What they didn't realize was that they could go online at that very moment and learn for themselves the precise gene or chromosome responsible for a whole shitload of diseases. If a mechanic said their car needed a new starter, they'd replace it without a second thought. If enough starters went bad on a particular model, the manufacturer would either issue a recall or install a better starter in future vehicles. This was how the industrialized world worked. Living things—particularly plants—had been improved upon since the days of Mendel. Yet, no one cried foul when a turf grass engineered to be drought-resistant helped athletic fields use less water. They didn't seem to mind that corn-based products were tasty and dirt-cheap as a result of genetic modifications that made the plant more resistant to pests. Fucking hypocrites.

It seemed like a long time ago that he'd been featured in the journal *Science* as a 17-year-old prodigy about to pursue a simultaneous PhD and MD at the University of Wisconsin, though it had only been three years. On paper, he'd lived up to the hype. He'd authored or co-authored more than 40 peer-reviewed articles since then and held 14 bioengineering patents, any one of which could make him a very wealthy man overnight. But very little of that was common knowledge, and he almost never talked about it because he almost never talked to anyone besides Baz, Dr. Biermann, and the research assistants in the lab. Very few people in the world could understand what he was working on, let alone what it could lead to.

He finished his coffee, zipped up his jacket and headed back across the quad to the Genetics Biotechnology Center where his lab awaited. The wind off Lake Mendota carved smooth ridges into the powdery snow. Long, white fingers reached across the sidewalk as though trying to crawl toward shelter. It stung his face through his scraggly beard, prompting him to ask himself yet again what he was doing there when he could've gone anywhere he wanted.

The answer was Biermann. His doctoral advisor was close enough to the work to add legitimacy but not close enough to notice the siphoning of funds from multiple grants into his little side project. For example, he and Baz were working together on three of them, so if they had a working lunch, they could charge it back to any of the three. His proposals were based on timelines that didn't really apply to him. By spending less than they needed in less time than they forecast, he bought himself some room for his pet project. The results were all that really mattered to the funding authority.

The building was warm—too warm compared to outside. He immediately removed his jacket and folded it into the crook of his arm as he made his way upstairs, his footsteps echoing through the empty stairwell. When he opened the heavy door onto the main genetics floor, he was greeted by the sweet perfume of lab work, a persistent antiseptic sort of smell that Geller never tired of. The building was almost always silent this time of day, yet he heard a commotion from the end of the hall. And was that … music? He quickened his pace and pushed into the lab.

It was a party. All the grad assistants were there and a few brought their significant others. The "dirty room," as they called it, was festooned with tissue paper and Christmas lights. Relish trays and plastic cups covered nearly every square inch of horizontal space. Several people were even dancing, including Biermann himself. No chance of un-seeing that.

Geller stood in the doorway for several seconds before anyone noticed him. A young grad assistant named Kalpana noticed him first, and her broad white smile collapsed. One by one, the partygoers realized he was there and paused their revelry to see how he would react. Someone turned the music off. After a moment, Baz pushed his way through from the back. Geller saw Baz's girlfriend, Lucia, keeping a safe distance.

"Brent!" Baz said. He held an open beer in one hand and an unopened one in the other. "We expected you a little sooner."

Baz held the unopened beer out to him, but Geller indicated his coffee.

"What's this?" he asked.

"Didn't you get my message?"

Geller shook his head and pulled out his phone,

which he rarely checked. A raft of messages filled the screen.

"Doesn't matter," Baz said, clearly tipsy. "We're celebrating because we cured liver cancer."

Interesting choice of pronoun, Geller thought.

"What do you mean?"

"Your protein binds perfectly to the carbohydrate," he said, beaming.

"Show me," Geller said.

Baz turned around to the group, all of whom were trying to interpret Geller's reaction. "Party on, people!"

The music came back on and the hum of conversations returned. Geller followed Baz through a door and into the main part of the laboratory. A single workstation was illuminated with a screen saver running on the computer.

"I knew you'd want to see," Baz said.

Geller sat and moved the mouse to wake the screen. A 3D model of a protein appeared, which looked like a mile of ribbon blown by the wind into a hopeless tangle. To Geller, it was the secret language of God—an impossible system of folds and loops that combined to do one specific thing in one specific way. He clicked through a series of images and tables, his brain processing the data as fast as it could be displayed.

"What about the rats?"

"Clean. Like it was never even there."

"Lymph?"

"Normal."

Geller felt a little jolt of adrenaline. The idea was to isolate the sugar molecule the cancer cells needed for fuel and change it into something useless yet harmless, like turning a baloney sandwich into a rock. If the cells starved, the body's own immune system could easily destroy the cancer. The last protein they'd tested caused massive lymphedema that killed the rats in days. But what excited Geller most was the retroviral delivery system that programmed cells to manufacture the protein. It had been extremely effective.

Geller pushed his chair back and sat for a moment, staring out the window. He never dreamt they'd be at this point already, but it seemed they were. It didn't matter that it took just two years to get to this point in a five-year grant. The plan was always the same. He had the time and the resources, and he definitely had the vision. Now he had to try and sell it to the most ethical person he knew.

"Let's get back in there," Geller said, forcing a smile. "The party's waiting."

2

Lyle Merriweather felt a lump. Softened as Laura's breasts were by age, it was easy to distinguish. He'd thought little of it right then. Five years previous she'd had a scare with a benign cyst, but the doctor cautioned it probably wouldn't be the last. She had found that one during yoga and didn't handle it as calmly as he'd come to expect during their 36 years together. Breast cancer had grown in adjacent branches of her family tree, so her anxiety was justified then. But because of that, and since it had been such a painfully long time since they'd made love, his focus remained in the moment.

It was a little much to call Lyle and Laura soul mates, but theirs was a pretty good story and not many people knew it.

While they were dating, Laura's father, Chet, cracked a piston on his tractor a couple days before heavy rains accelerated the wheat harvest. Lyle cast a replacement from a die he made himself and had the tractor up and running the next day. Chet would later give Lyle the seed money, at great personal risk, to start Merriweather Tool and Die. On the same day Lyle repaid his debt, he asked for Laura's hand. When the very same tractor— still running like a champ—rolled over on top of Chet three years later and crushed him to death, the inheritance helped expand the business and branch out into other parts of Kansas with other ventures. Eventually Merriweather Industries evolved into the country's second-largest company, with its fingers in many pies.

It was uncommon for a captain of industry like him to remain genuinely faithful to one woman, but faithful he was. There had been so many opportunities to stray, but what more could he have wanted? His billions meant nothing to her. Laura saw his whole self. She'd expected him to build a comfortable life around her and nothing more. She'd have dispensed with the rest without hesitation.

The next morning, she poured his coffee for him and sat down to a bright red half-grapefruit.

"I need to tell you something," he said.

"Oh?"

"Last night I felt something in your—"

"Yeah, I noticed it last week," she said, casually. "In fact, I already went in."

"Really?"

"They took a biopsy. They said they'd have results in a few days."

Either her first experience with the cyst had steeled her, or her insouciance was just an act. Either way, it didn't make him feel any better.

"Dr. Fagan?"

She nodded.

"Did she seem concerned?"

"Meh. You know how doctors are. I'm not thinking about it until I have to and neither should you."

"I'll do my best."

She smiled her slightly crooked smile at him and eased a wedge of grapefruit between her lips. He returned it and checked his watch. It was getting late—there was a board meeting he couldn't beg off.

"I have to run, but obviously—"

"You'll know when I know," she said. "'Now. Cervantes' foil.' Five letters, ends in 'a.'"

He thought for a moment, and said, "Panza?"

She smiled and tapped in the letters. "You've served your purpose," she said, and shooed him toward the door. "We're here for dinner."

He kissed her on the cheek, a gesture she received with a practiced stretch of her face toward his lips, and he left her.

· · ·

THE DAY PASSED SLOWLY. Two hours tying off on the shareholder meeting, then a short lunch at his desk, then an afternoon of conference calls. During the drive home he turned his phone off—something he never did—with nothing but the thin, hermetic hum of the Mercedes to distract him, thinking of Laura. He knew he never took her for granted, yet worried he did. She was the context for his wealth and success; without that, it had no meaning.

The Merriweather Foundation was like the daughter they hadn't lost. When Molly died in her crib all those years ago, Laura poured herself into getting the foundation off the ground. She'd chaired and appointed the board of the fledgling organization herself, allowing him to handle the business particulars while she courted donors. Initially it was established to help coax great ideas into life. They both knew they'd simply been in the right place and time, and that there were others out there who could benefit from money and validation.

In this spirit, the foundation courted the interest of well-resourced people. A college dropout in Iowa came up with a way to mix pulverized corn stalks and husks with an organic resin to create cheap, durable building materials akin to cinder blocks. The foundation gave him $50,000 to build a prototype home, and four years later HusKey Homes was helping transform third-world villages. Special legislation made it possible for farmers to put their regular subsidies toward the program in exchange for tax credits, and they were happy to do it. There were millions of other great ideas, of course, but the foundation breathed life into a select few and the world had benefited. Over time, Lyle had come to see the foundation's myriad pursuits as a more noble calling than running the business. It was necessary to remain involved at a high strategic level—mostly as the public face of corporate governance and to help launch new spinoffs or products, but the foundation wasn't just a reflection of his company's success—it justified it.

Young people had the best ideas. Oh, what a gift idealism was! To pursue a thing with single-minded resolve, out of a crystalline notion of what was right, or fair, or necessary. He'd always felt and acted younger than he was, and he liked that about himself, but it had been many years since he'd had that kind of clarity about anything. It was like that old movie *Being There*, when the gardener, Chauncey, walked on water because he didn't perceive it as an obstacle. These days, all he knew were obstacles, and all he ever seemed to do was negotiate them. In a way, his approach to the foundation was a little patriarchal—in the sense that it was his, but more so the vicarious thrill of enabling a dream.

The drive from downtown to Mercer Island gave him time to put things in perspective regarding Laura. If she was sick, they would simply deal with it. He had access to the best medical care on Earth, and plenty of true friends who would stay with them through anything. Not that it would come to that.

But he hadn't heard from her one way or the other, and that was disconcerting. It seemed certain that she would call or send him a message if everything was fine, and she hadn't. He half expected to find her Range Rover gone when he pulled in, but it was in the garage as always and the hood was cold. The kitchen was dark when he went inside, and smelled of the meal she made hours earlier but had long since moved to the fridge. Chicken, maybe. The only light in the living room was the lamp Laura liked to read by. She wasn't under it, but her favorite blanket was, open like a seed pod. He headed upstairs.

Soft music wafted from the bathroom—Liszt. He pushed the cracked door open as he rapped gently on it.

"Babe? Can I come in?" he said.

"Mi casa es su casa," she said, a little slurred, trying to sound Latin but coming off more like Natasha Fatale. "*Tu* casa, I mean. We are *familiar*, after all."

She was in the tub, a pair of scented candles lit on the little table. She was facing away, her hair up, neck and shoulders glistening with moisture; in the flickering half light, she could have been 25. A glass of red was in her right hand. He smiled, thinking this was all a good sign. She'd taken a bath after dinner, overindulged a bit, and was just enjoying herself.

"Where's mine?" he said.

"I brought you a glass," she said, nodding toward a wine glass on the sink. "Unfortunately, it was rather good …" She reached down over the side of the tub and swirled around the dregs of her empty bottle of cabernet. "Sorry, Dahling."

He moved in front of her and sat down on a tile platform under the bay window that overlooked Lake Washington, moonlit and cold.

"So either you're celebrating or you're not."

She guffawed. "I am celebrating. I'm celebrating *life*. This time is for rumination and reflection."

"What did they say?" he said after a moment. It felt dumb, knowing the answer as he suddenly did, having just thought it was the opposite. Perhaps he just wanted to hear what she'd say, and how she'd say it.

"What did *they* say? Well, *they* said plenty, and I learned a *lot*. For example, I didn't truly understand what 'metastatic' meant until this afternoon. You feel kind of smart throwing words like that around."

A knot formed in his throat.

"Where?"

"Same place that has been metabolizing this delicious vintage the past few hours. When it comes to destroying my liver, however, this thing has met its match. It's a race to the finish. Cheers."

She drained her glass. This conversation was like so many they had—more implicit than explicit, a verbal shorthand streamlined by time. She liked that he could fill in the blanks she left him, and he liked trying to read her intent. He didn't like anything about this.

"What's next?" he said.

"Oh, a whole parade of horrors. Radiation. Chemo. Surgery, maybe. But in the end?" She made a farting sound, then sunk up to her nose in the water.

He rose and slipped off his tie, his shoes, his pants —everything—and eased himself into the water facing her. His girth pushed a few gallons of water over the side, but it didn't matter. Nothing did then, except for her. Laura was a fighter, but she wasn't an idealist like the people the foundation worked with. She was the kind of woman who wouldn't think twice about cutting her foot off if it was hopelessly stuck. Hell, that might even be her first choice.

No, she would try some of the treatments, but unless they started showing results in pretty short order, she would start tidying up her will and give him her blessing to start looking for someone else as soon as she was gone. That was just Laura. He wasn't much better, which was why he so admired people who were.

She handed him her glass, with its one last swallow of wine, and he downed it, warm and awful.

3

**From *The Perfect Generation: A Memoir*
by Dr. Brent A. Geller**

Winter 2019 was extraordinarily cold, even for Madison. My roommate, whom I'll call Martin because of his birdlike features, worked part time on city road crews, usually flipping a sign that said SLOW on one side and STOP on the other to wrangle traffic through a lane closure. He went to Fleet Farm and bought an actual snowsuit to wear during his shifts, for which I gave him no end of grief. My grants kept me comfortable without an outside job, but it's important to note that Martin's father was the used-car czar of Indianapolis. His lifestyle was already subsidized to where he no longer bothered to deposit my rent checks (it was his place). I give him credit for taking those gigs, but how he stood outside for four hours at a stretch in 20-below weather was beyond reckoning.

The cold is significant in my memory of that year for two reasons: First, it kept me inside a lot more than usual. It was much easier to spend extra hours in the lab when the alternative was walking ten blocks home with your nostrils stuck together. And when Martin worked the late shift, he would usually swing by and get me on his way home.

I was a known quantity in the scientific community by then, at least on the academic side. My advisor, Dr. Horst Biermann, had been principal investigator on several studies with me, many of which turned some heads. The journal *Science* profiled me, and I appeared in a few small documentaries about the future of medicine, genetics, etc. My ego loved the validation, and so there were few opportunities I wouldn't take or quotes I wouldn't give.

By that time, most of my postdoc research had coalesced around gene therapy and molecular genetics. I was finishing up a simultaneous MD, as well, to maintain as much control over my future treatments as possible. Few people did this, with good reason, but I found the more macro world of medicine to be much less mysterious than the micro world of genetics. Gene therapy is a process by which defective genes are replaced with good ones, but early attempts weren't successful enough for anyone to take it very seriously. I was determined to change that because of my sister, Jennifer.

Jennifer had Down Syndrome, a.k.a. trisomy 21, a random defect in one of every 1,000 random couplings that adds an extra copy of the 21st chromosome. In addition to several characteristic physical traits, Down Syndrome is marked by mental impairment. I was six when Jen was born, by which time I was doing college-level work in math and chemistry.

The mechanics of her disease weren't a mystery to me, but I never tried to understand her as a person. As our realities diverged, I distanced myself. I loved her, but I had no interest in learning how to deal with her. That was my parents' job. To be honest, her very existence was an embarrassment. Here I was, absorbing my studies with ease, while she literally took the short bus to school. We were far enough apart in years that I couldn't stand up for her when she got picked on, but I wouldn't have anyway. I was selfish, entitled, and driven, while Jen was funny, empathetic, and determined. I admired her, but only in secret. In reality I wanted her as far away from me as possible.

It remains my greatest shame.

She died three days shy of her 17th birthday, which was the second reason I remember the cold so distinctly that winter. My mother called to tell me that Jen died of heart failure, a call I expected after learning she was in the hospital. I didn't go home to see her.

Mom called when I was just about to leave the lab and Martin was off that day, so I walked home in the cold. I was just two blocks from the apartment when I noticed someone in a sleeping bag, tight against a property fence that faced an alley. I noticed no fogged breath and thought myself magnanimous for nudging the figure with my foot. Nothing. I did it again, harder. Still nothing.

I reached down and pulled back the bag to reveal the face of a man in his fifties who had frozen to death. His eyelids and lips were blue, and I remember realizing that Jen's lips would have been blue just then, too, from the cyanosis that likely preceded her death. In his face it was easy to imagine hers, and in that moment I realized how completely I had failed her. I also realized, however, for the first time, that she'd inspired me to follow this path. What happened to her was random, but preventable. And I would be the one to prevent it.

A few weeks after Jen died, my phone rang. It was Baz, my former associate, better known as Dr. Basilio Montes. Though older, he'd settled into the role of de facto assistant on our projects for Biermann. Our NIH grant work was overfunded, so we funneled some of it into a little side project that was far more audacious. The going was slow because we still had to spend almost half our lab time on the boring grant work. I offered to supervise the plebes that night because he was going to propose to his girlfriend, Lucia, who was visiting from Spain. Again, I viewed this as selfless until I realized he'd excused himself to the men's room at *L'Etoile,* where he'd taken Lucia, in order to call me.

"You need to get online right now," he said.

He explained that Lyle Merriweather was making whatever secret announcement they'd been hyping for weeks. I'd heard about it but hadn't given it much thought. All I knew about Merriweather was that he was an industrialist with a hard-on for social justice and Third World causes. That wasn't the sort of thing that impressed me so I wouldn't have crossed the street to meet him. Baz didn't go into much detail, saying he had to get back and pop the question before he lost his nerve, but something in his voice persuaded me. So, I went back in one of the offices to check it out.

What he said that night changed everything.

4

———

"I don't like him, Basilio," Lucia said.

Baz sighed. "Take a number."

Lucia was radiant and exotic—two things he was not. They'd been on a schedule of seeing each other every six months since they met as undergrads, while Baz was studying in Barcelona. It was not enough, but there was something satisfying about how much he burned for her when they were apart. The day would come soon enough when they were together all the time, and he wouldn't feel it anymore.

L'Etoile was trendy among the university crowd, but not poor doctoral students so much as long-tenured professors and administrators. As Baz studied the menu, sneaking furtive glances at Lucia, it occurred to him he could eat for almost a week for the price of a single entrée. Suddenly, he wondered whether this was all too cliché.

"What are you thinking about?" he asked.

"That you should find another research partner."

Baz laughed. "No, I mean to eat."

"Oh," she said, giggling. "I stand by my answer."

"Enough about Brent. Tonight isn't about him. It's about escargot, and bouillabaisse, and a bunch of other things I can't pronounce. Which brings us back to your food selection."

"Well, the wild mushroom risotto sounds amazing."

It better be for $36, he thought.

"I was looking at that, too," he said.

"But?"

"But I'm leaning toward the scallops."

"Where's that?"

"The coquilles St. Jacques. They're scallops."

"Mmm, that sounds good, too."

They went back and forth like this for a while, eventually both returning to their first selections but opting to start with the lobster bisque at $18 per bowl. Baz was keeping track of the bill in his head so he could fake indifference when it came.

He would later recall that the soup was worth every penny, tasting and feeling in his mouth for all the world like something that could start or end a war. The entrees were both exquisite, but they were harder to enjoy because they drew him nearer to the moment when the waiter would bring them a signature dessert on the house—a little tree made of chocolate ganache that would have a ring perched on top, and while Lucia took it all in, he would drop to one knee …

She excused herself to the bathroom, and rather than fret about what came next, Baz checked his phone. One of his grad assistants had texted him an article about something called the Merriweather Prize. He skimmed it long enough to understand why it was important.

"Oh my God, the bathrooms here are almost too nice to use," Lucia said from behind him, sliding back into her chair.

Baz's heart felt like it might explode. He couldn't have said whether it was because the big moment was drawing closer or because of what he'd just seen. In either case, there was only one thing to do.

"I guess I'll have to see for myself," he said, folding his napkin and placing it on the empty table. As he rose, he made eye contact with their server, who subtly twisted his hand back and forth between thumbs up and thumbs down. Baz raised his splayed fingers to indicate he needed five minutes, and the server signaled back OK.

Lucia was right; the bathroom was too nice to use. He did, in fact, have to pee, but it wasn't clear where that was supposed to happen. Where he might have expected urinals there was just a wall of polished stone tiles beneath a gentle, even flow of water that vanished into a bed of pebbles. It was impossible to tell whether it was a decorative feature or a place to piss, which seemed like an important distinction. Just as he was debating whether to use the toilet instead, an older man entered, strode confidently up to the waterfall and relieved himself into it. The man looked vaguely familiar, perhaps some faculty emeriti he'd met at a banquet. Universities were like that.

"I did the same damn thing first time I came here," he said, as Baz ventured forward to take a spot a couple feet away. "You'd think they'd put a little sign up or something."

"Or one of those peeing cherubs you see in Europe," Baz offered. "To show you the way."

"Now you're talking," the man said, chuckling.

Baz finished first and went to wash his hands. The man joined him a few seconds later.

"Special occasion?" he asked.

"I think I'm getting engaged," Baz said.

"Married 45 years," he said, drying his hands. "And happily for at least half of them. You'll do great."

"Thanks," Baz said, taking his sweet time. His mouth was dry.

After the man left, he dialed Geller.

"You need to get online right now," he said.

"Why? Where?" Geller said, annoyed by the call.

"Anywhere," Baz said. "We'll talk later."

Baz hung up, fixed his tie, and stared at himself in the mirror. He wanted this, or he wouldn't be here. Lucia wanted this as well, or he wouldn't be asking. He wasn't sure if she truly understood the life of a researcher, and if so, what it could mean that his reputation was entwined with Geller's.

Geller had no living peers. Pauling, Salk, Curie, Pasteur, Jenner—that was the company he would keep if they were around, though they wouldn't have liked him either. He was a lousy collaborator; Geller loved the notion of one scientist, working alone in some hidden lab for years or decades, emerging with some insight that would turn everything on its ear. But that wasn't how it worked anymore. He needed funding, and that meant suffering colleagues. Baz was the one who Geller seemed to choose, for whatever reason, and so he either had to reject their partnership on principle or play a part in making bioscientific history.

It was an audacious and ethically dangerous idea Geller had: Don't *fix* the disease—systematically eliminate it from the gene pool at scale. It smacked of eugenics, but in a different spirit. While Baz shared Geller's interest in the actual mechanics of it, he was alone in his concerns about morality. Geller was not about to veer off that track. Baz was on the train or at the station, and he climbed aboard. Geller was one of the worst people he'd ever met, but Baz believed he was coming at the work from a good place, buoyed by a preternatural intellect and instinct. If pressed, he would have admitted that wondering what Geller might do was part of the fun.

When the door opened to another patron, it jolted Baz from his musings and back to reality. He dried his hands, opened the door, and with a deep breath, took his first of many steps into the unknown.

5

By the time Geller got online and found the live stream it was snowing again—the powdery, moistureless snow of a Wisconsin deep-freeze. The browser window was on CNN with MERRIWEATHER ANNOUNCES HISTORIC PRIZE in the bottom crawl.

Lyle Merriweather stood alone at a podium dripping with microphones. His name and title—Chairman of the Board of Merriweather Industries—splashed across the lower third. Camera shutters fired like little machine guns. His hands curled around the edges of the podium like part of him wanted to pick it up and throw it at someone. It was clear he hated stuff like this. Even so, he spoke evenly and clearly.

"Thank you all for coming. I'm here to make two related announcements. The first is that my wife of nearly 30 years, Laura, is dying of cancer. The details of her sickness are no one's business but my family's so I won't entertain questions about her condition or prognosis, now or in the future. The only reason I'm sharing this news with the public is because it's closely related to my second announcement."

He cleared his throat, swallowing some obvious emotion.

"The mission of the Merriweather Foundation is to help enable people with extraordinary ideas and abilities bring them to bear on the world for the good of humankind. Some of those ideas and people have changed the world for the better, and their achievements are a continued source of pride, for the foundation and, hopefully, the nation. However, we mustn't forget the countless millions whose own ideas were cut short by disease. The human cost of that loss, and the losses to come, is immeasurable.

"But the real tragedy is that so many of the best and brightest among us are engaged in empty pursuits. Somewhere, a brilliant chemist is reformulating hair gel. An engineer is designing the world's scariest rollercoaster. In other words, they're following the money. I want them to keep following it.

"Today I am announcing the Merriweather Prize to Reduce Human Suffering. This award will go to any individual, team, institution, state, or country who can produce a viable, long-term cure for one or more of the most insidious human diseases. If such a cure is presented to the satisfaction of the committee I appoint, the Merriweather Foundation will commit an initial investment of one billion dollars toward the refinement, testing and eventual FDA approval of that treatment, and more as results merit."

Geller didn't hear the gasp of the press corps over his own. His hands were sweating.

"My wife will not be saved by any treatment we now have. If it's even possible to develop a cure for these diseases, it will be many years away. I'm a patient man, but I have lost my patience with our society. A society that seems satisfied with incremental advances and half measures in the pursuit of truly revolutionary science. A society whose brightest minds are valued more for their commercial potential than for the boldness of their approach. We're looking for the thing that changes everything. We're looking for a panacea."

He paused to let those words hang in the air for a moment.

"More details about the Merriweather Prize will come soon, but for now I offer my apology to any industries whose scientists choose humanity over hairspray."

That story ended and a panel of pundits readied themselves to weigh in. Geller's mind raced; Merriweather might as well have descended from Mt. Olympus to lay this at his feet. What could he accomplish with a billion dollars of capital? The possibilities washed over him. He saw a grand research center, elegant and clever in its architecture. He saw dream teams of scientists from around the globe, tripping over each other to impress him. Adulation. Celebrity. Clinical trials and entire walls of framed patents. Most importantly, he saw himself leaving an indelible mark on history.

News of the prize spanned the globe in minutes. Engineers and architects whined about the prize's medical focus. Within weeks, thousands of researchers either quit their jobs to go it alone or formed teams to chase the prize together. Geller decided he would continue availing himself of university resources, correctly assuming Biermann would keep him on a very long leash. He'd only have to move up his timeline on the side project.

Traditional gene therapy was fraught. First, you needed to design a vector—usually a modified virus or an engineered nanoparticle shell—to deliver good genes into cells with bad ones. But viruses didn't always cooperate and nanotech was hard to produce at scale. A patient's immune response was unpredictable and it was maddeningly difficult to target the exact right tissue in the exact right way. Plus, it mainly worked to replace a single gene; no one had figured out how to replace several at the same time. There was the size of the vector itself, which had to be small enough to enter a cell nucleus and potentially cross the blood-brain barrier. But no challenge was more vexing than the unpredictable long-term effects of a gene vector on cells other than the ones being targeted. If a vector replaced a broken gene in one area—say, the brain—but inserted its DNA into a different place in another group of cells, there was no telling what would happen, or when.

In the days that followed Merriweather's announcement, Geller mused whether he should target cancers or other genetic disorders. The techniques were essentially the same, but there were a few ways to tackle cancer through gene therapy. You could instruct the cells to produce a specific cytotoxic protein, as some had tried in the past, or you could program them to commit suicide. It had been shown that you could also reprogram lymphocytes to target cells with a specific RNA signature and re-introduce them into the bloodstream. Promising, but none were magic bullets. Better progress had been made toward curing genetic disorders like Huntington's or sickle-cell anemia.

Geller's idea wasn't so much a cure as a guarantee against getting sick at all. He'd have to replace all the problem genes in all the cells at once, and that was only possible when there were relatively few undifferentiated cells. That meant introducing the vector in-vitro.

Stem cells were the raw materials of human life. They could become virtually any differentiated cell. All they needed were "instructions" and the right conditions. Geller thought that a vector "cocktail" inserted into an embryo could replace *all* the genes associated with a raft of genetic disorders, whether they were defective or not.

But even if theory became reality and he received FDA approval for such a treatment, most diseases with genetic links were still rare. But so were car crashes, and people still had insurance. He'd seen how parents were about keeping their children safe, even from factors over which they had some control. He suspected "disease insurance" wouldn't be a hard sell if proven safe.

Baz was a game partner in the research, rarely in a position to disagree. His core research was understanding the autoimmune process that destroyed pancreatic beta cells in type 1 diabetics. It wasn't sexy, but Geller needed a competent and fastidious wingman in this pursuit, and Baz was it.

The work was tedious, though by genetics standards it moved at lightning pace. One by one, Geller's gene-replacement therapies proved effective for congenital disorders in rats, and the red queens were having dramatic effects on the more environmental cancers. Taken alone, any one of them would've been on the cover of *Scientific American* and hailed as revolutionary but he bided his time and kept the circle tight. The lab assistants never knew exactly what tests they were running or why, and they rarely asked. Only Baz knew the whole truth; even Biermann was led to believe they were still struggling to develop a single effective vector.

Martin abruptly left college the next year. That left Geller homeless, so out of convenience and a desire to extend the workday, he moved into a cramped second-floor apartment with Baz and his fiancé. It was a dump, but he was often at the lab for 18 hours at a stretch so it didn't matter. Baz kept more normal hours, though Lucia continually bemoaned his workload.

It was an exciting time for the two of them, and it seemed like a new breakthrough was always just around the corner because it often was. Though not religious, Baz was still spiritual and he saw in Geller something almost godlike. His genius was so special, so prescient, that it made the scientific method seem perfunctory at times. By gut instinct or providence he would rule out combinations that anyone else would have had to test to know they didn't work, and it saved incredible amounts of time. And time was of the essence.

Yet for all his talents, Baz came to understand a great irony behind Geller's tireless pursuits to develop his treatment: He was a misanthrope of the highest order.

Occasionally, they would leave the lab to get lunch. One day they sat down to their Gordo's subs at a little table next to the sidewalk just a few blocks from their building. Three women came by having a loud conversation when the heaviest of the three tripped and fell.

Baz instantly sprang from his chair and hurried to her aid, along with a couple other people eating nearby. Geller paused chewing and looked on, bemused, while Baz gently helped the woman to her feet and verified that she was okay. She thanked him and they continued.

"Well that was something," Baz had said.

Geller chuckled and wiped a smear of mayo from the corner of his mouth. "Pretty big production."

"What do you mean?"

"She's a 35-year-old woman with no obvious impairments. I'd bet you a thousand dollars she couldn't lift 20 pounds."

"So what?"

"I'm just saying she's lucky she's not a gazelle, that's all."

"Someone falls, you help them up. It's what people do. Well, people who aren't you."

Geller shrugged. "Natural selection has failed us. More like we've failed *it*."

Baz stared at him, incredulous. "You're a horror show."

"Hey, if I ever trip and fall on a half-inch of sidewalk, you won't have to help me—I'll cull myself from the herd. Are you gonna eat your pickle?"

6

When Lyle was a kid, Pioneer Crest Cemetery was new. The labyrinth of narrow roads were the smoothest runs of asphalt anywhere in town, and he rode his bike there often. They wound around the hillside in a pattern that might have resembled church pews if viewed from above, and had great sight lines, so it was easy to jump off your bike when you saw a car and make like you were there to grieve.

In fact, Lyle did have a reason to be there, even as a kid. His great-grandfather on his mother's side, whom he never knew, was a wealthy businessman of some sort —shipping, if he remembered correctly. He'd purchased a substantial family plot with perpetual care so all his descendants could be interred together under a plain, authoritative black monolith bearing his surname:

FISCHER. As he wished, a community of stones marking the remains of Fischers and Carmodys and Ungers and Trevains now encircled it,

One day after school, his mother drove him there and they walked among the plot as she shared tidbits of information about every distant, long-dead relative under their feet. Some led interesting lives, some not, but he never forgot how much it mattered to her that she was the keeper of that information. Like each little piece of history was a handwritten note on a wrinkled piece of paper she kept in her pocket. It was both sad and beautiful, not unlike the cemetery itself.

Laura's grave was among the first in an entirely new section of the cemetery. She would've appreciated his thoughtfulness in choosing it, which was to balance convenience with seclusion. Their plot backed up to a stand of Douglas firs, with a fence on one side and a bend in the little road on another so only one side could be next to another plot. There was nothing to see except more of the cemetery, technically the back side, which rose to the eponymous crest before spilling back down toward Triad Parkway. When it rained hard, it was possible that not even the elaborate system of culverts and French drains crisscrossing the cemetery would be able to direct all the water away from Laura's corner, but there again she would've appreciated Lyle's logic: She loved the water.

But this day was sunny and beautiful. Chilly, but

that was the trade-off for a clear February day in Seattle. He removed the folding chair and fleece blanket from the trunk and walked it over to her gravesite, setting the chair atop his own plot. He felt a little bit guilty about choosing burial over cremation, but there was something more dignified about a cemetery. Her absence was a presence. He talked to her like he wanted, but not with the casual freedom he envisioned. It still felt like she was there, listening.

Work was the only thing keeping him together. He had little to do with the day-to-day operations, focusing instead on philanthropy and certain special projects. These days that meant the Merriweather Prize.

He initially envisioned a true cancer cure, on account of Laura, and wanted to call it the Laura Merriweather Prize. But his committee of scientists convinced him to make it more general to include a spectrum of groundbreaking medical research, and to just use his surname. Lyle valued science, so it frustrated him to know how thoroughly it failed Laura. He believed humans ought to do better. He had the means and the will, and so he put things into motion.

Nearly three years had passed with no luck. The media had long since forgotten about it, and news of promising new submissions amounted to a cry-wolf scenario. The committee met semiannually to review both new submissions and the financial health of the Meriweather Prize Trust. A silver lining to it was that the trust had done exceedingly well—so well, in fact, that they could award nearly double the promised amount to whomever came forward with the brass ring.

But none came.

There were flickers of hope. About a year earlier, a Norwegian team presented early research that might eventually lead to a cure for Tay-Sachs, a lethal nervous disorder in children caused by a defective gene on chromosome 15. Japanese researchers claimed to have cured cystic fibrosis in laboratory mice, but the committee poked too many holes in their findings to take them seriously.

The committee always met at the Emerald Club, a members-only club that occupied the top two floors of the Paramour Hotel. Lyle's company had a corporate membership but he rarely set foot in the place. It was pretentious and expensive, and he would've preferred a food cart in the park. But, they had a great conference room and it seemed more like neutral territory than his office building.

Lyle heard the patter of voices from the door of the open conference room and entered. Isaac Lindh, chair of the committee, had just removed his jacket. Four others were already seated.

"Hello, Lyle," he said in his thick accent.

"Isaac, good to see you," Lyle said, and shook his

hand. He did the same with the others who had beaten him there: Spivey, Alward, Ita and Djoumbe.

Lindh was a feisty Nobel laureate in genetics, and one of the top scientific minds in the world. His staff weeded out so many crackpot submissions that he and the committee had only ever laid eyes on the legit Norwegian and Japanese efforts. He and Lyle respected each other, but they never got on well. It made for some interesting meetings.

The remaining four greeted each other and exchanged pleasantries as they entered. McCarter was last to arrive, having missed his connection in San Francisco. They officially began 25 minutes late, which irritated Lyle to no end. The foundation paid the committee very well to do very little. Ramirez, Hyler, Abbott and Ramadi were more or less on time. Finally Sarika Hyler, the only woman besides Eileen Alward, read back the minutes from their previous meeting and everyone turned to Lindh.

"Yes. Well. My people flagged 13 submissions since our last meeting," he said, pausing to hand out neatly prepared little packets. "Unfortunately, they are unworthy of consideration. Abstracts and evaluations are in your reports if you're so inclined."

Lyle flipped through the pages, but most of it was over his head. This is how it usually went with Lindh; he poo-poohed anything of which he was not personally in awe. But Lyle knew to trust the scientists with the science, and the others trusted Lindh. They read through the packet in silence for several minutes.

"I've read about this jellyfish protein," said Noel Ramadi, a biochemist, tapping the printed document with his thin finger. "The initial research was extremely promising."

"Yes, I read about it as well," Lindh said, rubbing his eyes. "And in three or four years, we'll know more, but it's not ready for prime time and it's not the kind of … *panacea* we're all here to find anyway."

Lindh glanced in Lyle's direction as curled his lips around every syllable of "panacea." He leaned back in his chair and sighed heavily.

"Lyle, we believe in what you're trying to do. No one has ever sought to reward scientific innovation to anywhere near this degree before. But the parameters we're working with are simply impractical. In this report are 13 projects that, taken together, would move medicine forward a decade, if not more. Even if we chose 10 such projects to support, each of them is still coming away with nearly $200 million. Science doesn't move at the pace you want it to. In fact, if it did, it would be irresponsible."

"You're saying put the money to use, now," Lyle said, trying to match Lindh's tone.

"It's been nearly three years."

Lyle's eyes searched the others in the room. He

could see that most were inclined to agree with Lindh, but opted to test that theory.

"Is that the opinion of the committee?"

They exchanged nervous glances.

"I may speak only for myself, but it is a hard point to disagree with," said Ramirez. "The wheels of science turn slowly. Groundbreaking discoveries usually follow years or even decades of groundwork."

Nods all around the table. Lyle folded his hands on the table in front of him.

"Only a couple of you knew Laura. She was sort of this constant light source. For me, for everyone who knew her. Just brightened the room, y'know? I'm sure you all know someone like that. Anyway, as she got sicker and sicker, it was like this black thing snaked its way through her body and started to dim that light. I'm not talking in metaphors here; she was literally dimmed by it."

Everyone lowered their eyes.

"I don't deny the value of *treatments*. God knows, if I could've found anything else to extend her life, I would've. But what I *really* wanted was for her not to have this thing at all. What I wanted was for there to be nothing to treat in the first place. After she passed, that's all I could think about. If our sole focus isn't to keep these terrible things from happening to the people we care about, then what else is there? What else is worth spending time on besides that?"

He looked around. No one said anything.

"We stay the course for another year, then we have this conversation again. This was a dream I had for Laura, and even if I've let go of *her*, I can't let go of *it*. Not yet."

7

The lab was dark and silent, but not empty. Geller was there, checking on the animals and entering notes in a tablet. The last time Baz had seen him was at the apartment Wednesday morning, and it was Friday. It was likely he hadn't left the room.

It wasn't rational for Baz to think that Geller would ask whether Lucia had said yes. It wasn't rational to think that some small part of Geller's mind might have wondered why cake samples were in the refrigerator, or why he kept a spreadsheet of honeymoon options open on his laptop. And it certainly wasn't rational to think Geller might be concerned about changes in their working relationship. And because none of these things were rational, it was irrational for Baz to be as pissed off about it as he was.

Baz almost touched the light panel that would ignite the blinding fluorescents in the lab and send Geller into a rage, but he thought better of it and simply cleared his throat. Geller looked up with a start and saw him in the doorway.

"Hey," Geller said.

Baz walked down the long row of cages where dozens of rats were awaiting, or undergoing tests of their gene vectors. Some stirred and sniffed the air after him, and some curled up in little white piles at the corners. As of Wednesday there were 10 working vectors, but knowing Geller he might have added another.

"Thought I'd better check on you," Baz said, drawing close enough now to understand that Geller hadn't showered or changed in days, despite a small locker room and shower on that very floor. The faint smell of Greek takeout hung in the air. He half expected to find a cupboard full of graduated cylinders spilling over with Geller's urine. He didn't want to look in the garbage can.

"Oh. Yeah, I guess I've been at it for a while. The ALS vector is triggering a massive immune response and I don't know why."

Baz could have listed possibilities why this might be, all of which Geller would have considered. Sometimes he could help spin Geller off in another direction that eventually led him to a solution. But he said nothing.

"I thought we agreed this was a good week to take a break," Baz said.

"You said it would be and I said okay. I'm sorry if you thought that meant I agreed with you."

"I needed the break. I knew that about myself. You need the break, too, but you don't know it. I never imagined you of all people would need to work on your self-awareness."

"What did I ever do without you?" Geller said sarcastically, brushing past him to open a cage and remove a rat for a blood draw. He noted the number on the tag, unsheathed a tiny collection needle and got the sample in under ten seconds. "So Aruba, is it?"

Baz had, in fact, booked their honeymoon that very morning. Ten days, though he could scarcely afford even three.

"Yes," he said, trying to sound more surprised than pleased. "How did you—"

"Lucky guess," Geller said.

Geller was exceptional at guesswork, but Baz knew he hadn't guessed this. He knew somehow.

"You printed out your booking information for your records, just as the travel site suggested."

He was right. Baz had printed it, and it probably was still on the printer.

"I imagine you'll work the whole time I'm gone," Baz said.

"We're behind schedule. Someone's got to stay on top of all this."

"What schedule?"

"You think Merriweather's going to hang that money out there forever? He's a businessman. If we don't get our asses in gear he'll pull the plug."

"What we have right now is more than enough to win that money and you know it."

Geller dispensed a single drop of the rat's blood onto a slide and placed it into a digital microscope.

"Winning the money is a foregone conclusion. I'm already thinking about what comes next."

"Is that right?"

"Once we have capital, we'll have oversight. Accountability. What we have right now is autonomy, and we may never have it again. You want to squander that on piña coladas and sex, that's your business. I want to change the world."

Baz knew better than to let Geller, who almost certainly self-medicated in order to work these hours, suck him into his vortex. He had a way of making people feel extraneous, even unnecessary. But Baz knew Geller needed him. If Geller was a supercar, Baz was the brake. A car without brakes would eventually crash, no matter how good the driver was.

"If you didn't do the Marfan vector right now, we're at 10, yes?"

"Yeah." Geller typed a note into a tablet.

"So call what we have version 1.0 or something. Put it all together and physically set it aside."

"That'll take weeks. Why would I do that?"

"Because what's sitting in cryo right now isn't just a viable serum. It's a Nobel Prize."

"That's not the prize I care about."

"Let's say we hear tomorrow that the prize is shutting down at the end of the year. We only have data. It's like a proof of concept. You're not stopping, you're just leaving yourself some provisions for the return journey."

Geller pulled back from the microscope and his shoulders sagged. He was thinking about the work. The delay. But also the logic.

He shook his head. "There's no time," he said.

"What do you do when you're writing a research paper? You stop and save your work, often."

"Our progress is thoroughly documented."

"Listen, I share your ambitions for this. I do. But—"

Geller guffawed. "You don't share my ambition for anything, Baz. None of this is your doing. If it weren't for me, you'd be a footnote in some diabetes journal. We have a chance to make history here, and I'm on a fucking roll. Your concerns are noted."

Baz sighed and shook his head. That stung. He saw a flicker of guilt in Geller's eyes, then they returned to the microscope.

"Suit yourself," Baz said. "I know you will."

"Enjoy your honeymoon."

He left, and turned back as he opened the door. Geller didn't look up.

8

Emotionally, Lyle was running on empty. He was nearly ready to repurpose the money the foundation had set aside for the prize and try to put a positive spin on its failure. He was at a meeting of the foundation's board one fall afternoon, giving feedback on the press release, when a young senior communications manager whose name he could never remember entered the room lightly and leaned down to Lyle's ear.

"Mr. Merriweather, Dr. Lindh is on the line for you. He says it's urgent."

Merriweather checked his phone and noticed several missed calls from Lindh. His brow furrowed.

"Tell him I'll call him back as soon as we've wrapped up here."

"He said you would say that, sir, and to tell you—

these are his words, not mine—'Pick up the fucking phone, Lyle.'"

Lyle chuckled at that. Either Lindh had found something promising, or he was quitting. Probably the latter.

He ushered Lyle into a small conference room by the young man, who indicated he would transfer the call to the phone on the table. Lyle thanked him and sat as the door closed. Moments later, the phone rang.

"Let me guess," Lyle said. "You want out."

"There's a submission we need to discuss."

Lyle sat up. There was real excitement in Lindh's voice.

"Is it what we're looking for?"

"It's some of the damnedest research I've ever seen. If their data is accurate … I guess I'm saying that if this wasn't what you wanted, then I don't know what you wanted."

"Anyone you know?"

"Brent Geller and Basilio Montes from the University of Wisconsin. Geller was a young prodigy who I remember published a few interesting things but he's been under the radar for a long time now. Turns out he's been a busy boy. Montes, I've never heard of."

"So assemble the full committee?"

"Yes. Immediately."

Lindh was a hard man to impress, which was why his awe took Lyle by surprise. He paid Lindh to judge the science, but Lyle was just as interested in the man behind it. He looked forward to a meeting.

THE COMMITTEE CONVENED the following Tuesday. For scheduling reasons, they met in an executive boardroom at Merriweather Industries' controls division, a lavish glass cube atop a 72-story high-rise with a stunning view of the Sound. The LCD panels forming its walls could be made opaque with the flip of a switch, and they all had been save for the ones facing the water. The CFO of the foundation was there at Lyle's invitation, along with the usual committee members.

A cart of coffee and water was wheeled inside, and on its heels a female assistant held the door open for a man Lyle somehow knew to be Dr. Brent Geller. He was shortish—maybe 5'9"—and he hadn't gotten much in the way of sun, but otherwise he might've been an underwear model. His black hair was unkempt in a way that looked intentional, a trim week-old beard framing his otherwise smooth face. He flashed a disarming grin to everyone in the room and cast a sidelong glance at the young woman holding the door. Lyle supposed it wasn't entirely unwelcome.

Behind Geller was a much taller, rail-thin Latino, also with a beard, whose hair was pulled into a smooth ponytail. His Buddy Holly glasses were as suited to him as the crisp dress shirt he wore. Montes. He guessed him to be about 34 a fair bit older than Geller.

Introductions were made and Lindh set the stage for Geller's presentation. The broad strokes were outlined in the brief Lyle read over the weekend, but basically he reiterated that Geller's therapy had the theoretical potential to prevent, and eventually eradicate, a laundry list of genetic diseases with a single treatment. That much Lyle knew, but he looked forward to hearing more. He leaned back in his chair and gestured for him to begin.

Geller cleared his throat and set his smartphone on a glowing multipad built into the table. A screen integrated into the glass wall flickered to life, and he gestured toward the multipad. A sensor array overhead read his movements and he threw a presentation from his device onto the glowing screen.

Geller talked for nearly an hour and a half, but to anyone in the room it seemed like minutes. It was like a symphony. Every question Lindh and the rest of the committee posed was answered so skillfully that they felt foolish for asking. Never in his life had Lyle heard someone elucidate so effortlessly on so esoteric a subject. The science, he could see from the raised eyebrows and furtive glances around the table, was sound. By the end, he was ready to give Geller *everything*. Montes barely spoke—he studying everyone's reactions.

Lyle had no way of knowing whether the doctors and scientists on the committee truly understood everything they heard, or whether they followed him up to a point but got lost in the elegant, yet subtly condescending explanations of how and why. After Geller finished, he helped himself to a bottle of water and sat. The ensuing silence continued for several long seconds. It was Lindh who finally broke the spell.

"Dr. Geller, I'd like to delve a bit further into your plans for delivering this treatment in-vitro. Do you think expectant mothers will submit to an invasive and unproven treatment, FDA approved or not?"

Geller set his water on the table and shrugged.

"Beats me."

Everyone in the room did a double take except Baz, who smirked and shook his head. After what they just saw and heard, hearing Geller say this was like hearing an opera singer's voice crack. Lindh wasn't sure what to say, so Geller allowed a thin smile and continued.

"I mean, it's a risk—no question. But having a baby at all is a crapshoot. This could give mothers the opportunity to have a genetically flawless child. Not a designer child or a kid engineered to be super smart or beautiful, but a kid who starts life on a level playing field. A kid who won't require around-the-clock care when he's five, or 13, or 20. It's like applying Six Sigma to immunology and genetics—you're just eliminating defects. Over time, you get a whole generation of people with essentially flawless genes, and there aren't recessives or dominants anymore—no one gets the rug pulled out from under them. What mother wouldn't want that for her kid if it was practically guaranteed?"

Lyle turned to one of the two female scientists, Dr. Alward, whom he knew to be a mother. "Eileen, I believe you have a unique perspective on that question."

She raised her eyebrows and nodded reluctantly, like a politician conceding a small point in private.

"If the FDA blessed it, it would be hard to ignore. Every mother hopes for a healthy child, but there's always some fear there. Like you said, you leave a lot to chance."

"But regarding the cancers, there are obviously environmental factors," Lindh said, turning back to Geller. "Chemicals, free radicals—the sun. What happens to those people?"

"We figured out how to prevent 34 diseases with genetic links working off the fringes of a $5.5 million grant. What do you think we could do with a billion?"

Lindh instantly felt silly, and looked it. Lyle smiled —no point in playing devil's advocate anymore.

"What would a treatment like this cost?" asked the CFO. "I've got no frame of reference."

"Well, that's where we—" Geller began.

"Nothing," Lyle said, cutting him off.

The CFO's eyes widened.

"Edward Jenner gave the smallpox vaccine to the

world. No patent, no money. Today, smallpox is a dead disease. What would've happened if someone tried to profit from that?"

"That's different."

"Not really," Lyle said. "If this works the way Dr. Geller described, then you'd need nearly everyone to do it. A whole generation. It took a while, but now every parent who isn't crazy gets standard vaccinations for their kids. They can't even attend public school unless they do. No—doctors can charge whatever they like for the treatment, but the drug is free. Are we of a mind, Dr. Geller?"

"The more people who sign up for this, the better in the long run," Geller said, obviously pleased to have an ally in Merriweather. "Free helps make that happen." Baz was smiling too.

"Well, then," Lyle said, trying to read the look on Geller's face, "We'll be in touch."

9

From *The Perfect Generation: A Memoir*
by Dr. Brent A. Geller

Normally we'd have taken our five-year National Institutes of Health (NIH) grant and gone on a spending spree, hiring grad fellows, renting additional lab space, buying new gear— that sort of thing. But the grant was for something very specific: testing a retroviral delivery system for a gene therapy targeting liver cancer. I wanted to take that to the next level and beyond.

We worked on the grant-funded research just enough to satisfy its terms but used the equipment and the space, along with some of those grad students, to work on our treatment as well. The net result was that Baz's and my time was essentially free. Our stipends from the NIH grant covered our living expenses along with the personnel and extra equipment needed to set up experiments, so we were effectively sponsored in the work. Ethically, it wasn't exactly above-board, but our work was moving too quickly for bureaucracy. We had a billion dollars to win. (Don't worry, I've since made enough gifts to the university that they shouldn't feel too slighted. Also, it's important to note that Baz was never totally comfortable with any of it.)

The work itself was tedious and beyond most people's understanding. But I'll try and give you a layman's understanding of the science because it's important.

Genes are blueprints for building an organism and giving it traits. They contain DNA, which is unique to the organism. We have roughly 25,000 genes, each of which does something specific—mostly directing the manufacture of proteins. Manipulating genes is tricky (don't try it at home) because there are lots of them, they are complex in themselves, their products are also complex and interact in complex ways, and they don't always behave predictably. They can also mutate for a variety of reasons, which changes everything.

Imagine you're in a room with nearly infinite number of locked doors and 25,000 machines that spit out piles of keys when turned on. Every key unlocks at least one door—some perfectly, and some with a little wiggling. Behind one door are blue eyes. Behind another, cankles. Behind another, lymphoma. To manipulate genes you need to a) find the right key for the right door, and then b) figure out how to tell one machine to make keys that either fit another right door or don't fit a wrong door. Good luck.

Computers transformed the science, and quantum computing did it again. They can predict the 3D structure of a new protein produced by an altered or replaced gene, and whether it will bind or not to affect the desired change. They can do this billions of times per second all day, every day. In so doing, they can reduce the number of possibilities from a few quadrillion to a few thousand. That's impressive, but when real-world tests takes several days to complete, you can't deal with thousands. Sometimes you have to follow a hunch. Computers don't get funny feelings or have intuition or moments of insight. A good hunch can get you from a few thousand to a handful you can actually test. If there's one thing that separated me from my peers, it's a frequently accurate gut feeling.

I've said this before in interviews, but our ambitions were modest at the start. There was a small pool of disorders that we already knew were caused by defects in specific genes, and that's where we started. Working as a team, we developed effective therapies for these disorders in rats within a year. Emboldened, we kept trucking. One by one, keys slid into locks and turned. Though the treatment was becoming dizzyingly complex, our methods were achieving dramatic results more quickly than we dared imagine.

After the prize was announced, we heard through research channels that several teams, notably the Norwegians, were on the verge of huge breakthroughs. Biding our time, even if it potentially meant losing a billion dollars in funding, was maddening. But though I'd never met him to that point I felt like I knew Lyle Merriweather. When he said what he said about half measures, I got it. I mean, *really* got it. I knew he wasn't going to give that money away unless he felt in his very bones a sea change, and I wasn't going to stop until I knew I had that. So I didn't.

Many think Baz should've stood in my way, and been the voice of reason. That thinking is flawed for two reasons: One, neither Baz nor anyone else could have stopped me. I was at the peak of my abilities, highly driven, and highly productive. Two, continuing with our work was the only reasonable thing. Say you like to garden, but a stubborn weed takes over. Nothing you try to get rid of it works until one day, it just does. Would you stop before it was gone?

10

The call came a week later. Geller had spent the morning in the lab as usual, only he'd decided to take a break from the "Cure," as he and Baz called it, and instead helped Biermann supervise a small group of weary grad students assisting with Biermann's own immaterial research. No one was more surprised at this than Biermann, but he kept his mouth shut.

There was a message from Merriweather himself on his voicemail, with his private number. He eased into the couch, put his feet on the coffee table and turned on the news, muting it instantly. Mudslides in Sri Lanka, hundreds dead. He dialed.

"Dr. Geller."

"Mr. Merriweather. I didn't expect to hear from you so—"

"Have you eaten?"

"Um … no. Why?"

"I'm in town. I'd like to chat over dinner if you're free."

Geller tried not to laugh. One of the world's wealthiest men was calling asking if a meeting fit into his schedule.

"We might have a couple bean burritos in the freezer. Oh, I'll bet you meant go *out*."

Lyle chuckled. "My car will be there in ten minutes."

It was. Geller had his jacket on, looking out the window when a black Mercedes sedan pulled up in front of the house. Baz and Lucia were across town, having dinner on their own with Lucia's family so the house was unusually quiet. He killed the lights, ran down the steps and climbed in the back seat of the Mercedes, where Lyle was waiting.

They went to Elysium, an upscale place Geller had only heard about. A few people seemed to recognize Lyle, but he paid them no mind. Geller wore a sport coat and a dress shirt, but still felt underdressed. Lyle ordered a bottle of wine without consulting the list and made small talk while they waited for it to arrive. He approved of the wine once proffered and ordered for Geller, who was okay with that. After they ordered, Lyle took a sip of wine and smiled.

"I figure you know why we're here, Dr. Geller."

"Is it the consolation prize? Lemme guess—a box of Omaha Steaks."

He smiled. "You were … impressive the other day."

"I thought it went well. You might as well call me Brent, by the way."

"Lyle."

"Cool."

"So why do you do what you do?"

"What? Research?"

"*This* research."

Geller paused. "I guess I want to help people."

"Is that right?" He was skeptical.

"Yeah."

"I've noticed how you look at people. How you talk to them. They're cattle. Tell me I'm wrong."

Geller cocked an eyebrow. "I don't think that's quite—"

"I think it's pure ego. I think what you want more than anything is for the world to acknowledge your genius. To celebrate you. On fourth and long, and you want the ball."

Again, Geller paused. Lyle sort of had his number, and that was weird. "Would that disqualify me?"

"Only if you didn't admit it. In a way, it makes me that much more confident about you. I don't think you'd risk being wrong."

"Alright."

"If you pull this off, it will change everything. You,

me, the world, the economy, life expectancies. You realize that, of course."

Geller shrugged. "I don't think about it that way."

Lyle sighed. "I'm trying to convince myself that doing good for the wrong reasons is still doing good. I'm sort of a bleeding heart."

"I'm not interested in the money, if that's what you mean. Not for myself, at least."

"No one's interested in money. They're interested in what they can *do* with it."

"What I want to do will take lots of money."

"Why would you want more people, living longer? We already have overpopulation problems."

"It's the challenge. Something to match wits with. Human suffering is a clever opponent."

"Ah, now we're getting down to it. And what if you run out of those? Clever opponents, I mean."

"Maybe I'd learn how to fly fish."

Lyle smirked and took an experienced sip of his wine, let it tumble over his palate, and leaned over the table.

"You scare me, Brent. The people in the room with you last week are some of the world's best minds. You're so goddamned far ahead of your time here that I'm not sure anyone knows what questions are the right ones. Which angles are left to consider. They'd never admit it, but they barely knew what to tell me about what you had to say."

"Meaning?"

"Meaning I don't think you have many peers. If any. So either we wait until the world catches up with your mind so we can ask the right questions, or—"

"—or you give me the keys to a billion-dollar car. I get it. I'm a risk."

"It's not that. A billion is a lot of money, but as far as the foundation goes it's not betting the farm. Plus, if you do anything remotely interesting we'll make it back pretty quickly."

"So what's the problem?"

"You don't care about fame or money, you don't care about people, and I don't think you care about doing something good for humanity. I'm trying to understand what you *do* care about."

Geller didn't get intimidated, and he started to feel that this was Lyle's goal. He'd had enough.

"I care about being right."

"Now that I believe."

"You don't need anyone to ask the right questions, Lyle, because I've already asked them. If you want to keep auditioning wannabes for the next 10 years, go right ahead. I'm moving forward either way. And when I do what I know I'm going to do, we'll prove each other right and all this hemming and hawing will seem funny."

Lyle studied him for a long few seconds, during which Geller just stared right back.

"This is going to be your legacy, one way or another. After this, nothing else you do will matter."

"I'm good with that."

"Okay, then." He raised his glass. "To the Cure."

Geller raised his as well. "To the Cure."

11

The Billion Dollar Man

Dr. Brent Geller beat out thousands of the world's best scientists to win the $1B Merriweather Prize. Now what?

by Marcus Olivetti

(from *Time*, Oct. 18, 2022)

Brent Geller has a headache. He doesn't have any remedy and doesn't ask for any, but our photographer for the day, a freelancer named Dave, offers him a couple ibuprofen. Dr. Geller—Brent, as he prefers to be called—takes them without water (or thanks) and tries to focus on my questions. Less than a week after being announced the winner of the $1 billion Merriweather Prize, by far the largest and most ambitious reward in history for scientific innovation, he is playing the part of put-upon celebrity with aplomb.

The oldest of two children (his sister, Jennifer, died of complications from Down syndrome at 17), Geller was born to Julianne and Arthur Geller, owners of one of the last small-town pharmacies in Ohio. He showed an early interest in science, preferring his father's plastic molecule sets to toy cars or video games. At his seventh birthday party, he entertained friends by demonstrating the leidenfrost effect—a phenomenon where droplets of water in contact with a smooth, very hot surface dance around on it without evaporating. In the process he warped his mother's favorite steel mixing bowl. Emboldened by their wide-eyed reaction, he made a vinegar/baking soda rocket out of an empty 2-liter bottle and sent it flying almost a hundred feet into the neighbor's yard.

"It should've gone twice as far, but it was a rush job," he recalls with a rare smile. "I had people to impress."

He finished high school by age 15, college by 18 and completed his MD and PhD—simultaneously—in four years. His most recent post-doctoral supervisor at the University of Wisconsin, Dr. Horst Biermann, says Geller's mind doesn't work the way the rest of ours do.

"The scientific method is hypothesize, test, evaluate, repeat. Over time, you get closer to the answer by finding what doesn't work, like throwing darts and getting closer to the bullseye each time," Biermann said. "Brent has a way of hitting that bullseye on the first or second dart, every time. I've never seen anything like it. It's almost prescient."

That prescience led Geller and his research partner, Dr. Basilio Montes, to develop a gene-therapy cocktail of sorts that could treat nearly three dozen diseases with genetic triggers all at once, including several cancers with genetic markers. They just call it the Cure.

"To this point, gene therapies have been a bit like time travel—anything you change has unpredictable repercussions in the future," Montes explained. "Brent thought it might be possible to engineer those future repercussions to only be beneficial, like a desirable side effect."

Traditional gene therapies are reactive, using modified viruses called vectors to deliver new genetic instructions to defective cells. The cells can be instructed to do any number of things, from manufacturing a specific protein to block or encourage certain genetic pathways in the body, or hosting the vector while it makes copies of itself (which is what viruses do). The problem is that the problem cells are constantly dying off or multiplying. Regular treatments are required in perpetuity for the treatment to have any positive effect, if it works at all.

The Cure simplifies matters by proactively replacing all the genes tied to specific disorders, whether the flaw is present or not. If the gene was fine to begin with, then the DNA is essentially unchanged. If not, it's fixed.

For the genes to stay fixed, they need to be replaced while there are a small number of undifferentiated cells. There lies the rub of this already controversial treatment: It can only be delivered in vitro.

"No expectant mother can be dismissive about this," Geller says. "If they carry the gene for a particular disorder, they can guarantee their child, their grandchildren, and on down the line won't. This is their gift to the future."

Preventive gene therapy has never had an ally in the FDA. Even the scientific community has approached it with kid gloves because of the moral and ethical questions of "playing God." But if what Geller says is true, it may be the only way to do it right.

He adds that we've known for years—decades, in some cases—the genes that cause specific disorders.

"If we can fix those broken genes at the earliest stages of development, then only healthy genes are passed on," he says. "If we have the technology to change that—and we do—why wouldn't we?"

Geller's ambition is to equip an entire generation with flawless genes, heading off debilitating and fatal genetic disorders just as life begins and essentially freeing future generations from them. Mutations in those or other genes can still occur, for environmental and other reasons but he believes that by then, instances of the disorder in question would be extremely rare. Lou Gehrig's? Gone. Parkinson's? History. Huntington's?

Buh-bye. All together, the Cure would theoretically eliminate 34 diseases with clear genetic links from the American gene pool.

"We still don't know exactly how many genes are in humans, but we're close. It's around 25,000. We're looking to replace a few dozen that tend to cause trouble, and leave the rest," he says, making it sound both simple and obvious.

As details of the Cure and the Merriweather Prize have been splashed all over the web, religious groups worldwide have lined up to denounce it. Father Guiseppe Alarcon, a spokesperson for the Vatican, issued a statement on behalf of Pope Leo IX that read, in part, "We are gravely concerned about the moral and ethical implications of this treatment, which may interfere with God's Law. As has always been the case, we should be very wary of 'miracle' drugs."

But Geller's supporters happen to include President McMillian, who, ironically, is a devout Catholic. His closed-door meeting with Geller days after the announcement was followed by a brief grip-and-grin outside the oval office, during which he told reporters, "My grandmother always told me, 'An ounce of prevention is worth a pound of cure.' I believe that Dr. Geller's research has the potential to keep millions of Americans safe and healthy, and I look forward to seeing the fruits of his labor."

The implications of White House support are far-reaching. McMillan may be religious, but he's no fool; an FDA-approved treatment of this magnitude and scope could be just the sort of catalyst the long-suffering economy needs. Even though Geller has promised that The Cure will be free (more on that in a moment), the thought of an entire generation of healthy citizens begetting another would be tantalizing to any head of state, especially one riding the caboose on the recession train. Not only could they work harder and longer than an untreated generation, but they would be much less of a drain on the healthcare system and so would their children—at least in theory.

Interestingly, the religious right's moral issues with the Cure may be a much easier hurdle to clear than its planned price tag: free. The healthcare industry finds itself in the position of having to applaud the development publicly while shareholders of Big Pharma wring their hands.

"Sick people have always been good business," says economist Walter Horvath, a senior fellow at the Lewiston Institute, a Washington, D.C. think tank focused on the healthcare industry. "But the drugs they need are even better business. This is a game-changer, and the industry knows it."

Big Pharma depends on many of the diseases Geller's magic cocktail cures, especially considering the hefty price tag commanded by things like chemotherapy drugs. But when it comes to eliminating competitive threats, Horvath says they hold two aces: time and money

"First off, there are a lot of ifs. If the Cure gets FDA approval, and if it gets administered widely, and if it works the way it's supposed to, then pharmaceutical companies might have a real problem on their hands. But all that is going to take time, and you'd better believe they're going to try and figure out their own thing. If they don't or can't, they might come to Brent Geller with enough money to make $1 billion look like chump change."

But if what Dr. Geller says is true, he doesn't care about the money. And if time is money, he doesn't care about that much either.

"Edward Jenner gave the world the smallpox vaccine and he was hailed as a great humanitarian," Geller says. "Someone does that today and people think, 'What's the catch?' 'What angle is he working?' We've gotten very cynical that way. There is no catch, and there is no angle. This is the battle I was born to fight, and I feel uniquely qualified to fight it."

12

D
r. Biermann, principal investigator on Baz and Geller's grant, threw the two of them a party before they left. At that point, it was hard for him to get too worked up about the extent to which they'd taken advantage of his hands-off approach, because they'd tested and improved upon an effective gene therapy for liver cancer. All he knew besides that was that Geller had won the Merriweather Prize, and that it probably was because of work they'd done right under his nose. But issues of intellectual property could be debated later; it was time to eat schnitzel. And so they did. Baz considered himself a vegetarian but obliged Biermann with a small piece of the breaded pork. Geller's ratio of hefeweizen to schnitzel was about 4:1, which was just as well since Baz was driving.

· · ·

THE NEXT SEVERAL months were exciting and stressful. Lyle appointed a board to oversee the Merriweather Development Corporation, whose charge it was to build the literal and logistical foundations for what would eventually become their base of operations. They purchased 500 wooded acres in a remote part of Colorado, which had offered substantial tax breaks in addition to privacy and beauty.

Baz took great interest in this end of the planning, sitting in on board meetings and videoconferences and proving himself to be a savvy and enthusiastic administrator. Geller had some clear ideas about the lab spaces themselves and some interesting opinions about the overall architecture, but for the most part he remained in the background. It was an awkward and frustrating period for Geller, who was nearly mad with boredom. He no longer had the free reign he enjoyed under Biermann and had signed agreements with Merriweather's people saying he would suspend all work on the treatment, so mostly he read, wrote, and filled notebooks full of formulas and ideas for whatever might come next from a dingy temporary office at the University of Colorado-Boulder. Faculty regarded him with curiosity and awe until they met him, after which they gave him a wide berth.

During this time, a strange partnership developed between Geller and Merriweather. It wasn't anything like what he'd had with his old college mentor Jim

Robb; it was more like a mutual fascination. Merriweather understood very well who and what Geller was but believed in him anyway. His fundamental goodness could be important in the times to come, and Geller knew it. They did a press tour, spending the better part of a week together in New York doing talk shows and late-night TV, and another few days in LA doing the same.

Merriweather didn't care for the spotlight but was always ready with a sound bite or two. Geller, by contrast, came off as every bit the cynical, egomaniacal scientific genius he was. The Robert Ripley/World's Smartest Man dynamic played well on TV. Still, Geller grew tired of explaining the how and why of his work, and the ways in which it would change the world. He wanted to get going.

Baz and Geller were rarely together while their facility and staff were built. They communicated occasionally via video, with Geller deferring to Baz about any decisions he considered boring. He and Lucia had married just a few months into the process and went on their honeymoon as planned even though it put everything else on hold. When Geller's phone finally rang, it was the Kyra Broyles Show back in New York. With nearly 10 million regular viewers, mostly women, Geller couldn't afford to blow it off.

Around the time Baz was due back at the construction site, Geller was on his way to join Merriweather in

New York. Though they were years away from having a treatment that ordinary people could get, Merriweather felt it was important to get women on their bus because it could grease the skids for FDA approval. Geller felt like he was constantly defending the science, which was silly since only a handful of people in the world truly understood it. Lyle did most of the talking.

The studio was on West 57th, on the 22nd floor of Hearst Tower. Geller got in the makeup chair for a few minutes, and sat in the green room for almost an hour before Lyle finally showed up with maybe ten minutes to spare. The producer, Gwen, was so apoplectic by then that Lyle's arrival didn't calm her at all. He offered no explanation for being late. The same makeup person who worked on Geller entered in a huff with a small pouch and pointed to one of the vanities.

"Sit."

Lyle flashed a look at Geller, who shrugged and obliged the young girl who tried to eliminate the shine on his bald head, checking the clock over the door every ten seconds. It was 4:57.

"What're we talking about again?" Lyle asked.

"Construction progress, I'd imagine," Geller replied. "Maybe the studio audience can help us pick out window treatments."

"Business, me—science, you."

"I know the drill."

The makeup girl sighed and gave Lyle's forehead a

final dab of powder, undid the collar protector, and expertly restored his tie to its original position. She looked defeated.

"That's as good as you're going to get."

"I look twenty years younger. Thank you," Lyle said, and handed her a folded $100. "I'm sorry I stressed you out."

Geller watched this with great interest, then wondered if he would do the same when he was a billionaire. He doubted it.

The girl considered it for a moment, then shoved the money in her pocket moments before Gwen barreled through the door and held it open.

"Sixty seconds, guys. Time to move," she said.

Lyle rose, smoothed his jacket, and moved into the doorway as Gwen took off in a huff down the hallway. She was waiting for them when they arrived, glaring at them as though they'd stopped off for a sandwich. She put a finger to her lips and opened the studio door and ushered them toward another producer, who led them to the side of a large set piece crisscrossed with runs of electrical conduit. They could sense the studio audience and heard the applause when Kyra introduced them. The producer gestured toward the opening and they walked in.

The interview went as most did—a recap of who they were and why they were there, followed by a summary of what was going on now. As usual, Lyle did most of the talking. He was charming and authoritative, two of the many traits that made him a good leader. After a commercial break, however, the conversation turned toward the science. Geller talked generally about what their treatment would and wouldn't do, and then Kyra said:

"Dr. Geller, there are growing concerns in the religious and medical communities about an in-vitro gene therapy. Some religious leaders believe you're playing God, while there are medical researchers who believe your plan is too ambitious to work. What do you say to your critics?"

In the chair next to him, Lyle sucked in some breath and shifted in his seat.

"Well, Kyra, religious leaders like to tell their feeble-minded followers what they can't or shouldn't do, and my colleagues in medicine who fret over ambition either have none themselves or haven't bothered to read our research."

Kyra's eyes glinted in the studio lights as she leaned in.

"I'm sorry—did you say that people of faith are feeble-minded?"

"They prefer believing to knowing, so draw your own conclusions. Frankly, I don't know why they have a voice in this discussion. If you want to talk morality, then how about the morality of letting preventable diseases continue to exist?"

"So what about the medical community?"

"Most science takes baby steps. This is like the long jump. Not many of them can get their heads around it. It's fine to be skeptical if you know what you're looking at, but otherwise …"

He trailed off, followed by a pregnant silence.

"Kyra, we are so excited to talk about the facility we're building in Colorado," Lyle said.

Geller rolled his eyes and leaned back. Kyra took Lyle's cue and launched into questions about the facility, though she frequently looked past him at Geller, who no longer appeared to be listening.

After a while they concluded the interview and a production assistant removed their lapel mics. The same producer that rushed them out of the green room ushered them back out the studio door. Lyle thanked her, and the door auto-closed shut.

"What the *fuck*, Brent?!" Lyle hissed. Geller had never heard him swear.

"I forgot I'm supposed to be a set piece."

"She baited you and you took it."

"It was good TV. That's all these morons care about."

Lyle whirled suddenly, planted his big hand in the middle of Geller's chest and shoved him hard against the wall, like a senior to a freshman. Geller was stunned. Lyle leaned in close, his breath redolent of the pastrami sandwich he had at lunch.

"I know what you are, Brent. I've known since the first time we met. You're not the kind of man I would associate with unless I thought you were the only one— the *only fucking one*—who I thought was the real deal. Don't make me regret that any more than I already do."

Geller reached into his pocket, smirking, and proffered a stick of peppermint gum.

"Seriously," he said.

Lyle eased back on his hand and straightened his suit coat. He stared at Geller for a few moments, shook his head, and strode, fuming, down the hall. Geller popped the gum in his mouth.

13

The Geller Institute for Genetics, or GIG, opened its doors two years after the official awarding of the Merriweather Prize. Private investors footed the bill for the massive, state-of-the-art facility in the mountains west of Denver, which left Geller pretty much the full $1 billion (plus interest) to fill it with equipment, lab assistants, and a small army of lobbyists and lawyers whose only job was to lay the tracks that led to FDA approval. But once the dust settled, Geller's peers had become very doubtful of his success. Investors were still bullish on the whole thing, but to the larger scientific community it still seemed like science fiction. The net result was that Geller didn't have many people on his side who weren't on the payroll.

That was just fine with him. His team was small and

connected—mostly people he knew from earlier in his career. There was Baz, of course, and Biermann left UW to oversee lab operations. As a nod to Lyle, he even hired Kihn and Alward—the two geneticists on the prize panel. The long-term challenge would be to synthesize the Cure so it could be produced at scale. To that end, he'd hired a Dr. Li-Xiong Xu, who oversaw the production and distribution of the H1N1 vaccine in the 2000s.

Preclinical trials on animals tested the toxicity of the synthetic protein mixture Baz devised to carry the viral vectors. But the need for in-vitro delivery meant that Phase 1 trials had to use live embryos. Geller knew from stem-cell studies that his treatment would only be effective on embryos aged 60-90 days. There wasn't a huge population of mothers-to-be with family histories of genetic disorders willing to endure nine microinjections into their marble-sized unborn children when it would take years to know if it was safe. Geller's team found just 17 in the first year, and they didn't come cheap.

Phase II trials couldn't begin until they showed the FDA that the initial test group hadn't been harmed, cognitively or functionally, by the treatment. Phase 2 would have a much larger test group, and from there into phases 3 and 4, the number of subjects would continue to grow along with length of time between follow-ups. In all, Geller anticipated that full FDA approval of the Cure would take 8–10 years. That was a long time, but not nearly as long as if each of its 34 elements had been developed and tested separately.

The first person to receive the Cure was a young Hispanic woman named Veronica Veracruz, or Vivi. She'd literally been in the stirrups at an abortion clinic when her doctor mentioned the GIG trial and the six-figure stipend they were offering. It troubled Geller that her interest in the trial was purely financial, and that the chance to make history held no meaning for her. But she fit the profile of a young, healthy mother with at least one genetic Trojan horse: Tay-Sachs, a rare disorder that usually results in death by age four or younger and was addressed by the Cure.

A series of robotically guided microinjections were necessary because the embryo was too small for anything else. That was fine, because Geller had figured out that breaking the treatment up into parts and delivering it in a particular order would actually be more effective. Some of the injections went right into the embryo itself while others went into the umbilicus. The procedure had been practiced hundreds of times by Geller's surgical team, mostly on chimps, so everyone was happy but not surprised when Vivi's treatment went flawlessly. Over the next few months, 15 others received it; one freaked out at the last second and changed her mind on the table. It was a very exciting time at GIG, but it didn't take long for everyone to realize that, at least when it came to the

Cure, there wasn't much for any of them to do but
wait

PHASE 2 TRIALS began the following year on the heels
of Phase 1's unequivocal success. Vivi's son, Perfecto,
was a healthy 10-year-old who joined his Phase 1 cohort
(6 other boys, 9 girls) on the cover of TIME ("The
Cure: 10 Years Later"), smiling and fairly glowing with
youth, as a follow-up to its first article about Geller.
GIG's PR department had planned it that way to rein-
force the safety of the treatment. DNA tests, the results
of which were published with the article, confirmed the
absence of recessive or dominant disease genes. Any
random sample of 16 10-year-olds probably would have
shown the same thing, but just the fact that they were
all healthy was enough to silence many of Geller's
former critics.

The same couldn't be said about Vivi, who died of a
heroin overdose when Perfecto was only two. He
became a ward of the state for about three months,
before being adopted by Baz and Lucia. They were
unable to have children of their own.

Geller was 37 and firing on all cylinders. Their FDA
fast-track plan was working. The Phase 2 trial would
expand to nearly 200, and thanks to all the publicity
about the 10-year anniversary, there was all kinds of
pressure to make the Cure available to the public.

However, the economy was still foundering. Joblessness and political instability at home combined with unprecedented unrest in Europe and Southeast Asia to create a global mess. China and the US were the only superpowers left standing.

While Phase 2 continued, GIG churned out hundreds of patents, on everything from new lab equipment to food additives that sped the absorption of minerals by dairy cows. Geller kept his inner circle tight and hired many of the world's best scientific minds away from other places. GIG was slated to have 13 regional clinics, spread around the country in order to make the Cure easy to get.

Geller kept mostly to himself. Baz was usually the top executive at any company function, or if Geller showed up it would be for an awkward couple of attaboys before disappearing back into the lab. Some days he would hike up the ridge behind the building and not return for hours. He'd been inscrutable and odd since anyone could recall, so no one thought much of it. Mostly he left everyone to do their job, and no one had much of a problem with that.

President Art Dixon was re-elected to a second term in 2036 by the narrowest of margins—a fortunate outcome, considering his support of the sciences. GIG was both a productive startup and a research center, garnering support across the political spectrum. Geller's notoriety ebbed and flowed, more or less in step with

GIG's. His intuition about new models and ways of thinking was undimmed by time. He already had started planning future embellishments to the Cure that included more forms of cancer and rarer genetic diseases like the blood disorder porphyria and the enzyme disorder phenylketonuria. Each enhancement added several orders of complexity to how the treatment was designed and delivered, but considering how long it would be before any of it came to pass, he figured he had time to sort it out. He held enough patents by then that he didn't have to worry about money, either.

Perfecto and his fellow test subjects were regular visitors to GIG. The general health of the volunteers was of great concern to GIG, so it was part of the deal. Of course, most of the blood tests and scans wouldn't have been standard procedure for a hometown clinic, but parents didn't seem to mind. Everyone really was quite healthy, and any lingering fears they had about the Cure's safety had ebbed.

Late that summer, a former professor of Geller's named Jim Robb called. They hadn't spoken in years, so he favored Geller with news of his undergrad alma mater, Laird College. Once the small talk petered out, Robb revealed his real reason for calling, which was to invite Geller to the grand opening of the new science building he'd contributed the final $20 million to build. Appropriately, it was being named Geller Hall.

To Robb's surprise, he agreed without hesitation.

14

Professor Robb was the reason Geller chose Laird, a tiny liberal-arts college on Michigan's beautiful western shore, over the many Harvards and Princetons that offered him everything. For those scientists and donors who had followed his career and wooed him to attend their institutions, it came as quite a shock. There was no legacy connection to the college, which was better known for its chamber choir than for the sciences. But anyone who knew about Geller would have understood why Professor Robb succeeded in recruiting him where so many others did not: He appealed to his ego.

In an e-mail to Geller, Robb explained he had a problem. A species of Costa Rican frog he'd studied for years was dying out because of diminished reproductive success. He'd eliminated environmental factors such as pesticides, yet smaller and smaller numbers of eggs were hatching. He hoped Geller might have a theory why, and whether anything could be done about it. There was no mention about visiting Laird, scholarships, student life or the usual pablum—just a small-town PhD with a problem he couldn't solve.

Geller responded to that on two levels: One, he had done extensive, graduate-level work on frog reproduction as part of an 8th-grade science project. Two, he knew and admired Robb's work. In a sense, their relationship already felt collegial. Everyone else's pitch was based on what great minds he could learn from, and all the dazzling things *they* would help *him* do. But even at 14, Geller knew he needed people smart enough to get out of his way. It didn't matter where he did his undergrad—he'd only be there a couple years anyway. A tenured, widely published expert asked a kid prodigy for advice on a real-world problem. That was good enough for him.

Within a month of matriculating, Geller accompanied Robb to Costa Rica to spend two weeks in the rainforest studying the frogs. Three days in, Geller identified a mutation that made their eggs' outer walls slightly too thick for most tadpoles to break through, or for the water to break them down in time. He designed a cross-breeding program to slowly eliminate the mutation from the gene pool, ultimately sharing authorship of the resulting paper with Robb, who got a big NSF grant out of the bargain.

Geller left Laird with a BS two years later and started grad school at the University of Wisconsin immediately afterward. Robb sent him a note of congratulations after the Merriweather announcement, which Geller didn't see because he never read his e-mail. Other than that they hadn't been in touch for about 17 years, so Robb was a little surprised when Geller accepted his invitation to attend the grand opening and contribute to the time capsule.

The college spent the next few months figuring out how to get their wealthiest and most reclusive alumnus back to campus. Geller's check for $45 million was an ordinary bank note that came in the mail by itself, with "science building" typed in the memo line. An awkward series of phone calls, letters and emails between the college and Geller's administrative assistant followed, during which they only learned that Geller was "fine" with having his name on the building if that's what they wanted. He didn't attend the groundbreaking ceremony, so Robb's successful efforts to land Geller made him something of a hero; his sabbatical request for the spring semester was granted without hesitation.

Robb, along with Laird President Ryan Humphries, met Geller's jet at the airport. For all his faults, Geller was still as unpretentious as they came; he emerged wearing faded Bermuda shorts and a plain T-shirt. Robb warned President Humphries to expect as much, and couldn't help but smile a little at knowing he still knew a thing or two about the inscrutable Brent Geller.

Mrs. Humphries prepared a gourmet feast at the president's house for the four of them, plus select members of the board and three science professors emeriti. After a few glasses of cabernet, Geller was downright garrulous, even to the point of sounding interested in the long-retired professors' accounts of their own research, and what they could have done with more funding, and the Internet, and so on. He endured the trustees' faked understanding of his work, and even shared stories from his and Robb's exploits in Costa Rica. Eventually the evening wound down and everyone departed except Geller himself, who tipsily accepted Humphries' invitation to stay in the attached guest house for the night. Arrangements were made for the ceremony the next evening.

THE FOLLOWING day was busy for everyone. Geller ate breakfast with a long tableful of community leaders, then visited a few science classes, from a freshmen chemistry class to a senior seminar in holographic inter-ferometry. In each instance, he spoke little and dove into whatever projects were underway. He easily summoned chemical and biological formulas and tech-niques he hadn't personally used in 20 years.

The previous evening, Geller learned that a student with a similar academic pedigree to his was enrolled at Laird that year. Erik Heiser was a third-generation student at Laird and never really considered going anywhere else, though, like Geller, he could've gone anywhere. He was doing some surprisingly advanced work with tissue regeneration in cardiac muscle, and Robb arranged for Geller's day to end with Heiser presenting some of his research 1:1 to Geller.

Robb suspected that Geller was hard to impress, and he was right about that, but Erik captivated him. After introducing his work and answering a few probing questions from Geller, he stepped up to a smartboard and started scrawling his latest growth-factor findings, unaided by notes. Robb watched, fascinated by both Erik's erudition and Geller's visible appreciation as he silently judged the kid's methodology. They'd budgeted two hours for Geller to meet with Erik, shower and change before the gala, but in the end he had to cut them off just 20 minutes short of the opening remarks.

Geller Hall was a big coup for the institution, which hadn't seen an all-new construction on its small campus since 1978. A centerpiece of its glass-and-metal design was a cavernous front lobby, featuring a 100-foot tall rotunda with a seamless glass hemisphere at the top. During the day, the photochromic glass ceiling acted like a sunglass lens to help regulate the temperature inside. At night, the same panels rendered the night sky over Laird in real time, clouds be damned, so students could relax or study in the atrium with a sense of awe and wonder. A circular infinity pool at the floor level perfectly reflected the image overhead, so someone leaning over the railing on one of the three classroom floors could still enjoy the view. For this occasion, most of Laird's 2,000 students and half the community had crammed themselves into the atrium. Many—students, especially—were there just to catch a glimpse of their most famous alumnus.

The cornerstone had been laid nearly two years before, so the time capsule would be sealed inside a giant black monolith behind the reflecting pool that recognized the building's major donors. The monolith was a nod to Stanley Kubrick's *2001: A Space Odyssey*, which complemented the astronomy-heavy entrance. An assortment of students, faculty and staff members, community members and schoolchildren had been selected to contribute an item to the capsule, along with Geller and a few other major contributors. No one, including Robb, had any idea what Geller was going to put into it.

After the hors d'oeuvres and champagne, it was time for the remarks to begin. Humphries gave the opening welcome and invocation, then asked the newly appointed dean of faculty to introduce the time-capsule contributors. Each explained what science meant to them, then explained how their items related to science and the times. They included the remains of an inciner-ated model rocket, a compass, and a jar once used to catch fireflies before they went extinct. As the final speaker of the evening, Geller was met with a seemingly endless chorus of applause that filled the atrium like thunder. He carried a small plastic bag onto the dais and set it down behind the podium, and began:

"Thank you, President Humphries, Dean Whelden and distinguished guests. I know you all are anxious to take your first tour of this amazing building, and maybe to get some fresh air, so I'll keep my remarks brief. Before I begin, however, I'd like to quickly address some of the rumors you may have heard about me.

"For those of you who don't know who I am, I won a little science contest a few years ago."

Appreciative, enthusiastic applause filled the atrium. Geller let it wash over him, then continued.

"Second of all, I don't save jars of my own urine in a secret underground bunker."

Polite laughter.

"The truth is, I prefer unbreakable plastic bottles, and I keep them in my living room for all to see."

Raucous laughter. Robb glanced over at Erik, who was rapt.

"The third and most insidious rumor about me is that I haven't been to the Laird campus since I gradu-ated those many years ago. That's not true. A few days after I won a billion dollars, President Jesseps kidnapped me and fed me the veggie burgers from Northrup Commons until I gave my address to the alumni office."

Again, the audience was charmed by their mysterious benefactor, most of whom were in disbelief that he seemed like just a regular guy.

"In all seriousness, I see this beautiful new building as sort of a monument to higher thought, particularly in the area of science. Obviously, that's very close to my heart. Please, indulge me a moment and look up at the canopy of stars overhead."

The lights in the atrium faded. Overhead, the universe itself unfolded in all its brilliance. Geller gave them a moment to appreciate it, and continued in a softer tone befitting the darkness.

"The ocean of stars and distant galaxies you see lie in the vast, unknowable vacuum of space. An incomprehensible abyss without end. Every object you see is receding from us, and each other. Yet there they are, as real to us as anything or anyone.

"Science endeavors to know the unknowable. It stares into that abyss and sees only a question: *Why?* But it does not know the answer. It knows what it knows, and based on that, it guesses.

"Think about that for a moment. Science—the whole of human knowledge about the world in which we live, and nature, and matter, and everything since the dawn of time is at our fingertips, but the best we can ever do when contemplating the endless mysteries of life is to *guess*. We know what we know, but because of that, we also know what we *don't* know, because sometimes we fail. Science, ladies and gentlemen, offers only this.

"But that is its beauty. We know what we don't know, yet we move forward, feeling our way through the long, dark tunnel of discovery. Reaching out into that abyss—that's courage. *Science* is courage. We don't know what will happen, no matter how much confidence we project to the world."

Geller paused for what seemed like a long time. Finally, he reached down and unwrapped the crinkled plastic bag as the lights came back up.

"I thought long and hard about what I was going to put into your time capsule. All they said was that it should be something meaningful and significant to me yet germane to the occasion. The stuff that's gone in so far has been really clever and personal, and I feel like this doesn't measure up, but anyway … Among other things, I'm a geneticist, and one thing we geneticists study are gene pairs. So, I thought it might be fitting to bring one of my own personal gene pairs."

He reached into the bag and removed a faded pair of blue jeans with holes worn through. It took the audience a moment, but finally polite chuckles rippled through them and some soft applause. It wasn't that they didn't get the joke—it was surprise and perhaps a little disappointment that the most celebrated scientific mind of their time didn't come up with something weightier than an old pair of jeans. Sensing this, Geller continued.

"Now hear me out. I bought these jeans my freshman year at Laird, and wore them basically every day. Dr. Robb probably remembers. Well, up until about two days ago they were in the same box I put them in when I moved out of my dorm. Every discovery I've made, every patent I hold, owes a debt to these old jeans. But that isn't the point.

"The point is, these are who I am. I am not this sport coat, or this expensive building, or whatever notoriety I have. I'm a ridiculously comfortable pair of jeans, and a lab, and fluorescent lights, and Chinese takeout. We all have something like this in our life. Whatever it is, my advice is that you hold onto it. Don't forget who you are, and never apologize for it. Thank you again for the honor of helping bring this amazing building to Laird, and thank you to all—well, most—of my former professors, especially Professor Robb, for never asking me to be anything other than what I am."

Geller received appreciative applause as he carefully rolled up the old jeans and placed them into the oblong concrete box. President Humphries invited everyone in attendance to check their tickets to see what tour group they were in, and pointed to student tour guides wearing color-coded vests. As they filtered out of the atrium, Robb inched his way toward the dais and found

Geller chatting with a couple donors. They shook his hand and joined a tour group.

"Well?" Geller asked.

"You were … surprising," Robb said. "If I didn't know better, I'd say you enjoyed holding court."

"I rise to the occasion," Geller said. He joined Robb on the floor and they fell in behind their own tour group.

"Listen, Brent, I need to ask you something …"

Robb pulled him out of the hallway and into a small study area, then checked around to make sure no one was in earshot.

"I'm going to be a grandfather."

"That's great, Jim. Congrats."

"The thing is, Hannah carries the gene for ALS."

"You want her treated."

"She's not convinced, but if she agrees, I'd feel better if you were the one to do it."

"Sure. Yeah, whatever you need."

"I believe in what you're doing, and I trust you. I know her risk is low, but she's having my grandchild. I want it to be zero."

"I understand," Geller said.

15

From *The Perfect Generation: A Memoir*
by Dr. Brent A. Geller

I owe a debt to Laird College, even though I'm persona non grata to them. It's the kind of place you don't appreciate or even understand until well after the fact, like grandma's meatloaf or losing your virginity. Much has been made about my relationship with the college over the years, but when I was shopping for colleges at age 15, it wasn't enough to have my ass kissed. Everyone was doing that. But when Jim Robb came to me with an actual, specific problem he thought I might be able to help solve, it intrigued me. I knew I was only going to be there for a couple years while I applied to graduate schools. Plus, they considered undergrad research to be a focus so once I visited and hit it off with Jim, that was that.

We studied frogs in Costa Rica for most of my first year, during which we became pretty close. Jim was working off grants from the Costa Rican government and some international wildlife concerns, and we flew down there often enough for us to figure out why their reproduction rates were dropping—a few weeks each semester. I had never been to Costa Rica and my Spanish was lousy but Jim was like a native. He taught me that science wasn't about labs and white coats—it was about asking the right questions, obsessing about the answers, and getting your hands dirty. And boy, did they get dirty. Frogs, as you know, enjoy areas we consider swampy or mucky. I spent more time in chest waders during that year than I did until I started fly fishing about 40 years later. It was great fun.

In the spring of 2030, Ryan Humphries, president of Laird College, called me to talk about the science building, Erdmann Hall. I remembered it as one of many overbuilt, boxy classroom buildings, and it had been showing its age even when I was there. It was built in the late 1980s, and though it had been well-kept and scrupulously maintained, it had become an eyesore. He candidly admitted that my notoriety as an alumnus would help boost enrollment if they had a new building.

I listened to his pitch about naming opportunities in that kid-gloves way that fund raisers like to talk. I hate phone calls, so I asked him to prepare a proposal and send it to me. Long story short, a $20 million lead gift would get my name on it and they were pretty confident they could raise the other $40 million. Now, I know how this sounds, but at that point in my life I don't know if I would've gotten out of bed for $20 million. I personally held about 60 lucrative patents by then, mostly techniques for protein synthesis that had agricultural and medical applications. The point is, I didn't care if they named it after me or not. I really didn't. In fact, I even asked Humphries if they could name it something awesome like Kickass Hall but he didn't seem amused. I had my admin look over the proposal for anything weird and signed it without reading many of the details.

Laird's campaign was successful and so they built Geller Hall. I kicked in a few million at the end to get some extra bells and whistles, like the cool star thingy in the main atrium, but I asked them not to publicize it. I thought it would be good for the college if it looked like they got a lot for their money.

The grand opening was in 2037. I carved out a couple days to return to Laird and help dedicate the building. It was nostalgic in a way, though I was only there a couple years and spent so much time out of the country that very few people even knew me. The morning of the dedication, Jim took me into the new building, which had been holding classes since the start of the term, and introduced me to a freshman named Erik Heiser. The kid was doing incredibly advanced work, pioneering a way to regrow cardiac muscle over a nanotube substrate. It was a mystery to me why he wasn't at Hopkins or somewhere like that, but I could guess at his reasons, having followed a similar path.

Erik was hungry and smart. He asked good questions and knew what he didn't know. We talked about his work, my work, stuff we were working on at GIG, and the Cure. He was curious about its development, its potential, and its potential complications. By the time Jim practically yanked me out of the lab, there was barely time to throw on a jacket and join the crowd gathered in the atrium.

Jim pulled me aside that night and told me his daughter, Hannah, was pregnant and interested in being part of the trial. I'd met her only once or twice, but she sounded like a pretty good fit. It was clear that Jim wanted this for her, but I never could figure if it was because of what the Cure offered her or because he trusted me. I wanted to think it was a little of both.

It was a classy affair by Laird standards, and the mood was high. It's hard for a small college to start and build momentum compared to bigger institutions, so the whole thing had a great energy. We all said a few words, I cracked a couple jokes, and the honoraries put some knick-knacks in a time capsule. My contribution was a pair of jeans that I actually brought with me from Colorado. I'm not certain that I had them when I was at Laird, but I wore them almost exclusively while we were working on the Cure and never had the heart to get rid of them. What no one knew then, and didn't know until I wrote this, is that the pockets weren't entirely empty.

16

Baz and Lucia surprised their adopted son, Perfecto, on his 25th birthday with a 14-day cruise around the Mediterranean for him and his fiancé, Sophie. They not-secretly wanted to come along, but didn't press the issue. He carried all their hopes for grandchildren, so he delighted in teasing them with scant or misleading information about their wedding date.

The Cure (formally the multivector in-vitro selective gene replacement battery) received FDA approval in 2032, 18 years before Perfecto and Sophie were clinking glasses off Malta. Nearly 22 million mothers would eventually received the in-vitro treatment by then which, true to Geller's original plan, was completely free. It had attained nearly mythical status, perceived by many to be a bulwark against <u>all</u> disease, which wasn't true. That didn't stop the tidal wave of interest from expectant mothers, many of whom had been hearing about the Cure since their formative years.

By the time Phase 3 trials were completed, none of the 1,300 kids they'd treated had developed any of the 34 specific conditions it was designed to prevent. The numbers were pretty compelling, considering their risk factors. Some of Geller's "desirable side effects" were also evident: Clear skin, bright eyes, great teeth and above-average intelligence and physical stamina were pretty much the norm, so when a writer for *The Atlantic* dubbed them "The Perfect Generation," it stuck.

GIG's 13 regional facilities treated an uninterrupted stream of expectant mothers. By then, they had expanded the treatment window by 30 days, from 60–90 to 30–90. As a result, many women who thought they might be pregnant just went straight to a GIG center to be tested and, if the test was positive, received the treatment immediately.

The program had plenty of detractors. Scientists in the newly reconfigured Soviet Union routinely used genetic manipulation to "design" children for wealthy couples, a shady practice often conflated with the Cure. Religious groups continued to decry it as playing God, and the medical community was split on whether the benefits outweighed the risks. But it was hard for anyone to argue with the results. The Perfect Generation, by many objective measures, was.

Two days before Perfecto and Sophie were flying back to Denver, Baz received a panicked phone call from Sophie. She said Perfecto had taken suddenly and violently ill on their cruise, and that the ship made an unscheduled port stop in Barcelona to get him into an ICU.

Baz immediately arranged a flight to Barcelona, but on his way to the airport less than an hour later, Sophie called back to say he was dead.

THE NEXT DAY, Baz met with with Perfecto's doctor, a thickly accented woman named Velasquez, at Hospital de Sant Pau in Barcelona. Between the long flight and the suddenness of what happened, none of it felt real. During the flight, Baz had time to contemplate the lie he told Lucia about the reason for his trip. Perfecto acquired some strange bug acquired during the cruise and was in the hospital, he'd said, but he couldn't say the rest. Not until he knew what happened.

"What do you know?" he asked.

"His liver and kidneys shut down first, then his lungs filled with blood. It all happened at once. Any family history of disease?"

"Nothing like this. In fact … he was the first child in the world to receive the Cure."

Baz gave her a moment to understand that the man

in her hospital was *that* Perfecto Montes, the one she'd read about in medical school.

"I see. Well, again, we don't know much right now. The cruise line is aware of the situation, but they've been advised that a pathogen probably wasn't responsible. I was told that no other passengers have taken ill. Still, we're taking every precaution. The CDC is here."

"I'd like to see him."

"Of course."

He wasn't as confident as Dr. Velasquez about a pathogen. What she described was eerily similar to Ebola. He wondered about an engineered virus or a new strain as they exited an elevator on the 5th floor. Almost immediately, he recognized Dr. Cassidy "Dee" Harding, a senior director at the CDC he knew well. Her presence spoke volumes.

"Dee."

"Baz, I'm so sorry," she said, her voice heavy.

They embraced warmly.

"Walk with me."

He followed her down a hallway toward a set of double doors.

"His room is BSL-2 until we know what we're dealing with. You can see him, but you're going to have to suit up."

"BSL-2? Dr. Velasquez seemed pretty sure it wasn't a bug."

"I don't think it is. But until we're 100 percent certain, we're being safe."

"Where's Sophie?"

"The fiancé? We took her to a hotel and gave her some Ambien. She's been through the ringer."

A few minutes later, they entered the quarantine area. Baz suited up and followed Dee into the safety zone.

A couple lab workers huddled over Perfecto, taking additional samples from his arm. His skin was Kabuki white. Thin rivulets of blood were dried and black around his nose, eyes and ears. Only the small mole under his left eye betrayed that it was him, a vigorous young man who had just turned 25 a couple weeks back. The lab workers turned and stared at Baz like he shouldn't be there, but Dee explained who he was. They nodded grimly and put their samples in a box, then filed back out. Perfecto's eyes were pure red and staring at the ceiling.

His hands and elbows were bruised and scratched. He assumed there were others under his gown somewhere. He had convulsed or seized, probably on the ship, and went unconscious. The final moment may have come quickly, but by the looks of it, his last moments were horrifying.

Baz fell to his knees and wept.

17

Geller's phone rang, interrupting his dictation. He saw it was Baz.

"Answer," he said, and the device picked up. "Hey, Lindh is looking for you. Where the hell are you?"

There was a long pause.

"He's dead," Baz said, his voice hoarse and tired. "My boy is dead."

Geller picked up the phone.

"What?! My God, Baz, are you— What happened?"

Baz explained as much as he could bear—the cruise, the presumed stomach bug, the CDC, and all his systems turning to mush while everyone watched, helpless. Dee had been right; there was no pathogen.

Geller's mind raced. If it wasn't a bug, the list of

possibilities was awfully short. He had a theory, but he couldn't share it. Not yet.

"I'm having his body sent back to the States right away," Baz said. "I need you to find out what happened to him, Brent. Please."

He remembered Perfecto as a little boy, coming to GIG with Baz sometimes to hang out at the back of the lab. Lucia stayed at home, so Perfecto liked to get out sometimes to be close to his dad. Baz even had a kid-size lab coat made with "Dr. Montes" embroidered on it, along with the GIG logo. It seemed fitting that the first member of the so-called Perfect Generation was a fixture there. Everyone loved him.

Perfecto remained interested in science, and was about to start his career as an engineer. He came to treat Lyle Merriweather as sort of a great uncle, and became inspired by all the amazing projects the Foundation was supporting. He dreamt of eliminating the need for petrochemicals in building and packaging materials, and was about to apply for his first patent. Now, Geller was being asked to cut him open.

Geller said, "Everything stops until we know. I promise you that."

THE CDC HELPED ARRANGE for the immediate return of Perfecto's body, still under strict quarantine protocols, and Baz accompanied him on the plane. Geller took the

GIG jet to Atlanta and was waiting at the CDC when the van arrived. Baz had gone home to Lucia, a reunion that Geller was glad to miss. No pathogen could have done the kind of damage Baz described, and not just because there were no other cases. He felt it in his gut, an instinct he had long since come to trust.

A Dr. Singh, whom he didn't know, assisted with the autopsy. Geller could tell he didn't appreciate playing assistant, but that wasn't his problem. He advised Singh there was no need to wear a positive-pressure suit, but he did anyway.

Once they got Perfecto uncovered, Geller couldn't believe his eyes. His soft tissue and muscles, which should long since have hardened with rigor, were gelatinous and soft. They pooled beneath his bones in such a way that the entire front of his skeleton was plainly visible through his skin, which looked thin and moist, as though the fat layer beneath had begun to seep through. It was customary to team lift a body from the gurney to the examining table, but their hands slid into Perfecto's skin like a cake. Singh looked up at him in horror.

"Guess we're doing this right here," Geller said, taking up the scalpel.

THE AUTOPSY REVEALED little that a trained eye couldn't see by simply glancing at the body. Perfecto's systems hadn't just failed—they were almost completely dissolved. Dr. Singh's theory was a severe autoimmune disorder, which Geller agreed was a logical guess, but it didn't fit. Nothing worked this fast. Whatever happened was at a microcellular level, and no lab in the world was better equipped for it than GIG. It took serious persuasion and a call to the director of the CDC to let him take tissue and blood samples, which they refused to send until their own analysis proved there was definitely no pathogen.

It took the better part of a week to receive them, during which Geller didn't see Baz at all. He wondered whether he would even want to see his old friend after he knew something conclusive about Perfecto, or if it would be better for Baz to decide he'd rather not know.

With Baz's future in question, Geller needed someone to be his right hand. Erik Heiser, the bright young student he'd met at Laird, had proven himself up to the task. They'd hired him immediately after he finished his PhD at Johns Hopkins, and he'd been there ever since. Geller called him on his way across town and asked him to prep the lab for some tests. Being a Saturday, Erik was at home with his wife, Lucy, and 2-year-old son Lars. He said he'd come in right away.

GIG was fairly deserted on weekends, save for the occasional lab tech or project lead who was either catching up or trying to get ahead of schedule. On this occasion, the labs were completely empty. Geller found Erik in Lab B (microbiology), powering everything on.

"Nope—gen lab," Geller said.

"I thought we were looking for COD."

"We are."

The GIG genetics lab was the most advanced of its kind in the world. Though the mysteries of the human genome were still being unearthed, much of what we knew was the result of work done there.

By the time Erik came in, Geller was already dividing out blood samples for the centrifuge and labeling them. Erik took the tissue samples—heart, lung, liver, kidney, brain—and prepped them for microdissection. They worked in silence. The fact that they were there meant Geller suspected a genetic trigger in Perfecto's death. If there was such a trigger, it might be related to the Cure or it might not. Either scenario was disconcerting, but only one had implications for his young son.

They worked through the night. Most of the tissue was unusable, its cells and genetic material too damaged to analyze. They had to compare the genetic structure of those samples to a sequence from one of Perfecto's original blood and tissue samples, taken as a matter of course with Cure recipients, to know if Geller's theory was correct. Erik returned from a bathroom break to find Geller leaning forward in his chair with his head in his hands.

"What is it?"

Geller didn't respond. Erik got a closer look at the computer screen nearby and instantly understood. Flashing red lines on the display indicated a disparity between the two samples—two, in fact. Two of the genes on Perfecto's chromosomal DNA had switched places. Under normal circumstances that could lead to anything from an increased risk of birth defects in offspring to cancer. In this case, it led to something more insidious.

The Cure's complexity was almost impossible to fathom. There were millions of permutations and scenarios that had to be worked out, replacing troublesome genes with flawless ones, defective or not, should only have been beneficial. To that point, millions of genetically flawless babies had borne out that assumption. But despite all their advances and innovations, there was still plenty that even GIG didn't understand about the human genetic code. It didn't always follow its own rules. In other words, shit happened.

"It's programmed cell death," Geller said as he sat up. "Respiratory system, digestive, the brain stem …"

"Whoa, now slow down. Which genes are we looking at here?"

"It doesn't *matter*, Erik," Geller hissed. "The point is, now they manufacture an enzyme or a protein that destroys the cell wall, and in such quantities that it would be next to impossible to— It might as well be fucking acid."

"But what made them switch positions?"

"Something I didn't … I don't know—an enzyme, a bad pair, a mutation—it seems random. Something tied to physical maturity, maybe."

"It's one patient. We'll figure something out before it happens again. There's time. Geller, this is my *son* we're talking about."

"I know," Geller whispered. "Believe me, I know."

18

There was no sleep for Geller. Erik hit a wall after about 40 straight hours of running protein simulations and went home, vowing to return after a solid night's rest, but Geller kept going. His brain was activated, and there was no deactivating it. Not now.

He didn't know why two of the replaced genes switched positions, or why it had the effect it did, but he'd been right when he told Erik it didn't matter. What mattered now was the question of whether anything could be done.

The human body could spontaneously dismantle a tumor that had resisted all other treatments, or allow the tiniest mole to become a death sentence. It might live through unspeakable trauma but be undone by an infected cut. This nether region between science and "magic" is where Geller liked to operate. Math and chemistry were too black and white for him. What he'd made in the Cure was something like magic, so it was as though he'd been the sole architect of an elaborate illusion, only to learn that it didn't work as intended. Nature, it seemed, also had a trick up its sleeve.

Earlier in the week he received a text from Dr. Lindh about Merriweather, who had suffered a major heart attack. He needed surgery and was recovering from a triple bypass, but it was still touch and go. He said:

Pretty tied up right now. I'll get back to you.

And Lindh said:

He may not have long.

He checked his watch. It was 10:37 a.m. He could pack a bag and be at GIG's own landing strip by 11:30, and in Seattle a couple hours later. He'd be back well before sunrise the next day. On one hand, he didn't want to stop working, but on the other hand it was Lyle. Even Geller couldn't deny his debt to the man. He had to go.

The jet was in the air by 12:15. He poured himself a scotch and closed his eyes.

Turbulence jolted him awake just outside the city.

"Jesus fuck!" he reflexively said.

"Apologies, Dr. Geller," said the captain over the speaker. "That was bumpier than expected."

Fortunately his scotch was long since drained and

the glass picked up by the attendant. A few minutes later they touched down, and a waiting limo whisked him away.

Traffic was horrid, and it was mid afternoon by the time he stepped out in front of St. Ignatius Medical Center. He hated hospitals, even when he was doing his short residency. To him, they were places of bureaucracy, wastefulness, and death. He inquired about Lyle at the front desk and was instructed to go to the 14th floor.

To his surprise, the door to Merriweather's private room was open. Seated next to each other in the corner were his two sons, Avery and Mason, Avery's disappointingly plain wife, Tina (or was it Trina?) and Lindh, who appeared to be on a call. None looked particularly happy to see him. Mason smirked and stuck his open hand in front of Avery, who rolled his eyes and slapped a $20 into it.

"Didn't figure you'd show," Avery said. "Neither did Dad."

Lindh nodded at Geller, then brushed past him into the hall. Geller moved further into the room so he could see past the partition half-pulled around Lyle's bed. He was sitting up, but sedated and on oxygen.

"You came. The boys had a bet. Give us a few minutes?" he croaked through the mask.

His sons looked at each other and shrugged, then

Avery shook his wife awake. She did a small double-take at Geller, stretched, and followed them out the door.

"How you feeling?" Geller asked.

"Weak. Tired. Useless. All of the above."

"What happened? Lindh is being cagey."

"Ticker's not working at capacity. I think it's gone union."

Lyle chuckled at his own joke but it morphed almost instantly into a painful cough. Geller reflexively handed him water. As Lyle drank, Geller considered the possibilities. Most likely, his bypass was accompanied by blood thinners and statins, so the heart wasn't working as hard. That was good, but some people couldn't keep the cardiac muscle strong enough. If that was the case he might yo-yo months or years. Or, his heart might just say fuck it and check out. He could have a conversation with the cardiologist, but his speciality was internal medicine.

"I need to stop being hilarious."

"Lindh said you wanted to see me?"

"I heard about Baz's boy."

"How?"

"My brother's high up at the CDC. I told you that once, I think."

"Oh."

"Do we know what happened?"

Geller hadn't anticipated the question. Technically he didn't know what happened yet, though he knew more than anyone. Still, he thought it best to avoid causing Lyle additional stress.

"Erik's running tests as we speak."

Lyle looked hard at him, searching for a lie. Geller's face betrayed nothing.

"Could it be related to the Cure?"

The worry in his voice was unmistakable.

"It's too early to say," Geller said.

"What's your gut say?"

He hated lying to the man, but he had to.

"That it's something else."

He visibly relaxed.

"Well, call me as soon as you know anything. Or Lindh."

"Of course," Geller said.

They talked shop for a while, about GIG and various operational issues. Geller told him about the bad turbulence, and Lyle joked that Geller should get his pilot's license like a real man. There wasn't much left to say after that.

"I'm going to get back and see what Erik found out. We'll see you soon, okay?"

"Sure."

THREE DAYS LATER, just a few hours before he was going to be released from the hospital, Lyle's heart decided it had had enough. Avery and his wife had left, and Mason returned from the men's room to find his father encircled by frenzied doctors and nurses. They tried for several minutes to shock his heart, but Mason knew it wouldn't work. If his dad was reunited with his mother, he was never coming back.

19

Between the long hours in the lab and the flight, Geller was strangely tired. He wanted to fly straight back but didn't feel like it yet, so he got a hotel downtown, took a desperately needed shower, and collapsed into bed. It was dark when he woke, but he felt refreshed and hungry. He dressed and went down to the lobby, where he asked the concierge to recommend a lively spot for dinner, drinks and companionship, proffering a $50 to show he didn't mean some hipster place. The concierge wrote "Carter's" on a piece of paper and indicated Geller should map the six-block walk.

"This is what you're looking for," he said.

"Thanks," Geller said.

The concierge made a good call. Carter's was understated, dark, and oozed class. He enjoyed a sumptuous salmon dish, so fresh he'd have sworn it was thrown from the boat straight onto the grill. He paid his check and made his way to the bar, which by then was teeming with beautiful twenty- and thirty-somethings. A comely young woman with an elaborate floral tattoo on her calf delivered a rusty nail, up, and he handed her his card to open a tab.

Geller rarely socialized, but found the situation intoxicating. Surrounding him were the very people he had endeavored not to become—young business professionals, for whom being beautiful and rich was all that mattered. He was their age, basically, but felt so much older. So much more *material*. But they were laughing and drinking and being young, and he was *Geller*.

"Holy shit, you're that *guy*," said a man, perhaps 30, accompanied by a stunning blonde with flawless skin. A flimsy blouse fell across her tits like a theater curtain. She had that look.

"Am I now?" Geller said.

"Yeah, you're that scientist. I saw a clip of you on Kira Broyles."

"Brent Geller," he said, extending his hand.

"Ha! That's right," he said. "Holy shit. I'm Royce."

"Of course you are," Geller said. "And who's your friend here?"

"Brynn," she cooed, extending her hand. Smooth, tan hands that had never known a day's work tapered down to manicured nails in a suggestive shade of pink.

Geller took it and lingered just for a moment on her middle finger as she pulled it away, allowing his gaze to move slowly upward from her waist and directly into her bright blue eyes. He gripped the chairs to either side of him and pulled them back from the table.

"Well, let's all get to know each other better, shall we?"

GELLER DIDN'T BOARD the plane until almost 9. His head hurt and his mouth was fuzzy. Brynn was exquisitely eager to please, and Royce seemed content to watch. He participated toward the end, in a way that should have bothered Geller but didn't. The point was, everyone got what they needed.

He slept almost the entire way, and when he turned on his phone on the approach back to GIG, he had 7 new messages from Baz. The first few were of the, "What have you learned?" variety, but the rest were more like, "Where the fuck are you?"

There also was one from Erik. It was only a couple hours old.

"Call me back right away. I don't know what to tell Baz."

Baz. In his frantic rush to find out what went wrong and be at Lyle's side, he'd neglected to keep Baz informed about what was going on or even where he'd gone. Even he knew how shitty that was. He called Erik and said he'd visit Baz personally; he didn't bother asking if Erik had learned anything new.

LIKE ALL THE higher ups at GIG, Baz lived right on the sprawling mountain property, but not in the same area. His place was in the far northwest corner, in an area Geller considered unappealing. It was extremely modest for his salary, maybe 2,000 square feet, and fenced in by Douglas firs that blocked most of the light. Baz was enigmatic and a loner, but it was a bit much.

He pulled the Range Rover into a little gravel parking area at the end of the turnaround, near a fresh pile of brush Baz had gathered for disposal. He was the kind of guy who would leave GIG after a long day and look forward to the sweaty simplicity of manual labor. Moments later he appeared from behind the corner of the house wearing dirty jeans and a flannel shirt, dragging a train of dead branches. He wordlessly tossed them onto a pile, then pulled off his leather gloves as he faced Geller.

"That's quite a pile," Geller offered cheerily.

Baz looked him up and down. "I might say the same."

"Listen, I know I should've gotten back to you right away, but—"

"You were busy. Erik told me. Relaxing trip?"

"Lyle isn't well."

"I know. I'm sorry to hear that. But we have problems of our own."

"Erik filled you in?"

"As much as he could."

"Is there somewhere we can sit?"

Exasperated, Baz gestured for Geller to follow him around back. There was a large patio with a fire pit at the center, and they took chairs opposite each other with the pit in between. Over the course of the next several minutes, Geller told him the unvarnished truth: The Cure had caused two of Perfecto's genes to switch places, a behavior they didn't predict. Programmed cell death was taking place on a massive scale, across all tissues. They couldn't know for sure at this point if it was something unique to Perfecto's genetic makeup or another factor. Geller's guess was that it was linked to physical maturity, when cells naturally began to perish more quickly than they were replenished. But they couldn't know for sure until they ran more tests on more people.

Baz sat quietly, not reacting, staring down at the cold fire pit. Neither of them spoke for a while. Baz was doing the math, ruminating over all the times he had expressed concerns over the pace of their development. He was thinking about how he had been railroaded by Geller, as much in deference to his genius as by force of personality, and how he had believed so purely in the former.

"You need to tell the president what you just told me," Baz said, finally.

"I will, as soon as we know for sure whether—"

"You know for sure. Even after all these years, you can't be straight with me."

Geller sighed. He *did* know, or felt like he did. Baz was right: If Geller's gut was accurate, the world they knew had ended, and in the one that came next, they would not be heroes.

20

Much happened at GIG in the weeks before Baz finally returned to work. Geller sent tissue samples off to the handful of universities and institutes that had the expertise and equipment to corroborate their findings, which they all did. None knew the full context, however, since Geller didn't want anything reaching the president before he could get there. He had to brief him, the surgeon general and the CDC right away, but his first stop was to see a US Senator.

Constance "Connie" Earle was a political superstar, a black woman from Michigan rumored to be a front-runner for the next Democratic ticket. A woman of faith, she trusted in science, but never in the same way she trusted God. To a large extent, that understanding had helped get her elected to public office. It hadn't always been that way. When she and Stephen, her late husband, wanted to start a family they were told the prospects weren't good. Stephen was dead-set against adoption, and so they prayed. Months turned into years. Finally, her 40th birthday looming large, they sought out the best fertility doctor on the East Coast. It was expensive, rigorous, emotionally and physically taxing, and success was not assured. But after 18 months of shots and tests, it took.

By then the Cure was as common a shot as DTP, and after all they'd endured to conceive, it seemed like a smart insurance policy for the tiny, fragile life they'd coaxed into existence. Jayla was three months premature, weighing barely three pounds at birth. They'd been warned of that possibility, given Constance's age. For five agonizing months, Jayla was kept alive though respirators and the skill of the neonatal unit at Bethesda. Though she thanked God, she also knew science had done most of the heavy lifting.

Geller came alone to her office. He didn't look significantly older than the first time they'd met at GIG, when she was a senator and pregnant with Jayla, who was 11.

"Connie," Geller said, extending his hand and forcing a smile.

"Brent. You look like you just got off the slopes or something."

"It's the mountain air. Nothing so drastic as taking care of myself."

She chuckled and motioned for Geller to sit after he turned down her offer of water.

"Well, when I'm told that America's most famous mad scientist asks to see me about a matter of national security, I clear my plate."

"I do appreciate it. I know it's short notice."

"So what's going on?"

Geller outlined the situation carefully and thoroughly. It was along the lines of, *We made this thing to save everyone, and it looks like it's going to kill everyone instead. So, maybe reconsider your lunch plans.*

She scrutinized him for several seconds before responding, as though searching his expression for some hint of a prank, or a suggestion that what he'd just said was a worst-case scenario, not the truth. He was stone-faced.

"My daughter … "

He shook his head. "I'd love to be wrong, but she'd be affected like everyone else."

"But this has only happened to Dr. Montes' son so far, right? And he was the first one treated, so why can't we come up with a solution before it affects everyone who—"

"No, see, the reason the treatment was administered in vitro was because the cells were still forming. It was possible to alter the DNA then, but adults have trillions of cells, all specialized. It's the reason gene therapy hasn't proven very successful. Now, obviously we're working around the clock to identify the proteins that are causing this and synthesize a treatment, but even if we could, it would take … years."

"Years," she breathed. Behind her eyes he could see a tug of war between senator and mother. They became glassy for just a moment, but she blinked it away.

"You said, 'even if we could.' You don't believe this is fixable, do you?"

Connie worked in a bullshit factory all day, every day. Geller thought he should spare her more of it.

"No."

Geller felt compelled to go on, but remained silent. Constance rose and paced, her arms folded tight. He tried to put himself in her shoes, to appreciate the full complexity of her emotional pain at that moment, but he realized it was folly. He allowed her several moments to consider all he'd said. It felt like a long time before she spoke.

"They'll need someone to blame for this," she said.

"I know."

She shook her head as she moved toward a window. "They'll blame you, but you're not responsible. Everyone had a choice to make, and we messed with nature. If this is the price for that, it's … steep. How many, when it's all said and done?"

"If I'm right, and there's nothing to be done, we've treated almost 22 million people."

"Christ Almighty. That's an entire generation."

It was clear she was trying to be strong and senatorial, but all that was out the window. She was only thinking about one person at that moment.

"I'm on my way to brief President Randall at the White House, but I thought I should come to you first."

She said nothing.

"I'm so sorry, Connie. We'll do everything we can."

Geller left, and Constance Earle, who in six years would become President of the United States, fell to her knees.

PART II

2050 – 2067: THE LONG DARK

21

Constance silenced the evening news with a wave of her hand and laid on the bed, savoring the emptiness of the room. The number was a few thousand larger today. That's all they ever needed to say. Really, they didn't even need to say anything, because it wasn't news anymore. The news used to be the milestones—hundreds, then thousands. Now there was just the number, like a doomsday clock in reverse.

11,837,448.

They'd stopped trying to put it in perspective. It wouldn't—and couldn't—ever approach the 1918 flu pandemic's total deaths. But it was worse for the United States than that ever was. It didn't matter that it was man-made, and with the noblest of intentions. What mattered was the toll it would take. The mortality rate was 100 percent.

Right away, she understood that her faith in science had been misplaced. It had helped give Jayla life, but sometime in the next few years it would take her away. She blamed herself as much as anyone, but not so much for trusting in science as failing to acknowledge God's role. More than anything she was angry, but in some ways the anger was a comfort. It was something she could understand and control in a world that seemed divorced from reality.

It wasn't just that the Cure had already killed so many; it was their demographics. The youngest to die were about 23, the very oldest 26. The life expectancy for anyone who didn't receive the treatment was nearly 85. By the time it was all over, nearly an entire generation of Americans would be gone, and the next one wouldn't come of age for another decade or so. No one knew whether the defect would be passed on. If it was, the long-term effects were impossible to fathom.

The military was a grave concern. Congress initiated stop-loss measures immediately, and the draft was reinstated—to nonstop outrage. Any soldier discharged within the previous 10 years could be reactivated under a new law, and most were. Thousands fled to Canada or South America just to avoid that, say nothing of the thousands more who simply left the country out of fear. The mighty US war machine now comprised 30–45 year olds, expensive assets with everything to lose who generally resented being there—not a good combination —and an increasingly obsolete arsenal that was too expensive to upgrade or replace.

As a result of the US military's sharp decline, the country effectively became a protectorate of Canada and Great Britain. Acts of aggression against the United States, specifically an act of war, would be defended by all three militaries as though it were one country. About 300,000 Canadians came into the US to receive the Cure, a rare example of medical tourism in reverse. That was a lot, but it was only a small fraction of what the US stood to lose. America was wounded, weak, and vulnerable. It was peacetime just then, but how long would that last?

Dozens of industries either suffered or vanished altogether. The service sector was gutted. Amusement parks fell into ruin. Fairs, concerts, and festivals were rare, not only because they seemed indulgent and point-less, but because there weren't many people to run or attend them. States that relied heavily on tourism and recreation were demanding aid from a government on the brink of insolvency.

The effect of these things on the national psyche was profound. An already depressed and cynical public was moving toward desperation and hopelessness. Markets fell sharply. Manufacturing was down. Churches, mean-while, were enjoying their own second coming as many in the older generations either sought answers or took solace in fellowship now that everyone had at least this one thing in common.

The most significant legislation related to the Cure was the Exception Act of 2051. It essentially took most of the legal rights granted to 18- and 21-year-olds and rolled them back to age 13 for kids in the Perfect Generation, or PGs. That included drinking, voting, consent, and marriage. Even the most conservative Americans supported it; with so much living to be done in so little time, anything less would've cost millions of young people a chance at some kind of full life. If it meant that kids could drink, have sex, and make all the same bad decisions everyone else had to wait for, then so be it. Most PG children learned the truth around age 7 or 8, but few made it that long without realizing something was not quite right about the world.

The entire educational system had to be rethought. PG children were placed in a special curriculum designed to give them a baseline of knowledge and life skills. They attended four days per week with no summer break and received the equivalent of a high-school diploma by age 13. Anyone who was between aged 7 and 13 when the laws changed received private tutoring to get them over the finish line.

Thousands of colleges and universities closed their doors. Most planned to reopen at some point in the future, but their endowments had floundered and not many people believed they could come back. Very, very few PGs bothered with college. The rest were on their own.

The hardest thing Connie had to deal with were the regulations dealing with the disposal of PG bodies. She'd signed into law a federal mandate that only cremation was allowed for PGs, and steep taxes on burials made them prohibitively expensive for most everyone else. Federal crematoriums went up near all major cities to handle the volume. They looked like factories, but no one pretended they were. 10,000 people in their mid 20s died every single day.

The country was just too fragile for a political shakeup, which was also the case with lower offices. The Supreme Court suspended the 22nd Amendment and it seemed likely Connie would be re-elected for a third term in 2064. During the early days, the finger-pointing was directed at Geller, who had removed himself from public life. But despite weeks of Congressional hearings, they found Geller no more legally responsible than the creators of Vicadin were responsible for a dead rock star. GIG had very thoroughly indemnified itself through the Cure Program's reams of patient paperwork, all of which detailed the risks of genetic modification. In the end, parents of PG kids were forced to accept that they were as much to blame as anyone.

Jayla was only two when Geller came to visit her office, and now, in the eyes of the law, she was two years into adulthood. Their relationship wasn't great, but it could've been worse. She checked in every few months, usually from a different country each time. She still had a light Secret Service detail on her, which helped Connie's peace of mind. Often, when they spoke, Jayla would get her howling with stories about eluding or even pulling elaborate pranks on the agents. She treasured those conversations, and she hoped to have one tomorrow. Almost a year had passed since she'd seen her only daughter in person.

22

Trout, for all their qualities, were not smart. Many years ago, after he'd taken up fly fishing, Geller learned their estimated IQ was around 12. Once they found a good feeding lane along a bank or undercut in the river, protected by roots or a deadfall, it wasn't unusual for a trout, especially a brown, to remain in that spot until it died.

This was fairly unique in the natural world. Most creatures lived in a constant and mostly random search for food; they didn't have a conveyor system to funnel it into their mouths. The fact that other creatures had to forage meant there would be times when they were vulnerable. They would take risks that a hunter could exploit.

The only real mistake a trout ever made was to think a well-placed fly was an actual morsel of food. Guess at the size and nature of the food it was interested in and float it past the right place at the right time, and even the wiliest bank-hugger just might move an inch or two out of its way to get it. Geller was locked in a daily battle of wits with a creature that had an IQ of 12, and he lost more often than he won. He loved the irony.

He floated a size 18 Royal Wulff, a go-to pattern on Western streams which he'd tied himself, just a few inches from the edge of the bank where a sudden bend in the river had created a deep undercut. The sun was right; it was low enough to catch a bit of the white goat-hair wings and give the fly a good silhouette on the water. Because of the low angle, it would also make him nearly impossible to see since he was facing the sun, and it would make the surface look like a mirror from underneath instead of a window.

His shadow stretched out behind him, long enough to reach the flat stones on the far side of the creek. He knew there was a trout there the size of a marlin. *Knew.* All it took was the perfect cast: a roll of the tip just upstream, hopefully landing the fly on an overhanging blade of glass so he could perform a quick mend of the line and tug it gently into the water, like an insect losing its footing. It would help sell the effect.

There were only seconds to allow the fly to drift over the spot, because immediately after it was a downed aspen that would instantly snag him if he let it drift too far. And yet, he couldn't yank it away either, lest it pull free of the surface too suddenly and make the *ploop* sound that would spook a wary trout. He pulled the fly in, dried it, dressed it in floatant, and flicked it upstream. It missed the grass, but settled on the surface almost exactly where he wanted it. Nothing else existed but its white wings. He wanted them to vanish suddenly. He reminded himself to pause when the strike came, lest he pull the fly right out of the fish's mouth. *Patience*, he thought.

With less than two feet to go, a shadow fell over his spot. Startled, he looked up to see the silhouette of a person standing at the edge, not 15 feet away. His eyes returned to the water just in time to see the current pull the fly down into the tangle of aspen branches, where it would forever remain. Enraged, he grabbed the line with his hand and gave it a quick yank to break the tippet and leave the fly where it was. His carefully nurtured cover was blown. He shielded his eyes against the setting sun as he reeled in his slack.

"You're trespassing."

A young woman's voice responded, "Am I?"

She'd come from the direction of the cabin, most likely having followed the trail from behind the garage. He made a mental note to either hide it or gate it off as he waded downstream to where the river was wider and shallower, climbing up the bank on the same side as the visitor. He felt his 65 years in his knees.

"I'd be within my legal rights to shoot you right now."

"Wait a few years. It'll save you a bullet."

He stopped about 10 feet short of her when she said that, finally having gotten a good look at her. She was strikingly beautiful, a blonde wearing stretchy pants and a fleece vest. He also knew what she meant—she was a PG.

"Do I know you?" Geller said.

"My name's Heidi Robb."

Geller stared at her for several moments, trying to make the connection.

"Jim's granddaughter?"

She nodded.

"Well, well."

HE DISCOVERED a second mug at the back of the cupboard and noticed it had a dead fly and dust inside. He poured her coffee from a pot he'd just made, using his own clean mug, and distastefully washed the other for himself. The gesture felt magnanimous. He didn't entertain much.

"I'm curious to learn how you found me," he said.

"Grandpa told me you used to come on vacation out this way. I started asking around and looked at land records at the courthouse. Honestly, I got sort of lucky."

"How is old Jim now?"

"He'd've been 84 this year."

The news hit him hard—harder he could have anticipated. It gave her some pleasure to see his face change. To know he could feel. It passed quickly.

"When?"

"Two years ago. He was in for a hip replacement and threw a clot. They said it was fast. I was in Malaysia so I couldn't even make it back for the funeral."

"I'm sorry to hear it," he said, and poured his coffee. "They sort of stopped sending the alumni magazine."

"So was I, at first. But then I realized he wouldn't live to see me go."

"And your mother?"

"Breast cancer," she said. "The kind of thing she hoped to protect me from."

"Well you're certainly a wellspring of good news."

He took a seat across from her at the kitchen island, on one of the uncomfortable wooden barstools he also never used. She glared at him, shaking her head—a look he'd seen many times before.

"If you came here to unburden yourself of something, then get on with it. Otherwise—"

"*Unburden* myself?"

"You didn't come all this way to tell me Jim died."

"Maybe I just wanted to meet you. See if any of the stories were true."

She watched carefully for a reaction, but the comment just slid off like a lone raindrop. He smirked.

"Most of them probably are."

"You cared about my grandfather."

"Very much."

"So what about the rest of the world?"

"I knew Jim. The rest of the world isn't half as interesting."

"Do you even know what's happening out there? Twelve million people are already dead because of—"

"I'm well aware, Miss Robb. I came to escape public life, not the truth."

"And what have you been doing with all that time?"

"Writing a memoir. Fishing. Old man things."

"Why leave when you did?"

Shortly after the deaths began, foreign governments with entrenched US interests held a summit of top physicians and scientists to discuss the Cure situation. GIG had provided all its past research to the global scientific community in hopes they could stop, or at least slow the casualties. GIG offered $10 billion to anyone who could devise a solution, just as Merriweather had done. GIG was working on it exclusively by then, having closed everything but its headquarters. Geller, Baz, and Erik had worked on it for three years to no avail, and the foreign teams didn't fare any better. Geller pledged $1 billion of his own money toward the reward, then bowed out. Many thought he had either killed himself or gone mad. That was four years ago.

"We were out of options. I had nothing left to offer but money so I gave it and left."

"You were the only one even smart enough to create a problem like this. Don't you think you're the only one smart enough to solve it?"

"Starting a fire and putting it out are different skills."

"How well did you know my grandfather?"

"As well as I've ever known anyone. Like I said."

"He fought for you. When they decided to change the name of that building, he threatened to resign."

Nine years prior, the Laird College trustees voted to change the name of Geller Hall, in response to public pressure. It was now called Melvin Hall, after a professor emeritus who left his entire estate to the college. He knew about that, but he didn't know what had occurred behind the scenes. He felt a pang of regret for not having reached out to Jim for so long.

"He told them science was all about making mistakes. He said no one could have predicted any of this, and that there was plenty of blame to go around. It made him a pariah. They offered him an early retirement, which wasn't really an offer at all. It broke his heart. He wasn't home three months before he slipped on the front steps and broke his hip."

"He didn't have to fight for me."

"No, but that's just the kind of man he was. He loved you. I never understood it. Frankly, I still don't."

"If you have something else to say, I wish you'd just   "

"Have you been close to an actual PG?"

"Miss Robb, this isn't—"

"Answer the question. You say you know what's going on out there, fine, but do you *really* know? Have you ever watched someone start seizing, and thrash around while their organs dissolve?"

"I think we're done here."

"Have you watched them cough and sputter as they choke on their own blood, while you stand there helpless and just pray for it to just stop? Have you seen the faces of people who love as they watch it all happen?"

A memory seemed to pass behind his eyes, and his lips briefly parted as though to say he had, but then he said:

"I've never been in the room at that moment, no."

Heidi looked at him pityingly and sighed. His air of indignation had evaporated.

"My grandfather said you administered my mother's shot personally."

"That's right."

"Do you remember the year?"

"Well, it was just after that silly building was dedicated, so …"

He stopped short, a realization washing suddenly over him. Heidi sipped her coffee and waited. She'd expected it much sooner, considering his reputation.

"It was 2035," he said after a moment, staring at her as though she'd just stepped out of a dream. His eyes studied her up and down and his brow knotted with confusion. "You would've been born the next spring."

"Twenty-seven years ago last April," she said, sliding her coffee mug across the counter toward him. "Mind warming that up a little?"

23

Marius was seldom in town for long. Even before, it was a special thing for a group of like-minded musicians to cross paths, build a fan base and catalog en route to fame, but in these times it was nearly impossible. Most kids didn't bother learning instruments well enough to call themselves professionals. Even if they did, they rarely had the commitment to make a go of it.

It didn't surprise Rubin Beecher that his only son had managed to pull it off. Marius was a remarkable kid from day one. He and Ellie had decided not to start a family, owing to their grim medical legacies. His family had a history of heart issues and Ellie carried the gene for Huntington's Disease. But one day he was waiting to get his cholesterol checked and had a conversation with a very pregnant woman who had just had the Cure administered to her unborn baby. She hadn't planned on having kids either, but it seemed like a very attractive sort of insurance policy. Rubin hadn't put much stock in it before, but the more they looked into it, the more it sounded like it was just what they needed to set their minds at ease.

Later that year, they welcomed Marius into their lives—as perfect a child as there ever was. Their miracle had come courtesy of science, and for 11 years everything was as it was supposed to be. Marius learned he had a gift for music and pursued it with vigor. Ellie became symptomatic when he was only 8, but Marius adjusted to her new reality just like Rubin had to.

He was nearing the end of fifth grade when he learned the news about the so-called Perfect Generation. It took a long time for everyone to understand that it wasn't some sort of temporary condition, but once they did, everything started to change. They didn't know about whether the spontaneously activated genes would be passed on to the children of PGs (and still didn't), but it was all but certain that PG kids would die in their early 20s. Rubin and Ellie's beautiful son was doomed.

Ellie went into deep denial at first. She convinced herself that only the kids in Phase 1 trials would be affected. Marius was going to be one of the lucky ones. Deep down, Rubin knew better.

That Marius would die young wasn't even the worst part. It was that they'd treated his childhood as ordinary.

The vast majority of PGs learned early on about their fate, and so had tried to squeeze a lifetime of experience into 25 or so years. They hadn't learned what was going to happen until Marius was almost 12, by which time half his life had passed. Though it took a few months for the truth to finally erode their illusions, preparations for sending Marius out into the world could wait no longer. He'd have to get a crash course on life, and it started with explaining to him that he was going to die young.

The laws regarding the legal status of PGs changed shortly after Marius' 13th birthday. The fact of his mother's sickness coupled with his own tragic circumstance turned him into a bitter and angry kid for a while. He resolved to stay even though he was legally an adult, and even worked with him in the factory for a time. But when he was 15, they pooled his meager college fund together with contributions from their extended family and sent him off to a music festival for PGs. He didn't want to go.

His life changed that week. He met the boys who became his bandmates in the Clockwatchers, and the lightning in a bottle they caught together quickly gained the attention of a PG community desperate for heroes. Rubin knew then that Marius' time at the little country house had ended—whether he realized it yet or not.

24

The concert let out at about 11:30, but Lars Heiser didn't leave. Not right away. Red Rocks was always sort of a clusterfuck. It only had two narrow walkways on either side of the stage for ingress and egress. Years of seeing shows had taught him to wait until the crowd thinned and leisurely make his way out after that. That suited him anyway, because he liked the post-concert feeling to linger like melting chocolate.

He felt older than his 15 years—much older. He'd experienced as much of life as he could imagine for someone his age and he wanted more, but he felt a little weary, too. Like so many of his friends, he'd been on something of a world tour, taking advantage of the low airfares given to PGs and the almost universal kindness he experienced in his travels. People generally extended

PGs every courtesy and he could tell that many felt badly for America. He took some strange comfort in that.

After a while, the house lights came on and the cleaning crew came out. Stragglers finished their beers and made their way back to the lots, where the mood was still high. Lars' friend, Tom, called him over to an old truck, in the back of which was a huge cooler full of beer. He took one, sat in a folding chair and mostly listened. They were all PGs, not a one of them over 17. In 8 years or less they'd all be dead, yet they were laughing and carrying on like they didn't have a care in the world. He laughed, too—there wasn't time to waste being morose.

When he came in at almost 3, his father was waiting up. He could never sleep until Lars was in the house. He wondered what would happen when he was gone.

"Good show?" his father said.

"Amazing. I'm super tired, though."

"Who was it again?"

"The Level Bosses."

"That's right—I couldn't remember. I just wanted to make sure you got home okay."

His father patted him on the shoulder, smiled, and retreated toward the bedroom. Lars knew enough about GIG's history to understand why his father had stuck around even after everything that went down. After Baz finally retired, he would be in charge.

GIG had once been at the bleeding edge of not only research, but hope itself. The Cure aside, it had changed the world in profound ways. His father had very few peers, and fewer still who didn't work for him. The others were either Nobel laureates in complementary fields or former employees named Geller. The work, which had worn his marriage down to the nub, was all he had. He wanted nothing more than for his father to lay down the burden of guilt and pursue something more joyful, but it was an impossibility. As long as death waited at his door, his father would be bent over a microscope, looking for something that could keep it closed.

ERIK'S CLOCK read 3:48 a.m.—far too early to think about getting up. He hadn't slept well in years, so it was not unusual to be lying there in the dark, thinking.

His late wife, Lucy, reacted to his news about the Cure with the same calm objectivity he'd noticed at their wedding in Canberra. The caterer, who was late, undercooked the chicken and by the time the dancing was supposed to start, three-quarters of the wedding was either praying to the porcelain god or at the hospital— including him. Ordinarily, a new bride would freak out about that sort of thing. Lucy had been upset, but ultimately shrugged and said something like, "Mistakes happen."

At the time he'd admired her rationality, but during the intervening years he'd come to see it as almost a mild form of sociopathy. When the truth about the Cure came to light, Lars wasn't even three—a delightful, beautiful and obviously smart child any parent would envy. Lucy listened to Erik explain the problem and all its repercussions from across the table. You would expect a mother to immediately deny this kind of truth, or suggest new angles he hadn't thought of. Not Lucy. She said:

"Then our job now is to help him make the most of the time he has."

And that was that. It wasn't necessarily cold, or heartless, or insensitive. It just didn't suit the gravity of the situation. It never did. But Erik wasn't just some guy, powerless to do anything. He was *Dr. Erik Heiser*, wunderkind of GIG and protégé of Geller the Great. He was chief geneticist for the most powerful and prestigious laboratory on the planet. If he couldn't find a way to save his son, then who could?

He threw himself into the work. GIG had been his first and only real job, and he never wondered what might have been. Baz was a terrific mentor and friend, and understood all too well the heaviness of Erik's soul. Together they had continued forward while most of GIG was sold off or repurposed, and over the years rebuilt some of its reputation. The Cure aside, medical and pharmaceutical innovations driven by their research had *saved* millions of lives. Internally, they thought they might actually have saved more than they doomed.

Through the lens of time, however, the only thing about GIG that anyone would remember was it was responsible for ramming the Cure through FDA approval and delivering it at scale. That was what kept Erik up at night, what drove him through the day and what he thought about while brushing his teeth.

His marriage to Lucy was troubled and largely inconsequential to either of them, save for Lars, but it still carried the weight of time and memory. He'd encouraged her to take trips without him, needless of work as she was, and so she'd ended up on a catamaran off St. Kitts with her sister four years ago. There were different accounts of how she ended up unconscious in the water, but most of them agreed that she'd taken some kind of blow to the head, maybe from rigging and maybe not, and fell into the water at high speed. They'd circled back immediately but found only a single sandal. A search was undertaken, but they never found her. In the end she'd left him—just not in the way he expected.

Lars was still asleep. In a house so often filled with silence, he'd learned to distinguish one kind from another. The sharp silence that followed one of Lucy's thoughtless slights. The sterile sort that greeted him after a 17-hour day in the lab. The gentle, almost feminine silence of a new morning. But not this morning. This morning was different.

He padded over to the huge picture window that overlooked the valley, the firs lightly dusted with frost as the sun inched westward. His single-serving coffee wafted steam up into his nostrils, and he took a sip. There was so much beauty in the world—*his* world, even, despite its many flaws—and for a few precious moments he felt happy to be a part of it. The silence in the house just then was a hopeful one, so he moved slowly as he put on his jacket, as though the feeling might somehow follow him out the door.

25

Toward the end of her 23rd year, Heidi threw herself a farewell party. A good number of PGs did. For them, it was pretty easy to focus on living a full life, fear of death removed from the equation. For friends and loved ones, it was harder to understand. Harder to face the inevitability of it. So rather than saddle their families with the pain of a funeral, they'd wait until they were close to the end (but not too close), and through a big, raging party.

The past four years had gone fast, as years spent on the road often did. She was a decent musician and above-average actor with a strong singing voice. A few decades ago, that wouldn't have been enough to do anything or go anywhere, but artists were in high demand. For every person who thought creating art was folly now, half a dozen thought it was the only thing that still mattered. Outside the PG community, regular workaday people needed to tug free of reality, if only for a while. Or maybe they needed to watch young people be young, and beautiful, and joyful. In any event, Heidi was happy to oblige.

The role of music and theatre harkened back to Victorian times. Artists maintained loose associations at best. Theatrical performances were thrown together over an afternoon and largely improvised, not unlike the old penny dreadfuls. A whole culture sprang up around the care and feeding of PGs. Many of the same grizzled misanthropes who otherwise would've yelled at kids to get off their lawn now opened their homes to young strangers.

No PG ever said anything like, "Don't feel sorry for me," or, "I don't want your pity," because it wasn't true. There was great empathy for them. The years hosts recalled most fondly were those PGs could never hope to reach. That fact alone inspired kindness and hospitality on an unprecedented scale. PGs couldn't be expected to just get a job like their parents had. They needed help to live any kind of life, and for the most part, they got it.

Heidi had stayed with so many hosts over the years it was hard to keep track. But she did. Every single one of them received an invitation to her party, and almost all of them came. The Thompsons from Tulsa. Angela and Karen, from Santa Fe. Paul and Bettina from San

Bernardino. A few couldn't make it because they had a family member, often a PG themselves, whose time was up. Others couldn't afford the trip. But counting her extended family, which was already large, and all the hosts who made the trek to Middleton, nearly 170 people came to see her—some for the first time, some for the last.

Friends of her parents, John and Linda Westfield, owned a catering business and fell over themselves to make barbeque, her favorite. There was brisket, ribs, turkey, hot links, creamed corn, a few different kinds of beans, fresh rolls and blackberry cobbler. She couldn't remember seeing so much food in one place. The Westfields' son, Jason, was a PG who died three weeks shy of his 25th birthday. She knew him reasonably well when they were little, though not as well as his parents seemed to believe. Either that or she'd forgotten. *Remember when you and Jason tried to make milkshakes? Jason used to make you laugh so hard you couldn't breathe.*

Yes, she said, those were fun times.

About 20 people with whom she'd played or acted on the road came. Milo Sutton, a talented guitarist she'd met in Louisiana, presented her with a two-act musical based on what he knew of her life. What he didn't know he extrapolated; they all had similar stories. Despite her protests, she was forced into the audience, seated on rows of crisp, fragrant summer hay bales arranged in concentric arcs around the wagon that carried them there. The "pit orchestra" sat immediately in front. Heidi's father had rigged Christmas lights overhead. Her mother and aunt came around with drinks during the show like a hillbilly dinner theatre. It was pure magic. These were her people, and the only tears shed were from laughter.

As she watched the musical version of her life play out, it dawned on her, for the first time, just how much living she had done. The events depicted mostly involved Milo or his recollections of stories she'd told him, but she'd been to so many places, done so much, and met so many people it made her head spin. There, in the makeshift lights and the Southern Wisconsin humidity, she came to believe that her fate was equal parts gift and curse. A gift for the sense of urgency with which she lived, and a curse for how surely and violently it would end.

She finally joined Milo and the entire ensemble on the wagon to sing a dumb little ukulele song she'd written called "Honeysweet." He'd handed out lyrics so he could lead sections of the audience in an impressively complex round, eventually all ending on the same big note. By then, everyone had risen and locked arms across their shoulders, swaying back and forth like drunks in a pub. The company pushed her to the front of the wagon, where she received a warm ovation and curtsied, tears streaking her face. Milo came up and took her hand, flanked by the rest of the cast, and led them all in a final bow.

"Thank you," she whispered, and he winked.

It was well after 2 a.m. before the taillights of the last departing car disappeared into the night. Most spent the night in a tent city arranged on the vast lawn. Heidi made a point of saying goodnight to each of them, and Milo was the only one left. Words weren't necessary, so they didn't speak. Milo never had a party, and never would. He was 24 and seven months. His number would be up any day, and the young, talented man he was would be gone. She would never see him again, nor he her. He unzipped the side of his tent, and she followed him inside.

FOUR MONTHS LATER, Heidi received word of Milo's death. She was in Minneapolis at the time, deciding whether she would want his son or daughter to live. The very oldest children of a PG parent were about a year younger than she. No one, not even the geniuses at GIG, knew what would happen to them. It was as blind a roll of the dice as you could possibly take, and that definitely wasn't her style. It didn't matter what Milo would have said; it wasn't she who would have to raise a child—it was her family, and they had been through quite enough. There was only one decision she could make.

26

It was a good show. Not great, but good. Marius' standards were higher than his bandmates', but anyone who'd seen them a few times would've agreed. Some of it was the acoustics of Soldier Field, which were surprisingly bouncy for an open-air stadium, but Naldo's amp developed a buzz over the course of the show and Kris' harmonies were pitching sharp all night. Once, he might have sat everyone down and gone over such notes before returning to their respective hotel rooms, but those days were past.

Marius knew a less-than-perfect Clockwatchers with all six members was still better than losing one to his perfectionist nature. Marius could play any instrument in the band, but not all at once. Every time he thought about being hard on someone after a show or even at rehearsal he had visions of playing some little club by himself for a $50 and a place to stay, and he'd think better of it. Besides, it's not like they had a lot of competition.

To call music in post-Cure America an *industry* would've been generous. The handful of remaining labels mostly worked with foreign artists and distributed music digitally in markets where almost no one was still willing to pay for it. Clockwatchers didn't record anything; they just broadcast the mix wirelessly from the board so anyone could record it. This was how their music was distributed, and they didn't need any help to do it. Likewise, they didn't sell their own merchandise. Fans made their own and either wore it themselves or gave it to friends. If someone wanted to sell their Watchers stuff at a show, they simply paid a fee to set up shop and had to use a point-of-sale system that deducted 10 percent of all receipts. Between that and tickets, they made more than any of them could ever hope to spend in the time they had left. Mostly they were thinking about taking care of their families.

Marius was the oldest by a year. To him, there was a certain tragic beauty in the brevity of their journey together. They began as a quartet; Marius met JT, Yancy, and Naldo at a PG-focused festival in Nevada when they were barely in their teens. They jammed under some giant tents and got to open for a professional band. A short time later, they headed to Vegas in JT's van in hopes of landing a gig. The days that followed were a combination of luck, timing, and talent that launched their careers.

As the songs became more complex they brought in Kris on keys and backing vocals. Finally the added Billy, a multi-instrumentalist cut from the same cloth as Marius who generally played percussion, strings, and a third guitar on the big anthems. It wasn't long before they could afford a tour bus, and by then there wasn't a PG in America who didn't know the Clockwatchers.

Marius loved his bandmates as much as he'd ever loved anything or anyone. Making music was all he ever wanted to do. He was on this ride for as long as it lasted. After Chicago it was on to Minneapolis, Missoula, Boise, Seattle, Portland, San Francisco, Salt Lake City, and finally Denver. The last night of those three shows would fall on their 10th anniversary—June 3, 2063. Their agent came up with a whole 6/3/63 thing and persuaded them to do three nights at Red Rocks. Six guys, three nights—it was gimmicky but they all went for it. Their catalog was plenty deep.

They didn't always agree, but they had a pact: Clockwatchers was all of them or none of them. If someone left—voluntarily or otherwise—then that was it. Their chemistry was the only thing between them and bar mitzvahs. Without it, they would all embrace that life and not look back. Perhaps that was central to their mystique—a special thing that could, and eventually would, go away.

He packed a fresh bowl and smoked it on the veranda, peering out at the surprisingly quiet night. The metropolitan areas had done okay. Cheap housing and plentiful employment lured scores of thirty-somethings into (or back to) the cities, since the service businesses that held the suburbs together crumbled around them. From a hotel room, Chicago was still Chicago.

He wondered if he would be back to this place, or if this was his swan song—a middling show followed by a night alone. If he'd just been visiting, or working there for a few years, his last night in town would have been an event, with friends from work and drinks and a final, sweaty encounter with whomever. His real life was a string of nights, each with a greater chance of being his last. When he wrote, he wrote with urgency, and that came through in the songs. When he was gone, only the music would remain.

He went inside to fetch his notebook.

27

No PG lived to 27. *Nobody.* It wasn't possible that Heidi Robb—*that* Heidi Robb, the granddaughter of his mentor—was sitting across from him. Yet there she was, as much a medical anomaly at age 27 as 127.

"Are we going to have to go over all this again at some point?" she said, after several candid and slightly embarrassing answers in a row.

"Probably, but I'm trying to build a list of environmental and chemical factors so—"

"So you can ride in on your horse and save the day."

"—so I can see if anything in your history aligns with the subjects who made it to 26."

"How many of those are there?"

"Four."

The questions continued for the better part of an

hour, during which time Geller filled one notebook and started on another. Because there were only four PGs who made it to age 26 (as far as he knew), he knew their histories intimately. Nothing in Heidi's history correlated obviously to the others, and none of them had correlated to each other.

Heidi had led a rich and interesting life—not all that unusual for PGs. She left high school of her own accord, since the Exception Act hadn't been passed yet, and decided that her foreshortened life should be spent in service to others. Since traditional avenues like the Peace Corps hadn't changed their age policy yet, she started laying the groundwork for her own nonprofit organization, The PURE Project.

Her great uncle Pat, Jim's brother, had devised a very inexpensive and effective system for purifying water cheaply and on a large scale, like from a polluted well or dirty stream. His was a slight twist on an old idea, and though it was elegant and dependable he found himself with a warehouse full of units he couldn't sell. He showed one to her when it was just a prototype and she was 12, and she felt bad that he was just late to market.

So, when she left school she got about $10,000 in donations, purchased a handful of Pat's purifiers at cost and flew to Ethopia with him and a few Laird students to set up clean-water stations at small villages. She documented the entire process on video and was able to show how, after just a month of improved access to clean water, incidences of disease plummeted. After showing the documentary to potential donors in the US, it was off to the races for both of them. Heidi was effectively the CEO of a multinational nonprofit at age 17, and Pat couldn't make his purification units fast enough.

As she told the story, Geller couldn't help but think of Lyle, who had poured so much of himself into similar endeavors. He made them sandwiches while she talked, only half listening.

When she was done with the story, Geller said, "Take your time eating. I need to make a call."

Les Hilliard, GIG's longtime CFO, was going over highlights of the most recent financials in Baz's office. Baz was having trouble acting invested. If Les had said they were bankrupt, Baz would have nodded, shaken his hand and headed out to his car. The only reason he was still around at all was because he didn't know what else to do with himself. GIG was like a child into whom he poured all his hopes and dreams, only to be disappointed with how they turned out.

All he knew how to feel anymore was trapped. Perfecto's death shattered his marriage, and Lucia gave up trying to pick up the pieces. She was gone—happy, he heard, and in a relationship with some hotelier back in Spain. As for his work, it was just too late at this point to do much about it. Unlike Erik, who was still driven to find a solution, Baz was no longer actively involved in research. Occasionally he would answer questions from Erik's team about the Cure's development, but mostly he kept his head down and acted like the figurehead he was. If he'd had any idea what else to do with himself, he would've left years ago.

GIG's financials were a complex system of break-even ventures, massively profitable ones and others that hemorrhaged cash. They were still growing, though not at pre-Cure levels. Guilt was part of the company's DNA by then. It was remarkable that it even survived. Part of him didn't think it still should, but he never said so.

He was fighting a heavy pair of eyelids—and losing—when a pressure change in the room jostled him to attention. Wanda, Les' admin, had opened the heavy glass door and leaned her curly head inside.

"Sorry to interrupt, but I need to borrow Baz for a few minutes."

Les glanced at Baz and smirked. He obviously had seen him start to nod off.

"Something tells me he won't mind stepping out," Les said.

The look on Wanda's face was inscrutable, somewhere between gravity and confusion. Baz grabbed his empty coffee mug and followed her out. His back still hurt; he felt each of his 70 years just getting out of his chair, and assumed he looked it.

"What's up?" he said, still groggy. He found himself wondering if it was warm enough to take his lunch outside. Fresh air was what he needed.

"A call for you," she said, and led him into an adjacent conference room.

"Okay … " he started, encouraging her to identify the caller. "The suspense is killing me."

He settled into Les' chair—a much nicer one than his—and only heard her say, "I'll put it through on line one," as she pulled the door closed behind her. He guessed it was someone in Washington, perhaps the White House or the Pentagon. That happened occasionally.

Line one rang softly. He cleared his throat and answered as assertively as he could manage.

"This is Dr. Montes."

A familiar voice said, "Did anyone feed my fish?"

Baz felt his face flush. With what precise emotion, he couldn't have said.

"We dumped them in the Arkansas River," he managed, after a brief pause.

"They were tropical."

"They seemed patient."

Geller managed a chuckle. He sounded healthy, his voice clear and sure. *One advantage of a self-imposed exile,* Baz thought. *You never have to face anyone.*

"Long time, old man."

"Very," Baz said flatly, and waited for him to get to the point.

Geller explained matter-of-factly about Heidi, finding it odd that Baz wasn't more excited about it. Of course, Baz was too cynical himself to *think* of it as anything more than a curiosity that would quickly be explained. Still, he listened and thought about Perfecto, and what two more years would have meant.

"I'll make the arrangements."

"I'm coming with her," Geller said.

Baz stared at a painting on the wall for several seconds, trying to decide how he felt about that. Geller hadn't set foot there in more than a decade. Though he didn't endear himself to many people there (few remained who ever knew him), he cast a very long shadow. If there was anything to Heidi's longevity, no one stood a better chance of finding out than Geller and Erik. He hated that fact, but it didn't change the truth of it. He let go with a long sigh, right into the phone.

"Get her here in one piece."

28

**From *The Perfect Generation: A Memoir*
by Dr. Brent A. Geller**

My relationship with Baz would have struck most people as peculiar, when in fact it was just convenient. We were polar opposites in most respects. I'm messy, he's fastidious. I'm anxious, he's patient. We didn't like the same kind of food, so we'd often stop at two different places for lunch. I credit these differences with making us a good fit in the lab. For example, he could interpret my stream-of-consciousness rants and rearrange them into something we could eventually publish. Like so many rare and wondrous things, it wasn't evident on the surface. Still, it was remarkable that he could stand to be around me for any time at all. There's a reason I never married, and it's not because I'm gay. I don't like people and they don't like me.

I considered Baz a friend, but I doubt he would've said the same. Things changed after his son, Perfecto, died—even before we learned why. To dedicate your life to something that kills your adopted son is a hard thing to process.

His was never the most buoyant of personalities. As a first-generation college student, he took himself and his studies very seriously, as though knowing that what he lacked in intuition he'd have to make up for in hard work and tenacity. He could actually be pretty funny once you got him lubed up a bit, but mostly he was a buttoned-down, bookish guy who concerned himself with his work and the needs of others. But when Perfecto died, whatever light there was inside him seemed to die as well. He went away—so much that even his wife, Lucia, to whom he was singularly dedicated, knew that despair would forever be his mistress. They divorced amicably in 2053.

You might say he threw himself into his work, but in fact he simply had more time for it. All he'd ever had beside the work was Perfecto and Lucia, and they were gone. He had money to burn; he could've gone anywhere and done anything for as long as he wanted, but all he could think to do was show up at GIG sometime around 7 and leave right around dark. I couldn't tell you what he did on the weekends, but I imagine

him in a chair, reading or listening to NPR. He liked to
work in the yard, too. He even liked to remove snow

We poured millions into reversing or preventing the
fatal gene switch, but deep down I knew it was futile.
There was a very good reason we administered the Cure
in vitro, and without getting into the fine details of gene
editing, it's mostly a numbers game. The number of
stem cells in an embryo are manageable. If you can
change their DNA, then they'll retain the changes as
they divide. The closer you get to adulthood, those cells
—which are specialized by then—start to number in the
tens of trillions. That's a lot of editing. Plus, our cells
don't like to be fucked with, so you need to deal with a
potentially life-threatening immune response.

Baz and Erik both believed GIG had to keep trying
and I thought it was a wasted effort. Since that fundamental disagreement stood to become antagonistic, I
decided to remove myself from the equation.

Many still believe I ran away from the problem or
that my departure was a self-imposed exile. That's
understandable. In medicine, there comes a point where
a doctor realizes that all options for saving a patient
have been exhausted, and they make a call. I called it,
but only for my part. By then I was nearly 60 and had
spent about 35 years working on some aspect of the
Cure. No one understood it better, or its complications
more thoroughly. If I thought there were unexplored
avenues, I would have stayed until I couldn't work

anymore. But there weren't, and I didn't. If you want to call it giving up, nothing I say will change your mind.

Baz took over more of the business end of GIG, first as VP of laboratory operations, then R&D, then finally CEO. If I'm being honest, I'd say the business aspect suited him better than the research.

Between 2057 and 2063, I followed GIG's fortunes the same way anyone else did—by reading and watching. I kept up with professional journals and the news, though I didn't have much stomach for the latter anymore. Occasionally I'd be fishing or taking my dog, Crick, for a walk and have some flicker of an idea for reversing the effects of the Cure, but I always realized it either couldn't work, or would come too late to save anyone. Mostly I lived the life of a retired person who prefers solitude. The only people who knew where I was or how to reach me were Baz, Erik, my mailman, my cleaning lady, and probably the IRS and NSA. That all changed on a picture-perfect Tuesday afternoon.

Heidi Robb was the granddaughter of my friend and mentor, Jim Robb, from Laird College. She somehow found me at my ranch in Montana, as I suspected she someday would. I remember seeing her for the first time on the banks of a creek on the south end of the property, swaddled in golden prairie light. She was pretty in a wholesome, no-fuss sort of way that ensured she never looked bad. Sparkling white teeth, blond hair that fell just so about her shoulders, blah blah blah. A beautiful woman

I would characterize our initial meeting as uncomfortable. Her vision for how our conversation would go didn't comport with reality. She was there because she somehow knew that Jim had asked me to personally administer the Cure to her mother. Jim had died, she said, after defending me and my science against the growing number of Lairdians who found me contemptible. She wanted to hurt me with the news, and succeeded.

Heidi made the same incorrect assumptions about me as the general public. But she was right that I hadn't ever personally witnessed a PG die, and therefore hadn't been personally touched by the whole tragic story. I didn't see Perfecto suffer and die, and to be honest, I'd barely known the kid in the first place. Baz had been the closest thing I had to a friend for almost 30 years at the time, and I don't know that I could've picked his only son out of a lineup.

Of course, the most intriguing thing about Heidi Robb wasn't her looks, but her age: 27 years and counting—the oldest PG on Earth as far as anyone knew. I had a notion why that was, but until that played out, I needed to come out of retirement for a while.

29

The next morning, Geller and Heidi took a helicopter down to Missoula, where his jet was stored and occasionally leased out. Drawing him back into the fray was her goal from the moment she left St. Paul. Once the doors closed, he helped himself to a drink and placed a phone call to GIG. He wore the same khakis and sweatshirt as the night before, and still hadn't shaved. She felt silly for thinking he'd wear a tweed jacket and jeans with cowboy boots and a shirt unbuttoned too far for his age, but little about him aligned with her expectations. Brent Geller was both more and less than she imagined.

Stories about Geller abounded; the business world viewed him as a visionary genius who swept everyone up in his personal momentum and left them adrift when not at the till. Most everyone else thought he was a crackpot who had too much power and influence. She imagined that his return would inspire equal parts relief and dread, like a game that hinges on the team's best but streakiest player. Do you give him the ball or stand on principle? She didn't know.

Her own role in all this was uncertain. She hadn't given it much thought and wasn't sure what would be expected of her. She suspected they would draw blood and tissue, and that details of her life and family would be recounted ad nauseam. Beyond that, she had no idea.

Barely an hour into their flight, the plane banked west and began its descent into DIA. She had no idea she'd nodded off. Geller nudged her awake.

"Wakey wakey," he said.

GIG HAD SENT a black SUV to pick them up. A casually dressed young man came around for the door and looked positively awestruck to see Geller in person.

"Who the hell are you?" Geller said, as nicely as he could.

"Jason Chang, sir. It's such an honor to—"

"Jesus. Did you just get your license?"

"I'm twenty-one. I work in the comms office."

Geller studied him for a moment, apparently deciding how best to ask the obvious. The young man read his face and let him off the hook.

"My parents emigrated from China when I was two," he said. "I'm not a PG."

"Lucky you. Heidi here's the world's oldest PG," Geller said, gesturing toward her. "Get her there safely and she may give you an autograph. But grab our bags first."

With that, Geller got in the back seat and Heidi followed. Jason loaded their bags into the back and drove them out of the airport.

DOWNTOWN DENVER WAS visible through a tangle of ramps and overpasses to the south. Heidi thought she could see the top of a roller coaster at Elitch Gardens, one of the many amusement parks that had gone belly-up courtesy of the Cure. She happened to be in Denver a few weeks after they shut it down, and the community was still reeling. She'd never ridden a rollercoaster and probably never would.

Geller dozed off by the time they hit the freeway. Jason and Heidi made some small talk, but otherwise they rode in silence. Once they got through the Eisenhower tunnel on I-70, they drove another 15 miles or so then took an exit onto a two-lane road that wound off to the south. Twenty minutes later, the SUV slowed for a driveway with a surprisingly nondescript sign and a small guard shack. They were waved in immediately, and the guard leaned down to see if he could catch a glimpse of Geller before Jason's window closed.

GIG headquarters was a stunning piece of architecture. Tubular superstructures wound in a grand corkscrew shape along a central waterfall-fed pond, crisscrossing at four points that were home to diamond-shaped common areas, including a cafeteria. Around it were still more massive steel tubes, similar to the rails on Elitch Gardens' rusting thrill rides but much thicker, with beefy cables supporting the roof at key points. It was meant to evoke a DNA double helix, and it did so beautifully. The deep blue mirrored glass of the main structure reflected the sky of a perfect Colorado day. She nudged Geller.

"Wakey, wakey," she said, smirking.

"Good job, Jason," he said, coming out of the fog. "Let's use my old parking spot."

The color seemed to drain from Jason's face as he drove around the back side of the building and into a hole carved into the granite hillside that Heidi quickly understood to be a parking garage entrance.

"Of course," he said, unsure.

"I'm kidding—I never had a parking spot. Security risk. You don't have one, do you?"

"No, sir," Jason said, obviously relieved.

They stopped at a set of automatic glass doors and Geller hopped out.

"Need anything out of your bag?" he said.

"I don't think so," Heidi replied, closing her door.

Geller rapped on the bumper and raised a hand to Jason, who nodded into the rear view mirror and continued on around a cement wall.

"Well, welcome to GIG," he said. "After you."

THE MASSIVE DOORS slid silently open to reveal a moving walkway that angled down toward the main building, not unlike an airport. She stood, watching a row of displays showing scientists at work, including an image of a much younger Geller. He motioned for her to follow as the walkway leveled out into one of the common areas, some kind of welcome center. A tall, thin, slightly stooped Latino with salty hair peered down at them over a pair of conservative glasses. The corners of Geller's mouth inched faintly upward at the sight of Baz, but that was all. Anyone could see there was a complex history between these two men, and that neither was particularly thrilled to see the other.

They drew within a few feet of him and stopped. Neither made any physical gesture of greeting—no hands, no hugs. Only:

"Brent."

"Baz."

After a chilly two seconds, Baz shifted his attention to Heidi and warmly extended his hand.

"Miss Robb, welcome to GIG," he said. "I'm Dr. Basilio Montes. Everyone calls me Baz."

Heidi smiled and glanced sideways at Geller, who didn't react in any way.

"Nice to meet you."

"Everything went well with your trip, I trust?"

"Yeah, great," Heidi said. "Private plane and everything."

"Please," he said, gently placing a hand on the back of her shoulder and gesturing toward one of the arched hallways. "Let me give you the dime tour."

They'd barely gone ten feet before Heidi noticed that virtually every person in the area had stopped whatever they were doing to stare at Geller, who was taking in the updates. She knew plenty of people who didn't believe he was alive, or bought the very old rumor that he had been exiled by the government. Some younger employees asked older ones who they were staring at. A brave few introduced themselves and shook Geller's hand, which he obliged with some reluctance, but he kept pace with her and Baz as they walked. A few times Heidi caught him wrinkling his nose at something or frowning at another, but she tried to focus on what Baz was saying.

GIG was just as impressive on the inside. She didn't have to know anything about science to realize that everything from the lighting to the labs was still state-of-the-art. Eventually they came to a locked door with an odd-looking handle. Baz grasped and held it for a moment, then turned the knob.

"Most labs have advanced biometric access," he explained. "They use a combination of fingerprint data and pheromone recognition to authenticate."

"Cool," Heidi said. They went in.

"This is where we'll be doing most of the work," Baz continued. "I don't know what Brent told you, but most of what we need to try and learn about you genetically can be done with small blood and tissue samples, and simple questions. Your comfort and safety is my priority. You're our guest here for as long as you'd like."

They entered the main lab space, mostly separate rooms with glass walls. The dozen or so scientists she could see stopped what they were doing to stare at Geller. Baz cleared his throat to break the spell.

"Everyone, this is Heidi Robb. I know you're all very anxious to meet her and get started, but she's already had a long day. We're on her time now, understand? I believe you know our other guest."

Heidi expected to feel awkward and even a little embarrassed, but in the eyes of the whitecoats in front of her she saw something she hadn't seen much of in her life: intense, burning hope. They looked like bench-warmers finally getting their shot in the big game, and they were ready to form up behind the man with the ball. Until that moment, she wasn't entirely sure she wanted to subject herself to any of this, but suddenly she felt as eager as any of them. There was no way to know if she had anything meaningful to offer. All she knew for sure was that she'd just become part of something much bigger.

———

30

After dropping Heidi off in the lab, Geller took a stroll. His original office was now some kind of brainstorming romper room filled with beanbags. The giant windows framed a breathtaking view of the valley, interrupted only by the gray ribbon of the seldom-used airstrip at the edge of the property. It wasn't quite as good as the view from his living room in Montana, but it was as awesome as he remembered. Behind him, he heard the familiar voice of Jeanine, who used to be his admin.

"This area is off-limits," she said, with mock reproach.

Jeanine had been with GIG since the very beginning. She didn't put up with Geller's shit, and actually shed a couple tears when he'd left almost 13 years prior.

He didn't get that very often. They embraced awkwardly.

"How was lunch?" she asked.

"Better than I remember," he said.

"You're looking for Baz?"

"Yeah," Geller said. "I figured he'd be in my old office, but I guess not."

"Come with me," she said.

In fact, Baz's office was several doors down, almost across from the bathrooms. Unsurprisingly, it was small and nondescript. He was bent over typing, and continued to do so for several minutes after Jeanine left Geller in the doorway. Finally he finished whatever it was and looked up at him.

"What can I do for you?"

"Do for me?"

Baz shrugged and stared at him expectantly.

"I just thought we might catch up."

"Fine. Let's catch up."

"I heard you got remarried."

"That's right."

"What's her name?"

"Kalpana. We met at a conference in Mumbai."

"Congratulations."

"We've known each other for what—45 years? You've never had any interest in small talk. Especially not about my life."

"Listen, I know this is all a little awkward."

"Oh? Which part? The part where you walk away for 13 years, or the part where you swoop in out of the blue and act like a rock star? Help me understand."

"My presence was toxic. You know that."

Baz guffawed. "Indeed I do."

"What should I have done?"

"You could have manned up. You could have faced the pain you caused and swore to spend the rest of your days trying to fix it."

"It wasn't fixable. How many times do I have to—"

"All this time and you still don't get it. It didn't matter what you or I knew. What mattered was hope. There's never been a mind like yours. Everyone can hate you—and believe me, outside these walls, they do—but they also knew that you were our best chance. When you left, that all went to shit."

"That's a bit dramatic."

"Forget about the Cure for a second. What else could you have done in 12 years, with these facilities? What advancements could you have led in other areas? Did you ever think about that?"

"Of course. You should see my notebook."

"Every time I think you couldn't be more selfish, you go and prove me wrong. You're like a little boy who spills his cereal all over the kitchen floor then goes out to play while someone else cleans it up. There haven't been any consequences for you."

"Failure was my consequence."

"Poor Geller. Being wrong must've been such a burden."

"I knew you'd never understand why I left."

"I understand perfectly well, Brent."

Geller stood and moved to the window.

"I always knew what I was capable of. So did you. That's why we kept pushing the science forward. But when things fell apart, I saw the future. We would've spent the next decade spinning our wheels, and for what? False hope? I took the blame with me so you could do whatever you needed to do."

"Oh, so you're actually *selfless*."

"Think what you want."

"You left because you're a coward, Brent. Plain and simple. It doesn't matter if this woman has any of the answers; it only matters that she *might*. Hell, you'll probably even convince everyone you've been working out of some home lab all this time, and that you found *her*."

"I'm only here for her, and to consult. If you want me to leave, just say the word."

"If the Cure isn't fixable, then why is she here? What do you think is going to happen? For that matter, why are *you* here?"

"She's an outlier. I thought it was worth a closer look. If you disagree, I'll drop her off wherever she came from and go back to Montana."

Baz sighed deeply and leaned back over his computer.

"Do as you please. I have a lot of work to do."

Geller nodded and closed behind him. Jeanine lifted her eyes from her desk.

"Tearful reunion?" she asked.

"Picked up right where we left off," said Geller with a wink.

31

Hope could quickly become a problem, and Erik knew it. He needed to keep the circle very small, which was why the lab would only have a skeleton crew while Geller was around. Word would spread that he was there, which was bad enough, but few needed to know what he was doing there. Though they'd all been briefed about secrecy, they looked at him like he'd ridden in on a white horse. Erik came forward and extended his hand.

"Hey boss."

For a brief moment, Geller appeared not to recognize him. He had filled out a bit and kept his hair shorter, but other than that, he was just Erik.

"Well, I'll be damned," Geller said, looking him up and down.

Just then a very strange thing happened: Geller

hugged him. Erik never knew his own father, so for better or worse, Geller was the closest thing. He had unwittingly educated him in the ways of respect, business acumen, fastidiousness, candor and a million other positive traits by demonstrating the precise opposite. A hug was the last thing he expected.

"It's really good see you," Geller added, sincerely.

While Erik processed that, he cast his eyes for the first time upon Heidi Robb. She was a remarkably beautiful woman, tall and athletic. She was tan, with freckles on her cheeks and shoulders and long blond hair that made him think of organic cotton and trail mix. This was a girl who lived outdoors.

Behind him, the small team of researchers ventured forward, in turn, to introduce themselves to Geller. Erik extended a hand to Heidi, whose hands were callused from the playing of instruments. Somehow it made her all the more attractive.

"Ms. Robb, I'm Erik Heiser. This is my lab."

"Nice to meet you," she said.

HEIDI INDULGED Erik's small talk as they walked down to legal. They needed to sign off before anything happened and he couldn't think of anything smart to say. PGs had extraordinary protections under the law, so they had to be very careful when working with living subjects. Erik introduced Heidi to their lead counsel and promised to fetch her shortly. She thanked him and disappeared down the hall.

When he returned to the gen lab, he found Geller at a terminal, sifting through recent files.

"Learning anything?" Erik asked.

"Not really," Geller replied, and pushed back in his chair. "I could use some coffee."

THEY WALKED DOWN to a little coffee/break area at the intersection and ordered. Geller paid. The pimply young man working the counter didn't appear to recognize him, which was good. He handed Erik his cappuccino and sank down into an overstuffed chair nearby. Erik sat across from him.

"So," Geller said.

"So."

In the years he'd known Geller, never once did they go for coffee, or really even chit-chat. It was all business with him, as though polite conversation was beneath his intellect. Like the hug earlier, it was way out of character. He favored the old man with a recap of the last 13 years—Lucy, Lars, his work, the evolution of the company. Erik's life didn't have many moving parts. Even though he doubted most of the rumors about his old mentor, some were as plausible as any guess Erik could hazard. When he was done, Geller explained, with shocking candor, why he left.

Erik's role in the Cure was a small and blameless one —the kind you learned to live with. But until Geller spilled his guts just then about Montana, isolation, and the depth of his guilt, Erik couldn't have empathized. Now he did. Sort of.

The subject turned to Heidi. Once it did, Erik saw the old Geller fall over the new one like a shadow. His posture changed, his tone of voice—everything.

Erik knew the basics already: Heidi Robb, PG, 27 and healthy. Granddaughter of Geller's mentor from the little midwestern college that disowned him. Entrepreneur turned traveling entertainer. No unusual family history. No known exposure to radiation or chemicals. No drug abuse. No known physical defects. She shouldn't be alive, but there she was. He knew as well as Geller that even if she somehow held the key to everything, it was unlikely they could do anything before the last PG was dead.

They agreed that no one outside the circle of trust could know who or what she was, and why she was there. The thirst for a breakthrough was too great. Legal issued her credentials with a fake name, and gave her enough of a backstory so she could lie convincingly to anyone she bumped into on campus. She would stay in one of the executive guest houses, tucked away in a far corner of the property, for as long as she liked.

"Sounds like you have everything covered," Geller said.

"Not quite," Erik said. "I'm still unclear about your role in this. I mean, are you *here* here?"

"You're in charge," Geller said, taking the last sip of his coffee. "I'm here because of my personal connection to her, and to be a resource to you if I can. Otherwise, I'm only interested to see what the results show."

"And as of this moment, you have no idea why she's still alive."

Geller hesitated before answering—the kind of halted reply that could've meant anything.

"Only guesses."

He of the once-peerless ego was uncharacteristically deferential. Erik had been certain that he was here to seize the reins and steer this research—maybe even help clear his name. But if he wasn't here for that, then why? The company? It didn't add up. But then again, if Heidi led them to something significant, then Geller could take some of the credit. Maybe it made sense after all.

32

From *The Perfect Generation: A Memoir*
by Dr. Brent A. Geller

I t's silly, but one thing I hadn't considered upon returning to GIG was where the hell I'd stay. Despite it's notoriety, it's actually very isolated. When I was there on a regular basis I kept a house near Evergreen—about 40 miles away—but spent most of my nights in a GIG-owned house on-property. After we landed on the GIG airstrip and got picked up, I learned no one had arranged for a place for me.

The head of communications ended up coming to my rescue, which was nice of her. Truthfully I could have spent a night or two in the plane with no trouble, but my back appreciated having a proper bed. They put

Heidi up in one of the newer houses nearby, in a section used most often for international visitors.

As I indicated, I wasn't there to save the world. I was following a hunch about why Heidi was still alive. To do that, GIG needed to perform its due diligence. In so doing, they would eliminate enough possibilities to get us to the truth. In the meantime, I had to keep certain information to myself. I think Baz and Erik both knew I wasn't being completely forthcoming, but they probably were used to that.

Earlier that day, I used the plane ride from Montana to call to President Earle. News of Heidi's and my arrival would find its way to her, and I owed it to her to frame the situation very carefully.

Connie was an impressive woman. She was a centrist Democrat who'd stolen the election from a Republican ticket that obviously felt threatened by her black, Thai, and Latina heritage. She'd used her two doctorates from Columbia to start one of the most admired nonprofits in the world. That led her into politics, and when we met she was still a senator from Massachusetts. Shortly after the Cure received FDA approval, we shared a table at a big fundraiser in Chicago. It was one of these silly events where you write someone a check for $50 million and they don't know what else to do but give you an award. I never cared about that stuff, and I usually declined the invitations. After a time, though, I realized that awards were like funerals—they're not really for the honoree, they're for everyone else. So, I went along when my schedule permitted.

Even though Connie's degrees were in sociology and management, her questions about the Cure were insightful and challenging. She was trying to start a family at the time, but wasn't at all convinced about the treatment. It wasn't the science, she said, but the principle. I asked her why she would leave her child's health to chance, and she said that almost every good thing in her life had been a product of chance. I actually conceded her that point. But then I pointed out that chance was a fickle bitch. I had put my heart and soul into something that would nearly eliminate it, and that choosing "nature's way" was like choosing not to vaccinate.

At the time, we agreed to disagree and moved on to a discussion about her own work. She had no love for politics or politicians, but felt that leadership was a calling. I told her the political arena was no place for effective, humble, levelheaded people, and that if she really wanted to effect change she should double down on her nonprofit. Connie just smiled and raised her wine glass toward me and said, "History will prove one of us right."

Unlikely though it was at the time, I had made a lifelong friend.

Connie was on Air Force One when I called. Her chief of staff tried to tell me she couldn't be interrupted, but I thought she'd want to hear this. After a few minutes, she came on.

"Brent! My God, how long has it been?"

"Too long."

"A lot of people thought I had you killed."

"It would've elevated your standing if you had."

"What's up?"

"There's something I wanted to brief you about."

"You have my undivided attention."

She sounded tired, maybe even cynical. We hadn't spoken in years. I told her about Heidi's unprecedented age and that GIG was looking into it. She asked what it could mean, and I said I didn't think it would yield anything useful but that it was scientifically significant. Basically I knew she'd find out about Heidi but didn't want her to entertain any false hopes. I owed her an honest evaluation.

As it happened, Connie was due in Colorado in a few weeks for a fundraiser. She asked if she should take a side trip to meet Heidi and tour the facility. I was concerned about the optics of that, but I also thought it could be good for morale at GIG. The trick would be to not make it seem like there were any new developments. Connie understood PR as well as anyone, and said she'd think about it. That was pretty much where we left it.

A few hours later, she called back to confirm she could make it over to GIG, and that she understood the danger of spreading false hope. She never would've admitted it to me or anyone else, but I think she wanted to try a little hope on for size.

33

The drive from Boise to Seattle was more interesting than most tour hops. It was a straight shot through northeastern Oregon and some boring parts of Southern and Central Washington, growing more wild and diverse before the forest over Snoqualmie pass threatened to swallow the highway. Marius figured they'd circled the country about five times since the band formed, which didn't sound as impressive as it felt. Had he been a regular person, and if the whole thing hadn't happened the way it did, he'd probably still be figuring out what to do with his life while he pulled espressos in some hipster cafe. To paraphrase Robert Earl Keen, the road went on forever and the party never ended. This was church for him.

JT came out wearing pajama bottoms with the button missing on the fly, from whence his penis poked out. It was hard to know if he was oblivious or just uncaring—either was likely. Such was life on the bus. He sat in the huge passenger seat next to Marius, swiveled it toward him, and propped his feet up on the center console, affording Marius an on obstructed view of his junk.

"Well, I *was* just going to say how pretty it is through here," Marius said.

"Luke sleeping?" JT asked. Luke was their bus driver.

"Or something. He didn't feel so hot."

"Need me to take over for a while?"

"Maybe after we drop down toward the city. I don't want your cock in my chair."

JT smiled and began to sing, playing an air guitar: "Don't want your cock in my chair/Don't want my face covered in hair/I just want to … hug a bear."

Marius shook his head and laughed.

"This is why you don't write lyrics."

"Seriously, let me drive for a while. I'm bored."

"I'm good."

"You still don't trust me in the mountains."

"No, because I remember Tahoe."

"Fuck, dude, aren't we way past the statute of limitations on that shit? It's been like three years now."

"Drifting around a corner, in a fucking RV, with only a guard rail between us and a 500-foot drop never expires."

"Okay, first of all, I was doing maybe 20 and it was icy. Second of all, no one got hurt, and third, in spite of everything it *was* kind of epic."

Marius shook his head and smirked, feeling JT's eyes on him.

"The epicness of it is not material to the conversation—"

"Ha! So you admit it was epic!"

"I didn't say that."

"That's what I heard."

Satisfied, he swiveled all the way around to face the back.

"Are we the only ones up?"

"Dunno."

"Anything new on the whole stadium controversy?"

Marius shook his head. "Haven't been looking. Hopefully it's all blown over by now."

Seattle Park was a former football and soccer venue that had traded ownership got renamed several times since the decline of professional sports. Recently it had been converted into a shelter for Seattle's astonishing population of homeless PGs, who exchanged public services to the city for living there plus two square meals a day. In recent years, other cities had followed their lead. Seattle's other large venues, the old Tacoma Dome and a former baseball stadium, were gone. That left officials with a tough choice regarding Clockwatchers, whose presence had a major economic impact.

Since no existing outdoor venue would suit, they either had to figure out what to do with 20,000 homeless PGs for the show then make it somewhat presentable for 70,000 paying fans, or build some sort of Woodstock out in the boonies. It wound up being a huge controversy in the city, but ultimately promoters arranged to temporarily relocate the stadium's residents in exchange for diverting a big chunk of ticket sales back to the private foundation that supported the stadium's operations.

The band was conflicted about the whole plan. Kris' kid brother had lived in the stadium for almost a year, and they'd all heard horror stories about the conditions. They looked at the money that would go back into deferred maintenance and just improving the space, and decided it was a fair deal. No one wanted to talk about what might happen the next time they came to Seattle —if there was a next time.

Kris was ready to trade clothes with some homeless guy and go looking for his brother, but everyone was pretty tired from the road, so they sent Wes, their manager, to go find some ratty jackets and hats for them so they could go together. They left through the back of the hotel then boarded a train down toward the water. Kris was from Renton, so he knew his way around. No one paid them any mind.

It quickly became clear that the city hadn't lived up to its end of the bargain, or couldn't. A handful of warehouses and empty factories appeared to be overflowing with thousands of homeless PGs, but an equal number were camped out on the sidewalk. The guys in the band knew well that any city that looked kindly upon homeless PGs attracted more of them. It was the traditionally liberal cities that were victims of their own kindness. Phoenix, Houston, Birmingham, Miami, Charlotte—they had no PG problem because none of them wanted to live there. Boston, New York, Chicago, Denver, and Portland were like Seattle.

Kris said his brother, Kyle, was staying in a former cannery just east of the viaduct. They'd spoken about two weeks prior, but not since. The squalor as they walked was hard to describe; it reminded Marius of what medieval Europe must have been like. The sidewalks were a carpet of young homeless people. Some were under boxes or sleeping bags, but many had nothing at all. Gutters had become toilets, and the stench was eye-watering. A small row of porta-johns sat unused across the street on the edge of a vacant lot. One was tipped on its side and broken, excrement pooled around it. No one wanted to think what they were like inside.

As if the physical environment weren't bad enough, the anger and fear were palpable. Perhaps many of them had been there before, but it seemed most had been relocated on account of the concert. The guys didn't speak at all—they just kept their heads down and shambled along after Kris, trying not to draw attention to themselves. Finally they arrived near the touristy area where the aquarium used to be, and Kris nodded up the hill to indicate where they should go.

A piece of plywood was painted white and stenciled with a huge black number 6, apparently indicating the building number to which people had been assigned. Nearly everyone was outside. A wide door that once served as a loading dock was fully open, and they weren't even 50 feet inside before they understood why the sidewalk was more popular. The smell of human waste and body odor was hostile, oily, and stagnant. At a glance, little had been done to prepare the space for an influx of people. It was just a roof and a cement floor with some rusted equipment bolted to it. The only thing that differentiated it from the sidewalk was the shelter it provided, though it wasn't even the time of year when Seattle was getting its famous rain.

They wound between sleeping or passed-out bodies and bundles of clothing and plastic that may or may not have had bodies underneath. Kris showed everyone a photograph of Kyle on the train, disclaiming that it was almost two years old. He shared his brother's red hair and freckly complexion, which they hoped would help him stand out.

As they walked, more than a few people stared in

their direction. Marius was certain they would be recognized at any moment, and had no idea what would happen if they were, so he made every effort to cover his face. He wished he had a scarf.

They'd almost completed a circle of the warehouse when Kris suddenly darted toward the corner, grabbed the shoulders of a skinny young man with his back to them, and flipped him around. They embraced briefly then immediately began to talk. The rest of the band stayed put while Kris spoke to him in an urgent whisper. When he gestured their way, Kyle took notice of them and his eyes got big, but Kris whispered something in his ear and he calmed down. He gestured with his head toward the exit, and Kris looked to the band to head back out.

Only a couple restaurants remained open on the pier, which was being heavily patrolled by Seattle PD. They crossed the viaduct and headed toward a seafood place called Gilligan's, which had a vaguely Hawaiian-looking security guard standing outside. The policemen near the road eyed them carefully as they approached. The security guard rose and sniffed at them.

"Something I can help you gentlemen with?"

"Yeah, lunch," Kris said, annoyed.

"You got a reservation?" the guard said, stepping between them and the door.

Marius pushed past JT and Naldo, removed his stocking cap, and pulled down his hood.

"We were hoping you might squeeze us in," he said, checking to make sure no one nearby was looking their way. He didn't like doing this sort of thing, but sometimes it was necessary.

The guard's eyes widened. He looked to be in his late 30s. It was never a guarantee that non-PGs would recognize someone from the band, but just about anyone would recognize Marius.

"Holy shit," he said. "What the hell are you guys doing down here?"

"Lunch," Marius said, a bit irritated. "Like he said."

"Fuck yeah, brother," he said, offering his hand arm-wrestle style for Marius to take. When he did, the guard leaned in and put the other hand appreciatively on Marius' shoulder. They were bro's now, apparently.

"Thanks," Marius said, letting the other guys walk past ahead of him.

"Hey, I'll be there tonight," the guard said. "Section 104, row 30, seats 13 and 14. You point my way, alright?"

"Sure thing," Marius said, and followed everyone inside.

Kyle ate like he'd just discovered food. He powered through enough fried shrimp and tater tots to feed a basketball team, all in the time it took Marius to eat a single Dungeness po'boy. He then asked for a dessert menu and ordered two gigantic slices of cheesecake. Kris just let him do his thing and only started talking to him once it seemed he was running out of places to cram his barely chewed bites. Kyle was addicted to glitter, a dirt-cheap derivative of crystal meth that caused wild swings in mood and appetite. They'd all seen this sort of thing before. It was the reason Kris stopped sending him money.

Kyle said things weren't ideal at the stadium, but that it was the Four Seasons compared to what they had now. Initially the residents of "Stadium City" refused to leave, but city officials said they should actually *want* to leave because it would be far nicer when they returned. The Stadium City Council—a duly elected governing body recognized by City Hall—was leery but agreed to move everyone out a month ago, expecting to return two weeks after the show. But a rumor had started that the city had no intention of returning anyone to the stadium because a group of investors were talking about rebooting professional football, starting with the Seahawks. It wasn't very far-fetched.

Their server brought Kyle his cheesecake—one with cherries and one with chocolate sauce. He ate these more slowly, savoring every bite as though they might be his last. Kris looked uncomfortable.

"So what happens if the city goes back on its promise?" asked JT.

Kyle paused between bites for a moment, weighing this.

"It'll get bad, fast," Kyle said, matter-of-factly.

Marius tried to imagine several thousand homeless PGs and non-PGs alike, emptying their squalid shelters and terrorizing downtown. Thousands more would flood the city in solidarity—many of whom were already in town for their show. The city wouldn't have predicted this, and it would end badly. They were set to perform the very next day, meaning it would be impossible to determine beforehand if the rumor was true. If they didn't go on, they'd create a similar situation. If they were making other plans for the stadium, fine. In the long run it probably was good for the community. But if there was even a chance the city lied, then something had to be done.

He had an idea.

34

Connie knew better than to entertain false hope. Most PG parents clung to it in their grief and confusion, even now, and she knew better. But Geller was Geller, and he was there for a reason. GIG was the NASA of bioresearch. The world looked to them for the next revolutions in microbiology, agriculture and dozens of other areas, and they delivered again and again. But for all their contributions to global society, it was known more for its most spectacular failure than for its myriad successes. Its chief architect was probably the only person capable of doing anything about it, but if there was any real hope, he would've told her.

Jayla was arriving from Peru that morning, where she'd spent the past several months. Before that, Paraguay. PGs with the resources to do so often traveled extensively, taking inspiration and goodwill from a deeply sympathetic global community. So calming and welcome was the company of the non-doomed that some PGs actively avoided each other's company so they wouldn't have to watch anyone die. Jayla was one such kid; as far as Connie knew, she'd never lost anyone close to her and seemed determined to keep it that way. This aspect of Jayla's life made it that much more special when she did come home, which she'd only done twice since turning 13.

Very few people recognized her daughter, even in the US. She changed her look often—depending, it seemed, on local custom or fashion. Connie liked to think it was ordinary teenage self-exploration, though she supposed there were deeper reasons. She was arriving on a commercial flight into Dulles. She shouldn't have felt nervous about seeing her own daughter, but she was. Jayla was a wonderful girl—smart, funny, and kind. In any other circumstances, Connie was sure she'd have grown up to be a leader of people, perhaps a mayor or the head of a nonprofit. She had charisma, and a look in her eye that made you suspect she was somehow testing you, trying to figure you out. Yet for all her qualities, there was a darkness about her. Something that went deeper than just knowing she would die in the prime of her life. Something Connie never learned to address.

She wanted to take Marine One and meet Jayla

there personally, but sent a car to avoid attention. She used the time in between to read through a new immigration bill that awaited her signature.

There wasn't much of a protocol for picking Jayla up at the airport so a pair of Secret Service agents drove up in a plain black sedan and looked for her. One entered with a sign bearing her code name, Frankie J, and waited while the other circled mindlessly outside like anyone else.

Storms delayed her flight from Houston, making a long day even longer. By the time the escalator delivered her to the baggage area, she was so tired that the sign with her code name on it didn't register in her brain and she walked right past.

"Excuse me, miss," said the agent, who she didn't recognize, as he touched her shoulder. "Have you seen Frankie J?"

"Oh right," she said, and he gestured for her to follow. "My bag is—"

"We'll take care of it, miss," he said flatly, eager to have her away from the crowd. Outside she saw the black sedan pull up. Despite her aversion to luxury, the soft leather seats beckoned. She flew coach and her back was killing her. Her eyes were heavy. She followed the agent to the car, got in, and fell asleep.

.   .   .

AFTER WHAT SEEMED like 10 seconds, the back door opened and another agent gently shook her awake.

"We're here, miss," he said with the slightest of smiles. He was younger than most of the others, and nice-looking, clean and crisp—nothing like what she'd grown accustomed to seeing in South America.

Groggy, she shouldered her backpack and climbed out. She never got used to visiting her mother in the White House. Like the young agent, it looked whiter and cleaner than it was in her memory. She checked her watch—11:45 p.m.

Her mother was waiting just inside the door. She had changed, too: visibly older and bonier, a few extra flecks of gray in her hair. Her eyes seemed to protrude further than usual, and the wrinkles around her eyes had deepened. Still, she carried herself in the same way as always—purposeful and self-assured. She wore a track suit embroidered with the presidential seal—more casual than Jayla had seen her in years. She beamed and eagerly stepped forward to hug her. Jayla felt in her mother's slight frame a certain tightness, as though the transformation from mother to chief executive was finally complete. And yet, when she planted a big, enthusiastic kiss on Jayla's cheek, it had the same softness she always knew.

"Welcome home, baby girl," said her mother, wiping her eyes.

. . .

Jayla slept like the dead, only waking at the report of a very distant gunshot—hardly unusual in DC, but enough to yank her from her sleep. It felt like dawn, but it was nearly 11. It seemed strange no one had woken her, but then again, she knew her mother would have given everyone orders to let her daughter do as she pleased. For now, that was just fine.

First Daughter was a role she couldn't ever fully relinquish, even in the forgotten corners of the world where she preferred to be. In truth, there was never a moment where the NSA, at least, didn't have eyes on her. Important officials and their families were tagged with radioactive isotopes, safely embedded in carbon nanotubes, so they would light up on surveillance. So even when she managed to shake her detail long enough to get her rocks off or smoke up, someone was watching.

She stepped out of the shower after a very long time and found the large sink mirror unusable. She toweled off and stepped into the bedroom to study herself in the ornate full-length floor mirror—the first time, really, in months. Her hair was long, frizzy, and desperately in need of attention. She was too skinny. And she needed to shave her legs. The large butterfly tattoo on her hip looked garish in the bright light, and her skin a bit too Caucasian for her taste. She needed more time outside. But she was otherwise satisfied with her progress, physically. The curves were coming, and she welcomed them.

Her mother was sort of rectangular, broad-shouldered and narrow-hipped, though maybe that was the part of her that was one-quarter Filipina.

By the time she did some preening, pulled her hair back and dressed in her last clean-ish outfit it was pushing noon. An aide she didn't recognize was sitting in a chair across the hall. He rose nervously upon seeing her and tugged down on his sport coat.

"Miss Earle, your mother was hoping you would join her for lunch."

She regarded the small man bemusedly.

"Um, sure. No big plans."

"Excellent. Do you remember the way to the kitchens?"

"It hasn't been *that* long."

He smiled and turned to leave, but she stopped him.

"Hey, I have a little laundry. Do you think someone could—"

"Of course. I'll see to it."

"Cool. Thanks."

She watched him walk away and started to follow, then about-faced and stood for a moment, suddenly unsure whether to go right or left.

WHITE HOUSE FOOD WAS GOOD, but not as good as the appointments. Though her time in South America had curbed her taste for junk food, the potato chips that came with her panini were divine. She ate her sandwich then savored the chips while her mother peppered her with questions she already knew the answers to—again, courtesy of the NSA and Secret Service. Jayla played along, omitting the more lurid details involving men and drugs. She wasn't a "bad girl" compared to some PGs, but she also wasn't the girl her mother thought she was.

She nibbled at a shortbread cookie from the small plate where most of her mother's sandwich remained. Connie stirred honey into a fresh cup of jasmine tea and cleared her throat.

"Sweetheart," she said, "I was hoping we might take a short trip together."

Jayla sighed. "Mom, I just got here."

"Of course, and it wouldn't be for another several days, but I managed to clear my schedule for about 48 hours and I was hoping you could join me."

"Where?"

"Colorado."

"What's in Colorado?"

Connie dabbed at her chin with a cloth napkin and looked around to ensure they were alone, then leaned forward conspiratorially.

"Officially, I'm going to a fundraiser in Denver. Unofficially, I'm taking time to visit the Geller Institute of Genetics," she said, her eyes bright. "They want to brief me on their newest research."

Jayla felt resentment, bordering on hatred, for that name.

"What research?"

She sighed. "It can't leave this room, Jayla."

"Okay."

"I'm serious."

"I said okay."

Jayla listened as her mother explained about the 27-year-old PG in perfect health. Even if it was true, and she doubted it was, it wouldn't change anything for her. Hope wasn't a feeling she knew. Most parents seemed to think they had to have enough of it for their kids, and her mother was no exception. Still, if it made her happy to take a little trip together, she didn't see the harm in it. Besides, what was she going to do in the White House after a few days of R&R anyway?

"Sure mom. Let's go to Colorado."

35

Clockwatchers managed their own ticket sales. The days of brokers and label-owned ticket houses were long gone, and so the only way for the Watchers to constantly tour and fill the remaining usable big venues was to bring everything in-house. It was expensive, and that end of the operation barely paid for itself, but it was necessary. They'd tried pay-what-you-could shows when they were getting started, which was how 98 percent of the few bands out there still got by, but after a while they got too big.

Marius and JT sat in a sparsely decorated office across from the mayor of Seattle, Tom McManus, explaining this. He nodded politely and waited for them to finish.

"And that's why you think you can add a second show this late in the game?" he said.

"Tickets are easy—all electronic," Marius said. "The news will travel almost instantly. Event logistics is the tricky part—concessions, cleanup, security, additional staff—it'll be a long couple days for some people, but it's doable."

"But it's also another several thousand hotel rooms, meals, all that," JT noted.

McManus sized them up for a moment, apparently looking for holes in this plan.

"And you're confident you'll sell out again."

"Very," Marius said. No one under age 25 would ever ask this question.

"So why not always do multiple shows?" McManus said. "Hell, for that matter, why not stay here for weeks on end if you're just printing money? You'd be welcome."

Marius had anticipated this.

"Our fans are all over, and they don't have a lot of time, so we go to them," he said. "We're not interested in becoming a house band."

McManus leaned back in his chair and sighed. "This city was on the rise. Not that long ago—before all this happened. It was youthful, y'know? Electric. Movements started here that changed the world. Music in particular."

"Pearl Jam, Nirvana, Soundgarden, Mudhoney," JT said. "This was the epicenter."

JT was the band's unofficial musical historian. This

kind of thing was exactly why Marius brought him to the meeting.

"That was a little before my time, but you're right. Some of those guys were around a long time—did you know I saw Eddie Vedder's last show?" said the mayor.

"At the Off Ramp Cafe in 2037? Damn—that was supposed to be a legendary show," JT said, genuinely impressed.

Marius knew the mayor wouldn't tip his hand about the long-term plans for the stadium, but if he agreed to their idea it wasn't going to matter.

"You know, boys, a second night throws a few wrenches into a few machines, but if you can fill the place, it's good for the city. I'll grease the skids for you."

Marius and JT rose, beaming, and shook the mayor's hand.

"Thank you, Mr. Mayor," Marius said, and they headed for the door.

"Have a great couple shows," said the mayor, and they left.

Once they were down the stairs to the main floor, Marius placed a call and said one word:

"Go."

ON 4TH AVENUE, a ticket printer that hadn't seen action in more than 40 years was connected to an even older computer, whose cooling fan coughed up a puff of dust when powered up. In the corner of the garage were 14 boxes holding spools of tickets that said "Seattle Mariners" on them. A man in his early 70s, a collector of such antiquities, entered information into a form while Naldo helped him with the spelling of "CLOCK-WATCHERS" and clarified that it was one word. Once everything appeared correct, the man struck a key and the old printer started cranking out the first of 30,000 tickets that said:

Tick-Tock Productions Presents

An evening with

CLOCKWATCHERS

Sunday, May 20, 2063

SEATTLE STADIUM

General Admission

Naldo transferred a significant sum to the man's account and reminded him that the balance would be paid upon delivery, by 6 a.m. the following morning. Then he walked back to the hired car that was waiting, and asked the driver to return him to the hotel so he could get ready.

Kris had obtained a list of all the people who had, until a few weeks ago, called Seattle Stadium home. It wasn't hard to do, since the stadium was a city asset and had a legal obligation to keep such a list. It would be uploaded to networked devices carried by door security so they could verify that the ticket holder was, in fact, a displaced resident of the stadium. Once they were in, they would watch the show and simply stay after it ended. If the city had secretly planned to lock them out, they'd either have to abandon those plans. If they hadn't, then the city would have to return to business as usual, and that was good, too. Either way, Kyle and tens of thousands just like him would be back in the place they called home.

THAT EVENING'S show was among their best ever. It was one of those nights that felt like it would be special, and it was. No one in the band could've said exactly what it was, but the crowd was insane, the mix was perfect, their rhythms were tight, and Marius' voice rang like a bell. They also were thinking about the following night's subversive act, and realized it would almost certainly be the last show they ever played in Seattle. Not just because their plan was going to piss off a lot of powerful people, but because Billy and Marius were almost 25, and on borrowed time.

Early the next morning, Kyle and Kris went to meet with the Stadium City Council, whose resentment toward the band quickly gave way to enthusiasm about the plan to get them back inside. Each took a box full of tickets to distribute to everyone they could, along with a warning to keep things as quiet as possible.

Marius' post-concert guest was still in the shower when there was a knock at the door. He checked the time—9:15 a.m. He hadn't even gotten to the hotel until almost 4. Immediately he regretted not looking through the peephole.

"Mr. Beecher, good morning," said Mayor McManus, flanked by a lone security guard. "I hope I didn't wake you."

Marius turned and left the door open. "Lemme get a robe."

He entered the bedroom to fetch a robe from the closet, catching a glimpse of the girl as she toweled off in the bathroom. He closed the door behind him.

"You'll forgive me if I'm a little groggy," he said.

"I do apologize for the hour, but I had an urgent concern," said McManus.

"Oh?"

"I didn't mention it when we met yesterday, but an engagement last evening kept me from coming to the big show. Sorry I missed it—I hear it was one for the ages."

"We felt good about it."

"Well, after our chat I realized I *could* make the show you added tonight. So, I talked Mrs. McManus into joining me and asked my assistant to get us some good tickets. Funny thing is, she couldn't find any information about it anywhere."

Marius didn't count on this. Their rocket was lit, and there was no stopping it.

"Huh. The announcement definitely should've gone out by now. I'll have to look into that right away."

"I'm not the kind of man who uses his station to score tickets to a rock concert, but I guess that's sort of what this is."

It wasn't clear whether he knew something was up with the show and was trying to trap Marius in a lie, or if he really just wanted to know if there were tickets.

"You don't need tickets, Mr. Mayor. I'll put you on a list at Will Call."

"Are you sure? That would be tremendous."

"No problem. Anything else I can do for you? I kinda need to start coming alive here."

"Of course. I'm sorry to bother you for such a small thing, but I'm a fan. I'll be very curious to see who's able to drop everything to see a show at the last minute on a Wednesday."

"Probably people whose life is too short for an eight-to-five," Marius said.

"I suppose that's true. Well, you have a good show tonight."

"I'll look for you."

McManus smiled and nodded, his eyes lingering for a moment on Marius, then smirked and left.

36

Once she'd answered what seemed like a million questions and endured all the scans, tissue samples, and blood draws, there wasn't much for Heidi to do but hang out while they ran tests. She technically could've just left, but she didn't have anywhere to go. GIG put her up in a ridiculously appointed house about two miles away—a three-level monstrosity that clung to the side of a mountain, each level jutting out below the one above it in cascading terraces. The house was fully but unobtrusively staffed, with a professional chef, housekeeper and handyman.

Heidi was put off by the VIP treatment at first, but it grew on her. Her life was bohemian, but not as often in the romantic way as in the are-we-eating-tonight way. She intended to return to it if she lived long enough, but decided to try and enjoy this while it lasted. Either they'd get something useful from her or she'd be dead. Either way, nothing wrong with some sponsored hospitality.

She read, worked out, and caught up on television, three things that never seemed to fit in an urgent life. One show was a drama about twins, one of whom received the Cure and one who didn't. It felt phony to her. Instead she favored the shows of her youth, which were available on demand. But it was a one-way conduit only—one of the downsides of this arrangement. She could make calls and send messages to friends and family if she wished, but that was done from a special room at GIG, with the help of a communications officer named Brad, who helped make sure she created the impression she was traveling.

After finishing a gourmet sandwich, she pulled on some tights and a sweater and waited at the back of the living room until she heard her car pull up outside.

THE CAR DROVE her to a lower level in the parking complex, accessible only through a flip-up panel that opened a steel door. It closed immediately behind them. The narrow passage led to a turnaround in front of a cylindrical elevator. She got out and the driver indicated she should enter. Once she did, he pressed his thumb to a panel and the door hissed shut. She descended in silence for several seconds. The next door to open was behind her, where a small, pretty woman smiled at her from behind a curved desk.

"Good morning, Ms. Robb," she said, gesturing down a short hallway. "They're waiting for you."

The woman touched a panel and door in the hallway slid open on the right. Cautiously, she went in.

The room was a spare, official-looking boardroom, more angular and less comfortable than other rooms at GIG. Seated at a long table were Geller, Baz, Erik, and a man and woman she didn't recognize. Baz rose and greeted her warmly.

"Heidi, thank you for coming. I apologize about the James Bond routine, but honestly, the other secure conference rooms were booked."

Erik smiled. "This is mostly a safe room for biohazard emergencies, but don't worry—we're not having one of those."

Baz offered her a beverage, which she declined, then gestured for her to sit. He quickly moved to introduce the two strangers.

"This is Jill Nguyen, vice president of communications, and our media relations director, Ken Conlon."

They both raised a hand in greeting, as the table was too large to shake hands. Ken was a stumpy, red-faced man in his early fifties whose collar looked way too tight for his fat neck. Jill was a fashionably dressed Asian woman maybe ten years his junior.

"Are we team writing a press release or something?" Heidi asked.

Ken liked that one. He choked on his coffee a little.

"I'll let Jill explain," Baz said with a smile, then nodded deferentially to her.

"Thanks. Well, basically, Heidi, as you know, we've all worked hard behind the scenes to keep both your stay with us and Dr. Geller's involvement under wraps. Now, it was only a matter of time before the cat got out of the bag, and it has. We don't know how or who, but it doesn't matter. What matters is that we're prepared for what comes next."

"Okay …" Heidi said tentatively.

"The news is that Dr. Geller has come out of retirement," she said. "So far, it doesn't appear that anyone knows about you, but that could change."

"Dr. Geller is a polarizing figure," piped in Ken, who seemed much more grave than Jill. "The media are going to want to know what he's doing back and what it has to do with us, and that potentially could lead them to you specifically. You shouldn't have to deal with any of that."

"Our job is to get between you and them," Jill interjected. "We don't lie, but we don't tell the whole truth either. That's just how this works. Our priority is to protect you and the company."

"Protect us from what?"

"Anything. Rumors. Zealots. Competitors. Wackjobs."

"Congress," Jill said.

"Especially Congress," echoed Ken.

"This is just so you aren't blindsided by anything you might read over the next few days. The rumor mill's going to be very active. If your name gets out there, just know that it's our job to deal with that," Jill said.

"I appreciate that," Heidi said.

"We don't know for sure when this will break, or even how much information anyone has," Ken said. "With any luck, the GIG rumor sites will keep piling onto each other and it'll turn into a big game of telephone. Until then, nothing really changes for you. You're free to go anytime, but the less anyone sees of you, the less chance you become part of the story."

"No unsupervised contact with the outside world. Got it."

"Do you have any questions for us?" Jill asked.

Heidi surveyed the room, her eyes finding Erik's. He always looked like the calm center of a storm, and this was no different. He smiled, just a little.

"I don't think so," Heidi said. "Is that all?"

"Not quite," Geller said. By the looks of everyone else in the room, they didn't know what he was going to say. Jill looked especially concerned. "We're getting an under-the-radar visit from President Earle."

Jill raised both eyebrows. Ken's ruddy Irish face

looked like it might burst into a hot, purple cloud at any moment.

"You're serious?!" he said, activating a small tablet with which to take notes.

"Tomorrow, mid morning," Geller said, as casually as if his roommate from sophomore year was dropping by for coffee. The contrast of Geller's calmness and Ken's massive parasympathetic response was comical, and Heidi stifled a laugh. Only Jill seemed to notice, and smirked.

Geller said the president had contacted him the previous day, which caused Ken's face to ripen even further. She had business in Denver and was extending her stay for a private audience with him, and that was why he didn't see any need to trouble his staff. Heidi knew little of such things and couldn't quite grasp their panic.

"Dr. Geller, this is going to add fuel to the fire," Jill explained. "If anyone finds out she's here, they'll assume you have something so important to tell the president that she came to hear it herself."

"There's nothing to tell," Geller said, still implacably calm. "I promised Connie I'd keep her informed of developments. Heidi's a development. It's that simple."

"I appreciate that, but—"

Geller cut Jill's explanation short. "It'll be fine. They can't cover what they don't know anything about."

"Maybe you've forgotten about this thing called the

Internet," Ken said, incredulous and surprisingly condescending.

Geller's eyes swung over to Ken and wordlessly said *remember who you're talking to* before swinging them back to her. Ken shrank two shirt sizes.

"Heidi, I think you know what you need to know. Go home and relax. This'll blow over."

"We'll let you know when we need you," Erik said.

"Can't wait," she said.

37

Connie's official reason for being in Colorado was to attend a fundraiser in support of Colorado Governor Marcus Fitzwater, an old friend who could be on the Democratic ticket when her term was up in two years.

"What am I supposed to do for three hours?" Jayla whined, sounding very much like the teenager she was. "I don't know anyone in Denver."

"Dr. Geller said they'd send someone to pick you up and take you wherever you wanted to go."

"What, like a chaperone?"

"Mmm—I don't think so."

JAYLA STEWED for the balance of the long flight on Air Force One, drinking a hearty American beer and catching up on celebrity gossip with her headphones on. Her reaction was childish, and she was hardly a child anymore, but she didn't care. She was supposed to be petulant at her age.

Below them, the endless brown prairies of Middle America slowly gave way to shiny little neighborhoods with cul-de-sacs and tidy little parks. She'd been through Denver just a couple times, mostly on her way to Utah or Montana and never for long. Part of her wanted to explore it and part of her still wished she'd stayed in Peru.

The plane touched down at Buckley Air Force Base in Aurora, a middle-class southeastern suburb long since absorbed into Denver proper. The sun was just dipping below the Rockies and it looked like the start of a beautiful night. When she emerged onto the steps, it was a bit chilly but still nice. She left her jacket in the backpack, since she'd be inside one of the sedans lined up on the tarmac within minutes. She imagined being driven around by some middle-aged suit who didn't know any better than to act like she was on a bus tour. *And if you'll turn your attention to our left, you'll see the famous Denver Capitol, whose 15th step is exactly one mile above sea level …*

As she thought these things she almost forgot about her mother, who was standing at the bottom of the stairs looking impatient. They hadn't spoken in hours.

"Sweetie, I'm sorry, but I'm already running late."

Jayla descended to receive a hug. It felt nice.

"I should be back to the hotel by 10. Want me to knock on your door when I get there?"

"If you want," Jayla said. "I'm sure I'll be asleep by then."

"Okay, well … just make the best of it tonight. We'll have the whole day together tomorrow."

"Great," Jayla said.

Her mother's entourage got on their radios as they hurried her into the limo and drove away, along with three other black sedans. That left just two—one for her and the other for her Secret Service detail.

"Ma'am, we'll take your bags with us, if that's okay," said one of the agents. She thought his name was Scott, but it might have been Seth or Skyler or Todd.

"Sure," she said, and walked tentatively toward the other car. After a few steps the driver got out. The first thing she noticed was an unruly mop of sun-bleached hair that tumbled over a simple black sport coat with a T-shirt underneath. And jeans. He hurried around the front of the car, sliding his sunglasses over his bangs. He squinted into the sun, which turned deep red as it fell into the mountains. He appeared to be her age, maybe a little older, and he was utterly gorgeous.

"You must be the first daughter," he said, flashing a set of impossibly white teeth. He looked like an underwear model.

"Just Jayla," she said, sheepishly extending her hand.

"Are there snipers waiting to shoot me if I shake your hand too hard?"

"Only one way to find out," she said.

He took her hand. "I'm Lars, Just Jayla," he said. "You want to go find some trouble?"

It didn't take long for Jayla to learn everything she needed to know about Lars Heiser. He was a PG. He looked older, but they were almost the same age. He'd been to many of the same places she had, though never at the same time. He was fond of surfing and had the resources to go wherever the big waves were—Bali, Australia, Oahu. She'd been to Indonesia once and Australia twice and liked them well enough, but she was drawn to the warmth and vibrance of Latin culture. The East was too foreign somehow, even if they spoke her tongue. Plus, she didn't care for the food. Their families could hardly have been more different. Lars was much closer to his father than his mother, while Jayla's father died when she was very young. Her mother was charismatic and strong-willed, but Lars said his mother only aspired to be beautiful and alone.

They talked about travel and music, people they'd met, those they'd loved and lost. Periodically Lars would provide color about the city—famous bars and restaurants, major streets, parks, the teams that used to play there, like the Broncos and the Rockies. He parked downtown just a few blocks from Coors Field and they walked, stopping at a couple places for a drink. She liked Denver; there were many more PGs out than she had ever seen concentrated in one place. At one landmark (Lars' word) bar called Wynkoop, she met a girl who knew a lot of the same people in Cusco. Lars just laughed right along with them and their stories, as easily as though he'd been there himself. All the places they stopped had good drinks and good music, and were as unpretentious as she'd experienced anywhere in the States. There were more once, before all their frequent customers started dying. She found herself utterly uninterested in returning to DC, and already was thinking of ways to limit her girl time the next day.

They weren't able to ditch the Secret Service tail, but they kept a respectful distance and Lars didn't seem to mind their presence. They had nothing to protect her from here—especially not Lars. He was gentle and kind, with an almost tranquil way about him. Other than being first daughter, she didn't consider herself very interesting, but he made her feel interesting, and vital, and relevant. She liked him a lot.

After a while it seemed like she should be getting to the hotel. Plus, she was tired from the flight and getting a little drunk. She checked her phone, expecting it to be around 11, but it was nearly 2. When Lars found the door of a narrow bar called Squeezebox locked, she took it as a sign and asked if he wanted a ride to wherever he was going. Neither of them was in condition to drive, so they walked to where Scott and Other Agent were waiting in their sedan and got in the back seat.

She hoped Lars might be staying at the same hotel, but it turned out GIG kept several apartments downtown for executives who had meetings in Denver. He guided the agents to a high-rise near the 16th Street Mall and cracked the door. The plan, he said, was for them to leave after breakfast in one motorcade to drive to GIG's campus. In other words, he was going to be there in the morning. It wasn't in the way she'd hoped, but it would have to do. He took her hand and leaned over to kiss it, but she pulled it away, grabbed his face and planted her own on his lips. It took him by surprise, and she thought she might have blown it, but he just smiled and slid out.

"Well, Just Jayla, it's been real," he said. "See you tomorrow?"

"I hope so."

"Good night."

38

If anything, their ploy worked *too* well. Kyle and his friends had distributed all 30,000 tickets by 11 a.m., and as a result, the homeless PGs holding tickets started gathering outside the stadium around noon. By then, the secret was out about the show they'd added and some of the ticket holders were being offered exorbitant sums for their ticket. The temptation probably was too great for a few of them, even though all the tickets were really for was to help security know who they should check against the list of former residents. If someone got their hands on a ticket but weren't on the list, the ticket was worthless.

Marius was as good as his word and did, in fact, put Mayor McManus and a guest on the list. Since he would be wise to the band's master plan by then, it was hard to know whether he would actually show up or not. In all likelihood, he would never know.

BY THE TIME they left the hotel in discreet, hired cars, Marius wasn't feeling well. He rarely felt fatigue, even after long stretches on the road or endless sound checks. Presently, all he wanted was to crash out until morning, but there was a show to do. When they got to the stadium he found Phil, one of their roadies, who was more than happy to provide him with a couple of the yellow pills he always took on breakdown nights. By the time the lights came up and the crowd exploded, Marius felt right as rain.

THE SHOW WAS GOOD, if not quite as special as the previous night. Of course, the crowd wouldn't have noticed that they weren't super tight, or that Marius' voice broke a few times, or that Naldo was using his practice bass on account of a faulty plug—again—on his regular one. After they got back in the cars and headed out for the hotel, it was surreal to see that basically no one was leaving the show. They were home. Later, they found out several hundred appreciative residents helped break down the elaborate stage in half the time it would've taken otherwise. Marius ordered everyone to sleep in, so they didn't leave for Denver until around ?

Red Rocks was the last show on the current run. They would do three nights there, then rest before hitting LA and working their way down to Austin and New Orleans. Then, another break. Billy drove the first shift, so Marius took the opportunity to write. Had albums still been a thing, the band easily would've had enough material for two solid releases per year on account of Marius' prolific songwriting. He kept an ordinary Gretsch acoustic in the RV expressly for this purpose, and Kris a small Yamaha keyboard for the same reason. They didn't always write together, but when they did, they might bang out a couple songs per hour—the hook and the chorus, at least.

Marius didn't marvel at his own creative output, but there was no doubt the doomsday clock inside his body lent a certain urgency to his work. He didn't understand the science of what would happen to him, but he didn't have to. He'd seen it happen numerous times, starting with Naldo's older brother when they were kids.

There had been many since, but the most recent one had stuck with him.

It was less than a month ago in Indianapolis. They set up in the middle of the Indianapolis Motor Speedway, once a venue for car racing. Both the infield and the stadium filled with fans, swelling attendance to nearly 350,000. Marius had never seen that many people in one place before, and playing to that many was surreal—almost in a bad way. Even so, they put on a great show until about halfway through the first set, when Marius saw a commotion in the stadium a good 200 yards away.

Though he couldn't see exactly what was happening, it was clear enough that someone was in the throes of death. Marius signaled the band to just stop. It took a while before the people in the infield understood what was happening, but once they did it was almost utterly silent. Suddenly Marius decided didn't want *this person* to be one of 20 million like he and the rest of them—he wanted them to be known. And so he stepped up to the mic and said:

"Ladies and gentlemen, we just lost someone here. They were enjoying this shared experience with us, and now they're gone. I don't know about you all, but I want to know who they were. Hey, the people around them, could you please bring them down here? We're going to give them the biggest fucking sendoff in history. Can we get the house lights up?"

There was a murmur of solemn approval. The ten or so people around the fallen PG hesitated for only a moment, then took the body up and started carrying it down on their shoulders. The sea of humanity around them parted, then slowly closed behind the procession like a zipper. As they drew closer, Marius could see it was a young woman wearing a Clockwatchers shirt and jean shorts. One of her flip flops had fallen off. Blood still dripped from one corner of her mouth and her nostrils. Finally they reached the buffer between the crowd and the stage, and Marius indicated to the security detail that they should take her and pass her up to the stage. When they did, Marius and the rest of the band carefully took her and laid her down in front of his monitor. Marius again took the mic and knelt by her.

"Do any of you know this woman?"

Two of the people in the little procession, a teenage boy and a woman, raised their hands, tears streaming down.

"Would one or both of you please join me up here to say a few words about her?"

They looked at each other, then clasped hands as they were helped over the barrier and onto the stage. Both were sobbing uncontrollably.

"Thank you both so much," Marius said. "What was her name?"

"Emily Reser," said the woman, who appeared to be about the same age, maybe older.

"And you are?"

"Kendall. I'm her big sister."

"Thank you, Kendall. And you, my friend?"

"Greg. I'm her brother."

"Thank you, Greg. I'm so sorry for both of you. What can you tell us about Emily?"

For the next 15 minutes, the crowd listened carefully as Kendall and Greg told stories about Emily's life —where she'd been, what she'd done, what she still planned to do. Marius asked them questions, and comforted them, and did everything he could think of to celebrate Emily's life. Some of it was funny, some tragic. Mostly it was heartbreakingly sad. He asked for a moment of silence, and got two full minutes of absolute stillness. Finally there was little left to say, and the band lined up, three on a side, to take her away. Greg cradled her head carefully in his hands so it wouldn't loll to the side. After a time, the band returned to the stage, took up their instruments, and Marius leaned into the microphone.

"This one's for Emily."

39

After Geller dropped his bomb about the president's visit, Ken and Jill went into hyperdrive. By lunch they had a full communications plan and every employee briefed about what was happening and when. They were in touch with Connie's staff immediately. Her itinerary had to be included in her official travel record since it was likely the cat would be out of the bag by the time she arrived. The last thing the White House needed was rumors of a cover-up. Jill prepped and tested the press briefing area in case they needed it, while Ken honed talking points about Geller's return to GIG and how that related to the president's visit. It helped that the two of them were friends, having been photographed together dozens of times in years past, but the particulars were still a little dicey.

For security reasons, the president's motorcade was a group of SUVs of different makes and colors from the Denver field office of the CIA, which were bullet- and bomb-proof but had the advantage of being inauspicious. Somehow this fact was not communicated to the guards at GIG's delivery entrance, who initially refused to let them through. Eventually it was cleared up and the five vehicles proceeded inside. No press had shown up yet. The president's vehicles took a circuitous route over old fire roads on GIG property that had been smoothed out, the entrance for which looked like the overgrown entrance to someone's cabin. They were used so seldom that natural flora had maintained the illusion quite well, and during the winter they weren't used at all.

Connie fished around on the floor for her shoes, the same ones that killed her at the previous evening's fundraiser and she winced a little when she slipped them on her already swollen feet. Out of the corner of her eye she saw Jayla watch her bemusedly.

"We can't all get away with running shoes and yoga pants," she said.

Jayla put up her hands and smiled. "No judgment here."

Jayla pressed her nose to the window to see GIG's famous double-helix structure, the giant steel tubes gleaming in the Colorado sun like some alien mothership. There was no good reason for her to be there;

ostensibly she was spending time with her mother, yes, but now she cared only about seeing Lars again. Their night together in the city felt like the kind of romance she'd seen in old movies—two people from different worlds, thrust together by fate. She'd been in love before, once, with a Chilean college student named Valentino. It felt real, but Valentino knew his destiny was to grow old and have a career, and children, and loving a PG didn't jive with those plans. She'd felt foolish to think it could've ended any other way, and didn't understand why she was so taken with Lars, who acted as though they had all the time in the world.

AFTER THEIR CAR snaked through GIG's underground parking garage and through the blast door that led to the super secret entrance, the man who introduced himself as Geller's head of media relations ushered Connie and four agents inside the elevator. Jayla paused, unsure whether she was supposed to follow, at which point someone tapped her on the shoulder.

Lars.

"You can go for the dime tour, or we can go for a hike and see it from the ridge," he said. "Or you can sit in the car for about three hours. I guess that's a third option."

Jayla tried to suppress her joy and turned toward her

mother, who mouthed "Have fun," as the cylindrical door of the elevator hissed shut.

"Hiking it is," Lars said, and handed Jayla a bottle of water. "GIG owns about 20,000 acres, and it's full of trails. All the way to the top. It's about 3,000 vertical feet over three miles. You up to it?"

"You've got snacks?" she asked.

"First-daughter caliber snacks, in fact."

Lars tightened the straps on the small backpack he was wearing and started toward an unmarked door near the far side of the vehicle loop. Jayla followed and lifted her head to the two agents obviously assigned to follow her.

"Try and keep up," she said.

Two thousand eight hundred fifty-seven vertical feet later, atop a peak with no name, Lars removed his backpack and produced a bottle of cabernet, a bunch of red grapes and a pre-wrapped platter of sliced cheese. The two agents who had impressively matched their pace on the way up sat on a deadfall near a stand of trees at the edge of the rocky summit, jackets off and sleeves rolled, looking like they might die from thirst. Jayla would have left them to question the wisdom of following her, but Lars, upon noticing them, withdrew two bottles of water from his pack and trotted over to them. She expected them to wave him off, but after a brief look at each other they accepted the water with a grateful nod

She fished around his pack for a corkscrew and worked on the bottle as he made his way back. He'd even brought screw-together plastic wine glasses. She was just so-so on wine, preferring it cold and sweet if anything, but it sounded good just then. Lars was smiling broadly when he returned and appeared pleased that she'd proceeded without him.

"They sure were happy to see that bottle," he said. "I think they got more than they bargained for today."

She studied his face, trying to decide whether he'd taken the extra water for himself, her, or just anyone he encountered who needed a drink. Probably the latter.

Lars handed her the assembled glasses as he poured the wine.

"I didn't think to ask if you liked this stuff."

"Hey, nothing's better after a steep, hot hike, right?" she said, stammering a little.

"You said it." The second glass poured, he re-corked the bottle and raised his glass toward the sun. "What should we drink to?"

She looked around, tried to think of a worthy toast. Nothing came to mind, so she nodded toward the two agents.

"To Jeff and Scott," she said.

"Are those really their names?"

"Let's go with that."

He smiled and gestured in their direction.

"To Jeff and Scott!" He said, loud enough for them to hear. Jayla giggled.

For several minutes they ate and drank in beautiful silence. The wine was good—buttery, even. So was the cheese, and the grapes were just right. Everything about this was just right. She would've given anything for her entourage to get lost for half an hour. All around them were the Rockies, unspoiled forests, and natural splendor. It wasn't any better or worse than the Andes, the Cascades, or the Pyrenees. It had all been painted with the same brush, and it affected her the same way. The only thing different about any of this was him. For a moment she imagined herself as a grown woman, coming to this place for the first time or maybe even coming back. It wouldn't happen, nor could it, but she often pondered the adventures she'd had, and whether she'd have them again.

"You're headed back to Washington in the morning, huh?" he said, inspecting each grape before eating it.

"Yeah, early. Mom has a cabinet meeting or something tomorrow afternoon, so …"

"That sucks," he said in such a way that he knew the answer to this question already.

"Why?" she asked, curious to see where this was going.

"Well, it's sort of a big night around here," he said,

watching her face for some sort of realization. None washed over her.

"Yeah?"

"June third, 2063. Six three six three."

A very distant bell rang. The date was significant to her, but she couldn't quite place why. She could tell he enjoyed watching her try to suss it out.

"I know I know what you're talking about," she said. "I can't think of it, though. Remember, I've been in Peru the last two years, so I may need a clue."

Suddenly, Lars started whistling. She instantly recognized it as the chorus to "Flipsides," a song by the biggest band of their generation.

"Clockwatchers at Red Rocks!" she exclaimed. "Holy shit, that's tonight?!"

The Watchers had an enormous following among PGs. All six members were PGs themselves, which was pretty rare. Bands didn't tend to last, let alone form, but the main thing was the occasion for thousands of PGs to come together. Lately, though, they'd been playing a lot of dates and this one had a feeling of culmination about it, as it fell on the band's 10th anniversary. Six guys, three nights. 6/3/63.

"Red Rocks is 57 miles that way," he said, pointing to the southeast. "We'll be there by 7, easy, and they won't go on until almost 9."

He said this so matter-of-factly that it took her a few seconds to put it together.

"We?"

"Well I've got two tickets. Thought you might be interested."

Tickets for this show would've sold out in seconds. Lars may have had connections, but still.

"Are you serious right now?"

"As serious as Jeff and Scott over there."

"Well, shit, then what are we waiting for?! Last one to the bottom buys the first drink."

She sprang up from the grass, her butt numb from sitting, and quaffed the last of her wine. Lars looked up, smiling, and took the empty glass from her.

"Yes, ma'am."

Breathlessly, he chased her down the mountain.

40

After showering in an employee locker room at GIG, Jayla put on fresh clothes and met Lars outside, where he was waiting at the wheel of an expensive sedan. She guessed it was the sort they loaned to important visitors. She looked around for Scott and Jeff and saw them waiting in a government car just across the parking level, then climbed in.

"This is becoming a habit, me chauffeuring you around," he said.

"I can get chauffeured anytime I want."

"Not by me," he said, and wheeled around toward the exit, making the tires squawk.

About an hour later, they joined a parade of vehicles outside Red Rocks. People on foot were making far better progress, and after fifteen minutes of crawling along they came over a crest to see the line stretch another half a mile. PGs didn't do well with lines and waiting. She felt herself getting antsy, even though it was still quite early. Lars seemed to be taking it all in, as though waiting in the car was as much a part of the experience as the moment they killed the house lights. He produced a perfectly rolled joint from his shirt pocket and they passed it back and forth for a while with the windows barely cracked. By the time they finally turned into their lot, her head was swimming. She wondered aloud if GIG had a secret cannabis lab, but he just laughed at her, which made her laugh, too.

She'd never seen so many people her age, or even roughly her age, in one place. Thousands of PGs ranging from maybe 10 all the way to presumably 24 or 25, and many who were too old to be PGs, danced and laughed and sang poorly and made food, or begged for it. Some embraced old friends. Others—more than she ever expected—had babies. She saw license plates from virtually every state, and the swollen, dirty backpacks of the itinerant. There was even a valet for packs and bikes, the huge corral nearly filled. It was a dusty, hot, smelly sea of youth, and Jayla was enthralled. *Was this what it was like before? Did this happen everywhere?*

Behind them at least 100 yards were Scott and Jeff, dressed in shorts and camp shirts and looking as out of place as if they'd left their suits on. People less than half their age sniggered as they strolled by, duty bound and oblivious to their derision. She couldn't help but feel a little bit sorry for them this time, being so out of their element but helpless to do anything about it.

Lars seemed to know everyone. If he didn't, he acted like he did and that was good enough for them. They took a couple beers offered to them, which did little to center her, but it did help quench her considerable thirst a bit before they finally went through security and got inside.

Jayla had never been to Red Rocks, but she instantly understood its appeal. The amphitheater was carved out of the rocky Colorado hillside as though tectonic forces had pushed it up that way eons ago. The weathered eponymous monoliths framed a photo in which 10,000 people would watch their heroes take the stage. Lars took her hand and led her down the side stairs to row 9, seats 45 and 46—directly in front of the mixing booth. She couldn't imagine what they cost or how he got them, but suspected his connections were as deep as his pockets. Back at the security checkpoint, she could see her detail getting a hard time from a security guard who clearly didn't believe they were Secret Service. They would get in eventually and keep eyes on her, but there in the dark she would melt into the crowd. For a few precious hours, it would be just her and Lars.

He left for a few minutes and brought a jug of water back with him just moments before the lights went down. She killed half of it and instantly felt much better. The atmosphere was intoxicating, and now that the effects of the weed had leveled out she was utterly euphoric.

In the wings, under dim bluish purple gels, little flashlights lit up paths for the band, who entered before anyone's eyes had truly adjusted to the dark. Everyone went berserk. A few seconds later, the lead guitarist, JT Carnoy, plugged in and futzed around with a couple chords. The drummer, Yancy Reed, climbed behind his battlement of drums and thumped a little on the kicker before punctuating it with a *rat-tat-tat* on the snare. The bass player and keyboardist, whose names Jayla could never remember, did the same. She glanced at Lars, who just smiled and let out a whoop.

Still in semi-darkness, the tuneless sputtering of the four supporting players coalesced into a subtle order. No one recognized it, but everyone acted like they did. It went on like this for several minutes, during which anticipation for Marius Beecher, the famous and immensely talented frontman, reached a fever pitch. Finally, when no one thought they could stand it anymore, a chord pattern emerged from the unnamed song-in-progress and everyone instantly recognized it as "Further On." Right about then, a figure appeared from behind a curtain in the wings and joined his brothers in the dark. He shouldered his signature blue Gibson SG and struck the monstrous power chord that kicks off the song's initial verse:

Through the gray/The skies alight
We toast the day/And drink the night

The din of humanity was louder than just about anything Jayla had heard, and yet Marius' crystalline voice bored a hole through it and into her ears. Suddenly she got—really *got*—the Watchers like she never had before. It wasn't just how they connected with people, or that they'd played more shows in 10 years than many did in 40. No. They were just so fucking good it was hard to even conceive. No one had time to get that good, but somehow these six musicians had found each other and amassed a catalog of insane quality. The phrase "voice of a generation" was a little trite, but it was practically invented for Marius.

It could have been the weed, she supposed, but that alone couldn't have conjured the magic in of all this. The sea of life and vitality enveloped her, and Lars had led her there. *Great*, she thought. *What the hell do I do with this?*

On and on it went, each song forming the narrative of a grand rock opera in which the two of them starred. For the first time in a long time, maybe ever, she saw herself and her whole doomed generation from the outside. The futility. The rage. The unfettered joy. The story played out on the faces around her, on the hair tossed side to side, on sweaty, tattooed backs, on lips that moved with Marius' words, on her hand as it found

Lars' in the beautiful, barely contained chaos. An epic show in an epic place for a confluence of people attuned to the awful ephemerality of it all.

Marius Beecher poured himself into every song—so much so that he had to take long pauses between to gather himself for the next salvo of wounded, desperate notes and crunchy chords. When he performed, a bubble slowly formed around him and grew exponentially as the show progressed, enveloping everything and everyone in a sphere where there was no Cure, and no PGs, and no death, and anything was possible. It was a drunk sincerity of the best sort, and everyone was under his spell.

Late in the show, his bandmates set down their instruments and gathered around a condenser microphone in a semicircle, kicking off a short set of Opry-style numbers that would showcase their unadorned talent. They merely stood for a few minutes, looking solemnly outward, while they waited for 10,000 people to get quiet. It didn't take long. They began with an a cappella version of the very old gospel tune, "I'll Fly Away."

Some bright morning when this life is over
I'll fly away
To that home on Gods celestial shore
I'll fly away
I'll fly away, oh glory

I'll fly away in the morning
When I die hallelujah by and by
I'll fly away

By the end of the first verse, Jayla, who was only about 50 feet from the stage, noticed something was wrong with Marius. His dreadlocks, which customarily fell over his face in a ropy black veil, couldn't hide profuse sweating and a strange facial expression. Lars noticed it, too, and a low murmur began to gather in the crowd. After a few measures, his bandmates glanced over at him. On they pressed into the next verse.

When the shadows of this life have gone
I'll fly away
Like a bird from these prison walls I'll fly
I'll fly away

Jayla watched Marius' mouth form the word *I'll* after *walls*, and half a heartbeat later he was on the ground convulsing. He took the microphone down with him as he fell, sending a sickening screech of feedback into the amphitheater. There was a collective gasp, and several people ran out from the wings. Nearby, people loudly asked if anyone was a doctor. No one was a doctor who wasn't at least 40, and they probably wouldn't have been there anyway. Of course, it wouldn't have mattered. Fans knew that Marius had turned 25 just a few weeks ago.

Through a gap in the throng of people on stage, Jayla saw Marius' face slathered in blood, the heels of his shoes pushing weakly against the stage as though backing away from an attacker. Someone who might have been a doctor knelt over him while his bandmates tried to hold him in place. Around her, girls clenched each other and cried. Boys stood dumb, mouths hanging open. Nothing rose above a murmur. She squeezed Lars' hand so tightly she thought she'd break his fingers. He was a statue.

She'd seen a fellow PG die just once, on a plane from Miami to Cusco. She heard a commotion behind her and turned in time to see a young woman in a coughing fit, blood spraying from her mouth, her eyes as red as if the whites had been peeled off. She, too, went into violent seizures before her systems shut down. There was nothing anyone could do for her, and nothing anyone could do for Marius, either. Beautiful, talented, full-of-life Marius. He didn't deserve to go like this. No one did. It was an ugly, brutal, terrifying death and she couldn't watch it happen again.

Before she knew what she was doing, she yanked hard on Lars' hand and pulled him behind her as she shoved her way past horrified fans, many of whom had collapsed, stunned, into their seats. Others comforted each other as best they could. Lars seemed to understand immediately and followed close behind her. When they got to the side aisle, others had also decided that either it was all too much, or that they should find their cars and get out of there before the situation deteriorated. She was tempted to cast one final look back at the stage, but resisted. Out of the corner of her eye noticed Scott and Jeff still standing there in their dorky outfits, craning their necks to find her.

They were near the front of the first wave that spilled out through the main gate and into the parking lot. After about a hundred yards Lars placed his other hand on hers and spun her around. She hadn't realized her eyes were wet until she tried to focus on his face but couldn't. He pulled her into him and held her close as she cried and thumped her fists against his back. There was nothing to say.

41

Connie learned the broad strokes during a closed-door meeting with Geller. He explained how Heidi came to be at GIG, and that, as far as they knew, she was the oldest PG in existence. He said her longevity was extraordinary, and that they hoped to learn whether anything in her unique genetic makeup had made it so.

She listened carefully, asked questions, and understood the answers well enough to repeat them to key cabinet members if pressed. As long as she'd known him, Geller was enigmatic and obtuse when it came to sharing research information. But on this occasion he was oddly forthcoming. He said it was extremely unlikely that anything they learned about Heidi would lead to a treatment, and that it would be dangerous for anyone to believe otherwise. Geller was so clear on this point that it made her wonder how he could be so certain

She'd been to GIG once before, as chair of the House Committee on Science, Space, and Technology when she was still a Congresswoman. It was impressive then and still was, though it had changed. What began as a birthplace of radical ideas and world-changing treatments had morphed into a patent factory, focused mostly on agricultural and biochemical research. As the years rolled on, there was a feeling that if GIG couldn't reverse the Cure's effects, no one could.

The Cure's repercussions would play out over centuries, not decades. One of its most troubling casualties was a national reticence toward bold, brash ideas. America was a once bitten, thrice shy sort of country, and so innovations—especially in medicine—had largely stalled in the wake of the disaster. No one was willing to back the risky play. There were no Lyle Merriweathers anymore. If the US was still No. 1 in anything, it was fear.

When Jayla contacted her to say she was going to a concert and taking a commercial flight back to DC, she was a little hurt. Part of her wanted to say, *but I only have 10 years left with you—maybe less.* Instead she just told her to have a good time and be safe, and that she'd see her in a couple days.

Connie's visit to GIG somehow went unreported, much to the shock of their communications team. She left the way she came, via back roads in ordinary-looking FBI vehicles, and headed back to Denver. Jayla would meet her there after the concert and then, hopefully, they'd have some quality time together. She came looking for hope and time her daughter, but came away with precious little of either.

42

Jayla clambered up the hillside at the far south end of the parking lot and sat heavily on the smooth surface of Ship Rock, her gaze drifting across the sprawl of the city as tears flowed down her cheeks. She made no effort to wipe them away. Lars followed and sat quietly next to her. Many years earlier, from where she sat, you could still take in the whole of Denver, from Broomfield and Arvada all the way down to the south end of Littleton. Now, it was solid city as far as the eye could see in any direction. Down below them, a handful of emergency vehicles were still parked by the amphitheater entrance. The parking lots were dotted with mourners, campers and whoever else, many of whom huddled over tiny campfires or charcoal grills. Above the building wind rose an occasional flutter of laughter, and the tears would return.

During the long silence they shared, Lars came to understand that Jayla was about as innocent as PGs came. She had done things she probably wasn't proud of and fancied herself a tomboy rebel soul, but she still was the First Daughter and thus had been protected from the darker facets of PG life. He'd seen at least a dozen people go, some of whom he knew well. Like Marius Beecher, it was messy and violent every time. As hard as that was to see, it was worse if you knew them.

A good friend of his, Bobby Hardwicke, went into similar convulsions in his bivy at a state park in Vermont. The others came out of their tents and gathered around Bobby as he thrashed about, the blood he coughed coating the inside of the little bright yellow tent like grotesque abstract art. He screamed and made awful gagging sounds. He gasped for air. There was nothing to be done but just be there for him and say his name, along with whatever else seemed comforting.

We're here, Bobby.

It's okay.

Try to let go, Bobby. It'll hurt less.

We'll miss you, Bobby. You're a good person. Take that with you.

This only went on for maybe four minutes before he drowned in the blood and fluid that quickly filled his lungs, but it felt like an hour. Nobody went peacefully unless they took care of it themselves. No matter how ready they thought they were, or how much they'd made their peace with it, they all fought for another few moments. Marius almost certainly would have made his peace, but just as certainly would not have wanted to ruin a beautiful moment. A man like him would've found that worse than the pain.

After kind words were said about Bobby and stories shared about his life, they gathered him up in his bivy and carried him into the forest for a simple burial. It was illegal on multiple fronts, but most PGs, given the choice, did it this way. The government crematoriums were seldom nearby, and they all seemed just a little too reminiscent of WWII. Usually someone would anonymously message the family, if possible, with the coordinates of the gravesite. Lars didn't know what happened after that, if anything. He preferred to think they would simply leave wildflowers and say a few words, or perhaps leave some small, nondescript monument.

Jayla was too young and inexperienced to have come to terms with any of this. He was once, too—pretty much that whole first year after he turned 13 and struck out on his own. It was all too much for his young mind to handle, and he'd broken down just like she was now. She was a stone upon a stone, her face expressionless. Lars didn't know if he should sit by her, hug her, talk to her or just leave her be. They'd been up there almost an hour and a half. That was a long time for a PG to sit and do nothing. It was much too early to say whether he loved this girl, but he cared enough about her to stay, and that seemed significant. He got up to force the blood back into his legs and approached her slowly.

"Listen, I hate to say it, but I'm starving."

The first time she tried to speak, nothing came out. She probably hadn't had anything to drink since they were on the road from GIG, and that was a very long time ago. She swallowed and croaked:

"I know. Me, too."

She rose suddenly and started half-sliding, half-stumbling down the hill in the gloaming. Lars stared after her for a moment, then followed her back down to the main lot. She walked stiffly past the remaining concertgoers, eyes straight ahead, ignoring completely the invitations to eat, or smoke, or whatever. Lars had trouble keeping up, but eventually caught her near the far side and walked half a step behind down the short main entrance to Trading Post Road, where the car and a half-gallon vacuum bottle of ice water waited. He didn't see any signs of Scott or Jeff.

She drank most of the water herself. He finished what was left then drove out to find somewhere to eat. There were plenty of options just over the ridge into the city, so after about 15 minutes they pulled into a Vietnamese place and ordered heaping bowls of vermicelli and broth with a bunch of spring rolls. As they did, some of the color and life returned to Jayla's face. She really was quite beautiful, though her eyes were still puffy and her crisp braids had started to unravel. Eventually they ate their way through the entire meal and sat again in the silence, which Jayla eventually broke.

"I'm not going back to DC."

"Okay."

"Tonight ... changed me."

"I know."

"I'm not ready to talk about it yet."

"That's cool."

"We need to go somewhere. Tonight. Somewhere they can't find us."

"Scott and Jeff, you mean."

"Anyone. It has to be just you and me. At least for a while. I can't ... I can't deal with anyone else right now."

She reached suddenly across the table and grabbed his hand. He looked into her eyes and saw desperation. Loneliness. Sadness. Confusion. It was all there, and urgently so. He would've said anything to ease her mind just then.

"We own land in the mountains. I camp there sometimes, but only by myself. We'll stay in the city tonight and get what we need in the morning."

He saw some of the intensity in her eyes ebb, if only

a little. If what she needed was a few days to process everything, it wasn't a problem to give it to her. He was a little worried about what her mother—the president —would do, but he would deal with that later.

"I'd like that," Jayla said, with a faint smile.

The two Secret Service agents were acting grave, as though they expected Erik to share their deep concern when he really didn't. What he wanted was to go back to bed.

"He comes and goes as he pleases. I'm betting Jayla does the same. They're legal adults. They probably got a room somewhere."

Jeff (was he the tall one?) tapped a few notes into his device. It had gone on like this for nearly an hour. The agents came knocking at 2 a.m. and explained that they had lost track of the First Daughter, and that she was most likely with Lars. Erik explained repeatedly that his son didn't make a habit of checking in, and that weeks often passed without hearing from him. That he happened to have Jayla with him wasn't of any particular concern to him, and there was no reason for anyone to be freaking out. He was made to say whatever he knew about Lars' political affiliations (none), what countries he'd lived in (too many to remember) and who his associates were (no idea).

Finally, the short one (Scott?) said they were done and left information about how to reach them should Erik hear from Lars. He remained in the living room and read until he was confident he could fall back asleep. The sun would be up in less than an hour.

Though he intended to read, he mostly thought about Heidi. She was an enigma to him, in more ways than one. Firstly, she was a medical mystery. The actual Cure injection included isotopes that could show any lab whether an individual had received it or not. This was one of the first things Erik's team verified, and she'd lit up the screen, though not as brightly as usual. That was peculiar.

Knowing that, a separate team looked into her family history, going as far back as the late 1800s when her ancestors came over from Denmark. Her entire family tree was mapped and indexed, with impressively comprehensive details about who lived where, when, and what they did. The next most likely reason she was alive and healthy was due to some mutation that actually subdued or delayed the deadly gene switch. It wasn't uncommon for certain ethnic backgrounds to show unusually high resistance to, or propensity for certain genetic disorders. Though not every theory and trail along this line had been followed to its end, Erik knew in his gut it wasn't the answer.

Unfortunately, other than these two possibilities, the theories were few. One was that either her or her mother's blood chemistry had somehow rendered inert the complex cocktail of proteins, viral vectors and peptides that formed the Cure, leaving only the isotopes behind. Another was that the actual injection had been mislabeled, or hadn't been properly administered. These theories held water but were impossible to prove, and in any case they weren't useful because they couldn't lead to a treatment. That still was the ultimate goal.

Medical mysteries aside, Heidi was hard to figure. She was beautiful in all the ways Lucy hadn't been—earthy, practical, and warm. She had a quality—maybe it was all the time she'd obviously spent out in the sun doing stuff—that Erik thought of as golden. They didn't spend that much time together. Effectively she was little more than a neighbor of GIG's who lived in a lavish guest house in exchange for her time. As long as anyone believed she could be part of a solution, she seemed content to stay.

The time they did spend, however, was intense. He was drawn powerfully to her, and he thought it might go the other way. If it did, she wasn't the type who would let on anyway, which only magnified her allure. Still, he felt he caught enough lingering glances or subtle bits of body language to think that there might be more to their relationship. Unfortunately, he'd nearly run out of legitimate reasons to keep her there.

And then there was Geller. He was uncharacteristically hands-off when it came to their investigation, so much so that it felt odd. Maybe he was just being deferential, but that wasn't his style. He seemed confident from day one that Heidi had nothing to offer GIG or the millions waiting to die, so it wasn't clear to anyone why he was hanging around. He had a theory. It wasn't very likely, but he couldn't bring it to the fore until all other possibilities had been exhausted. That time was drawing very near.

44

L ars had to pull the car up by the front door of REI to load everything up. He got a 4-person tent, sleeping bags, everything they needed to cook, and a bunch of other stuff. Jayla stayed in the car for fear she might be recognized—especially if her mother had engaged federal resources to find her. She also wanted to protect Lars if that was the case. She remained in the car while he stopped at a grocery store, handing Lars a letter she'd addressed to a strange address and name in DC. She explained it was an emergency address she could use to reach her mother.

He studied it for a moment as though unsure what to do—the mail system had gone private many years ago and was passed around from company to company like a hot potato. He didn't even know who operated it now. It was generally quite expensive, but most grocery stores could still mail letters. Although it was clear she didn't want to be found for a while, it was smart to send word she was okay, lest half the government descend on Colorado to try and find her. All this went through his head in the space of two seconds, and so he took the letter into the store and mailed it. Thirty minutes later he returned with what looked like a month's worth of food.

They drove in silence. She didn't have anything to say just yet, and she could tell he was being respectful of that. They entered the mountains near Boulder this time, going west for a while on a winding road before angling north, until even the remote community of Nederland was a good hour behind them. Eventually, Lars turned into an overgrown drive blocked by a gate. He got out, unlocked a chain, pulled in and re-locked it behind him. She assumed they were close, but going was slow on the rough road. They drove what seemed like another 15 miles though it was probably closer to 7 or 8, and finally stopped when the road basically just petered out. Lars killed the engine and looked at her.

"We walk from here," he said, and got out.

It took some time to load their supplies into a huge pair of backpacks, though it would've taken longer if Jayla didn't know camping as well as she did. She even paused to show Lars a few tricks she learned about packing from a Chilean guide, and they smiled at each other for the first time since the previous morning.

They hiked in for about two hours, stopping once for a snack, and Lars led her over a small ridge that pitched steeply down to the most pristine mountain lake she'd ever seen. It was maybe 200 yards across and half as wide—basically a big rain barrel—and the bottom was so clearly visible through the glassy water that it looked fake. They hugged the ridge line to the left, eventually traversing downward as the grade softened. After a while they reached the edge and Jayla instantly removed her boots to plunge her aching, hot feet into the cold water.

"I call it Teacup Lake," Lars said, peeling off his boots as well. "I don't know if it has another name."

"It's incredible!"

There was only one logical place to pitch camp: a thinly grassed patch on the opposite shore surrounded by scrubby pines. She started to walk out further, but was immediately surprised by how deep it got. She stumbled a bit but Lars caught her arm in his strong hand and steadied her, saving her from an unplanned swim.

"Thanks."

By the time they circled around, figured out their new gear and set up camp, the sun had already dipped below the edge of the ridge. Lars gathered some firewood and she tried to put a meal together from their supplies, which she now realized would probably last about 10 days, give or take. It would be enough.

45

The car. Connie understood every detail of the timeline the night of Jayla's disappearance save for one thing: Why didn't the agents simply wait at Lars' car?

The way Scott and Jeff explained it, they lost Lars and Jayla in the confusion after that kid from the band died, then ended up following two people who looked almost exactly like them to *another* car, which they followed halfway to Pueblo before realizing it wasn't them. She failed to understand how such an egregious error was possible. Of course, she had to admit to herself that assigning a detail to Jayla probably wasn't necessary in the first place. Yes, she'd always had some sort of tail on her as long as she was abroad, but she knew how to take care of herself.

Jesus, she'd never gotten used to that. She thought

of herself at 15—a nervous, scrawny, outwardly confident but insecure kid who hadn't planned her high-school career beyond making the debate team and playing alto sax in the better of the two bands. She'd never even had a boyfriend. She had plans, and she pursued them with unwavering tenacity: Lawyer. Judge. State Attorney General. Senator. President. Her career—her *life*—had a trajectory. If this, then that. Then, if all goes well, that. She didn't and couldn't understand this life of artificial urgency, of trying to find meaning and purpose within its crowded bookends.

Many chose a hedonistic, indulgent, lawless existence free of long-term consequence. And really, why wouldn't you? Why choose restraint when you knew how and when you'd go? It was a problem—especially considering the great empathy that most people had for the Perfect Generation. For the bad ones, it made people easy targets; kindness was easy to exploit. Still, the overwhelming majority chose a life of travel, exploration, and brief but meaningful friendships. So it was with Jayla.

A soft rap came at the door to the Oval Office, and Ethan, her assistant, poked his head inside.

"Madam President, Jim's here to see you."

"Send him in."

Jim Dougherty was her chief of staff. A pain in the ass, but hard-nosed and a stickler for detail. She'd finally trained him to call her Connie, which had taken almost two terms. He carried an envelope.

"Thanks for seeing me, Connie. Security's been over this thoroughly and we verified the handwriting. I wouldn't bother you with it unless it seemed important."

"A written letter? Is it Jayla?"

"Yes, ma'am."

"Oh, thank God."

She donned her reading glasses and took the envelope, which bore a Denver postmark. Jim took a seat across the desk from her and leaned forward as she read, as though ready to spring into action at any moment. Constance hadn't actually seen her daughter's handwriting since she was in school, and there's no way she would've recognized it herself.

Mom,

As you probably know, I was one of the 10,000 people who watched Marius Beecher die. Lars and I had to get away from everything. We are okay.

Marius was an amazing talent and his music was important to people. But just as I felt I was part of a larger community, I realized that the thing we share isn't how we live. It's how we will die. It's violent and bloody. There's no dignity in it. To know and love someone is to risk watching them die. It's no kind of life.

Lars and I are young and in love. We are beautiful. Our time together is beautiful. We are surrounded by splendor. There is only one way to preserve this moment just as it is. So many moments will be taken from us, but not this one. I won't let it.

I am sorry. Just know that I am happy. This isn't your fault.

Love,

Jayla

She folded the letter and and tucked it back in the envelope.

"Jim, get me the FBI field office in Denver. Right now."

The sleek maroon SUV hummed along the winding gravel road, its electric motor no louder than the gentle breeze that stirred the encroaching firs and aspens. Erik didn't know exactly why he was going, or what he was going to say to Heidi when he got there. Whatever he said, it had to be enough to keep her from leaving.

At that moment, however, his foremost thought was of Lars. The kid was a free spirit with his own agenda. Sometimes he was around, but mostly he wasn't and that was okay. Erik always felt that he would've been a model father given a normal situation, cheering a kid on at soccer games and admonishing him for not studying hard enough. But the Cure had robbed him and millions of others of that normalcy. He'd felt that loss acutely, and it drove him to find a solution. Lars had something special to offer the world, and Erik owed him the opportunity. It didn't matter that he wasn't going to win any awards for parenting. The boy had turned out pretty well in spite of the icy relationship between him and Lucy. He wasn't worried about the fact that he disappeared with Jayla—in a way it was actually amusing—but he did worry a bit about the possible repercussions.

As usual, the immense house had a persistent look of emptiness, a dual function of its excessive scale and its dated architecture. He pulled in under the portico driveway and put the car in park, still unsure what he was really even doing there. After a few moments he got out and tentatively rang the bell. Heidi answered wearing yoga pants and a sports bra, her face flush and moist with sweat. Her hair was pulled up in a tangle that would elegantly undo itself the instant she removed a single strategically placed clip.

"Hey," she said, surprised.

"Did I catch you at a bad time? I can swing by later if you—"

"No, no, it's fine. Actually I was debating going longer, but now I have a reason to stop. C'mon in."

He'd been there dozens of times with other guests, but not with her. It felt more lived in, somehow, like she was the trophy wife of some absentee tycoon. She padded over to the built-in fridge.

"Want a smoothie? I make a mean one," she said.

"Actually, that'd be great. I haven't had breakfast."

"Most important meal of the day," she said. "Guess I don't have to tell you. So what's up? If you came for a urine sample, you're like five minutes too late."

She peeled bananas and sliced strawberries and kiwis into a giant blender as she talked, then started measuring out mysterious powders by the tablespoon. Then she started scooping in ice.

"Tempting, but no thanks," he said. "I just wanted to talk, I guess."

"Hold that thought."

She activated the industrial blender, which sounded more like a fighter engine than a kitchen appliance. Within ten seconds, the mixture was a silky pink froth. She flicked it off and poured the contents into two tall glasses, filling them perfectly. She proffered one to him.

"Monsieur," she said grandly. "Oh shit, wait!"

She dashed around the end of the huge island and rummaged around in a drawer until she produced two oversized straws, then hurried back around to give him one.

"Thanks," he said, grateful to have another few seconds to gather his thoughts. The smoothie tasted as good as it looked—fresh and sweet, with a little grit from whatever vitamins, bee pollen or whatever she dumped in there. She didn't seem like she needed an energy boost, but he did. He certainly needed something.

"Wow—it's awesome," he said.

"Right?" she said, smiling, and sucked down a few huge mouthfuls. Then she leaned on the counter and looked at him expectantly. "So, what brings ya by? Need to poke me again?"

"The genealogy work is pretty much done," he stammered. "They've gone back to two generations before your great, great, great, great grandparents landed on Ellis Island."

"Geez. That's … thorough."

"Yeah. And we've pretty much ruled out any mutations. In fact, your DNA is basically flawless."

"Hooray for me."

"Right, but …"

"But it doesn't get you any closer to a solution."

"Yeah."

"So what's next?"

"I don't know. We've learned about all we can about you. At any rate, we have enough samples that if there was something we missed, we could go back. The only thing left is—"

"Gee, Doc, It's starting to sound like you don't need me here anymore."

"Technically, no."

"What about non-technically?"

He looked at her for what seemed like a long time, trying to read what she wanted to hear.

"I guess there's a part of me that doesn't want you to leave."

She raised her eyebrows and took a long drink. "What part is that?"

He set his smoothie down and moved slowly toward her. She locked her eyes on his and didn't move.

"The part that wanted you to be the answer."

"Sorry to disappoint."

A tendril of her blond hair, still damp with sweat, clung to the side of her face. He reached slowly up and moved it out of the way, behind her ear. His mouth was dry and hot. He wasn't lying when he told her he didn't know why he was there, and yet in this moment he knew. Heidi was bursting with life, and so, it seemed, she could remain for quite some time. A few weeks back, she potentially was the most important woman in America. Now, she was almost free to be a tumbleweed again, unbound by anything and anyone.

But though her significance to the world had lessened, her significance to him had only intensified. She was like the knife that could finally cut the thin, but consequential thread between him and his late wife, and he realized now that he wanted her to. There was a certain intimacy to their relationship, but it had been professional and arm's length. Part of it was decorum, but part of it was out of some perverse notion that he was supposed to be alone.

He pulled her face to his and kissed her deeply,

hoping it would be like riding a bike. It wasn't that there hadn't been women since Lucy, but not like this. They weren't the kind of girls you kissed just to kiss. This was different. He wanted to get it right, and when her fingers curled around the bottom of his shirt and tugged it free of his pants, he figured he probably had.

DEEP INTO A WARM, ethereal sleep between impossibly luxurious bedsheets with a woman 19 years his junior, Erik's phone rang. He would've ignored it, and was kicking himself for even leaving it on, but the tone indicated a GIG emergency. Next to him, Heidi groaned and rolled over, balling the comforter up over her head. Her ratted blond hair splayed out from under it like it had grown from a seed in the pillow. He smiled and picked up the phone.

"This is Erik."

A calm voice said, "Dr. Erik Heiser?"

"Yes."

"Please hold for the President of the United States."

FIFTEEN MINUTES LATER, Erik's car skidded to a halt in his driveway. One of GIG's helicopters was being fueled; all he needed to do was grab a couple things, race up to the helipad and go. But for some reason, his circle drive wasn't empty. One of GIG's fleet vehicles was parked in it.

He found the front door open and, strode in a huff around the side of the kitchen to find Geller seated on the couch. Erik stood there for a moment, trying to look as incredulous and irritated as possible.

"I know what's happened," Geller said, standing. "And I know you need to leave right away."

"So why are you here? How did you even get inside?"

Geller ignored the question. "There's something you need to know about Lars."

"I know he's been brainwashed by that crazy bitch, so I have to go. We'll talk later."

Erik pivoted and started back down the hallway, only to hear Geller's voice call after him.

"He's not a PG."

Erik stopped in his tracks and slowly turned. Geller had moved to the end of the hall.

"What did you say?"

"He never was."

Erik stared dumbly at him.

"Lucy knew she carried the gene for Huntington's. So did you, so did we, of course. The chances of her passing it on were small but I think deep down she just never drank the Kool-Aid. Whatever her reasons, at the last minute she changed her mind. I only know because you asked me to administer it personally. She made me promise never to tell anyone."

Erik studied him for what seemed like a long time, trying to form words through his apoplexy. Geller had no problem with silence, and so he remained in it, staring back, hands in his pockets.

"You're telling me this *now*?! He might be taking his own life *as we speak* and you drop this fucking *bomb* on me?! What the FUCK, Brent?!"

"You needed to know. He's going to live a full life. Well, assuming he doesn't—"

"Fuck this. I have to go *right now*."

Erik wanted to tackle the old man, pin him down on the berber carpet and pummel his face into mush. His brain swam with questions—mostly ones he'd never be able to ask because Lucy was gone. But he pushed them and his homicidal thoughts aside and went into the bedroom to fetch his own med kit, a pair of boots, and a jacket. He also popped two motion-sickness pills for the helicopter. Moments later, he brushed past Geller on his way out.

"I'm very sorry," Geller offered.

Erik whirled and thrust his face right up to Geller's, fishing for some parting words to hiss, but settled for radiating pure rage. He about-faced and left, leaving Geller right where he was. He didn't follow. Erik jumped in his car and pounded his foot down on the accelerator, rocketing him straight across his perfectly kept lawn. As he drove, his mind raced. Was Geller for real? If so, why had he kept it from him even after Lucy was gone?

It didn't matter now. He couldn't *know* where Lars was; he could only guess. If he was wrong, he might be too late. Of course, he might be too late anyway. All he knew was that he had to get to Teacup Lake.

From *The Perfect Generation: A Memoir*
by Dr. Brent A. Geller

Lucy Heiser wasn't what you'd call likable. She was impossibly beautiful, one of those rare women who seemingly get better as they go. And her accent, from the upper crust of Adelaide, Australia, was the aural equivalent of Belgian chocolate melting on your tongue. I probably sound like a dirty old man saying that now.

Alas, she was decidedly less beautiful on the inside. She'd gotten more (or less, depending how you looked at it) than she bargained for with Erik. He was married first to the work and then her, and the arrangement was mutually unsatisfactory. I was shocked when Erik told me she was pregnant, but more so to learn that she agreed to the treatment. Frankly, validating Erik's work seemed out of character.

As the day neared, Erik pulled me aside in the hall and told me, with some hesitation, that Lucy requested I do it personally. That seemed odd, since there wasn't any logical or legal reason why Erik wouldn't do it himself. But he gave me his blessing so I accepted. The following week I arrived at the onsite clinic, gave her charts a quick scan, and was informed that she was prepped and ready to go.

Giving a microinjection to a developing fetus is delicate work. Our method was robot-assisted but that didn't make it easy. We used a local anesthetic and, once the patient was prepped and lightly sedated, it only took a few minutes. In fact, it took longer to explain the risks and the mechanics of the procedure than to actually do it. Among the thoroughly communicated risks were the unknown long-term effects of genetic manipulation. We made certain everyone understood what they were signing up for, including Lucy.

A few minutes before we started, Lucy asked to speak with me privately. I sent the nurse and an intern away, at which time Lucy told me that she didn't want it anymore, if she ever did. That happened sometimes; about 1 in every 200 patients changed their minds at the last minute.

What *didn't* happen very often was that the patient not only changed their minds at the last minute, but asked for our complicity in hiding that fact. That was more difficult than it sounded. With 3-6 people in the room, it wasn't ethical to ask anyone to claim they assisted with a procedure that didn't happen. We'd discussed this very scenario during clinical trials and had an unofficial policy that we would not lie on any patient's behalf. Whether she told her friends and family, or even her child, about the procedure was up to her. None of our business. Our records would truthfully indicate whether the procedure was completed or not, and if someone with a legal reason to see their medical records examined them, they would know the truth. This was the only ethical thing to do, and the only way to indemnify GIG.

Unfortunately, most patients weren't married to one of our senior researchers. Erik knew everyone who would be in the room and vice-versa. They needed plausible deniability. I didn't care what Lucy's reasons were, but I respected them. At the time, their marriage was already showing signs of cracking, and I knew how Erik could be about the work because he was just like me. He wouldn't have taken it well. I told her I would neither volunteer the truth nor hide it. That was good enough for her.

While prepping for the procedure, I swapped out the cartridge of Cure for a saline one, and we went through all the motions. The money shot, if you will, was just a series of harmless squirts of saltwater in the amniotic sac. Lucy's child would not be joining the Perfect Generation.

Only he did. One morning several years later, Erik confided that he had "the talk" with Lars where he explained what would happen to him, and how the world worked. Lucy never told him the truth and I felt bound by my word to her, loathsome though she was. He fell into a deep depression and I made him take time away, hoping that having him around all the time would practically force the truth out of Lucy, but it never did.

You might think it unconscionable that I wouldn't betray Lucy's confidence for Erik's sake, sparing him so much anguish even if it cost him his marriage. Goodness knows I held him in far greater esteem than her. But it was a *family* secret. Lucy's decision to forgo the treatment was easy to respect, whatever her state of mind at the time, but to leave Lars with the impression he was doomed and subject Erik to the same belief was cruel, even for her. I became convinced that there was something I didn't know about their dynamic, their history—*something*. I couldn't justify betraying her trust without knowing why, but the why was none of my business. So, I kept my mouth shut.

Hard as it might seem to understand, Lars' welfare was my chief concern in the matter. Let me explain.

By the time the Exception Act passed, childhood and young adulthood were virtually the same. Parents felt the need to protect their kids from the world for an unnaturally long time, and the kids didn't know any better. Not many young people even started their fully independent lives until they were in their mid-late twenties. Eventually Lars would learn the truth. He would turn 25, then 26, then 27 and realize that his fate wasn't sealed, for whatever reason. He could come looking for answers when he was ready to learn them, and only then would I explain the circumstances of his survival, if I was still around. I'd see that he understood. But by then he would have lived life so thoroughly that every extra day would feel like gravy and the truth wouldn't matter anymore. Though I can never know Lucy's reasons, I think she felt her life was on rails. She wanted Lars to feel free.

I knew Erik would suffer more than just about anyone at GIG, and he did. He bore not only the anguish of any PG father, but also, like Baz, the knowledge that he had played a role in it. I knew he would blame me most of all. I also knew that he would practically kill himself trying to avert that fate.

As he grew up, Lucy became less and less a factor in Lars' life and Erik more so. Lars was 9 when she died, by which point the two of them had a strong bond. Her death was ostensibly an accident, which I don't believe for a second. She was less capable of being a good mother than Erik was of being a good father, and I think she knew it. Whether she took her own life, was intentionally careless, or simply faked the whole thing, I'm convinced she did what she did for selfless reasons, and that both Erik and Lars were better for it.

48

It pleased Lars to be there for Jayla at such a vulnerable time in her life, and there was a frail beauty in her pathos that coaxed out something like love in him. He supposed he was falling for her a little. Yes, what happened at Red Rocks had pulled a shade over her, and six days at the lake hadn't made much of a dent. He'd expected it would take two or three nights for her to come to terms with what happened, but she still bore the haunted look of someone who had experienced something too terrible to process.

They'd eaten, drank, swam, smoked weed, talked, laid in the sun and fucked—all at altitude, mind you—pretty much since arriving. He was spent. He'd asked her what was in the letter he mailed, but she only reiterated that it was to let her mother know she was okay.

That would've satisfied him were it not for Jayla's fraught relationship with her mother. Something about that letter didn't sit right with him.

Though they talked for hours at a time, neither brought up Marius. It really had been awful, contrasted as it was with the joy and energy that surrounded it. It also had been more tortured an exit than others he'd seen, except for maybe poor Bobby Hardwicke in his tent—but that was more pathetic than tragic, given that Bobby was hardly a messianic figure. During the long silences, and as he drifted off to sleep, he thought about what he'd say when it finally came up. He'd tried to understand what she was thinking and feeling, and why her light had died. In the process her melancholy was slowly becoming his.

On the morning of their seventh day at the lake, he woke to see her sitting cross-legged on her sleeping bag with a warm smile. The luster of her sumptuous, dark skin had returned to pre-Red Rocks levels, and she looked utterly at peace with the world. They'd need a supply run if they were staying longer, which he would try to avoid, but something about the way she looked that morning made him think she'd come to terms with whatever she was going through.

"Good morning, sleepy boy," she said.

"Hey," he said, coming up on one elbow.

"I made tea," she said, and placed a hot mug in his

hands. He sipped from it, and the chill in the tent ebbed.

"Thanks. Someone's happy today."

"I am," she said, and leaned in to plant a slow, tender kiss on his lips. "It's a beautiful morning and I'm with a beautiful guy."

He ran fingers through his mop of blond hair and shook his head. "I need a real shower."

"I think you're perfect," she said.

They talked a little as he finished his tea, but mostly they just looked at each other—not just in the way that young lovers do, but as though they'd just been rescued. It felt strange, but nice. *Really* nice.

He dressed and they made breakfast together. He held the last of their eggs and toast over the burner with metal tongs, leaving a pale outline of the utensil on each side. They made more tea. When the sun got high enough, they swam. On the first day his watch fell off in the water and they had to swim around until they found it —not that hard with gin-clear water and a flat, rocky bottom, but it was actually kind of fun. That evolved into a game where they would turn their backs and he would throw it over his shoulder into the water. Then they'd count to three and jump in, each trying to find it first. Jayla was a faster swimmer and almost always won. They played this game several times throughout the day, pausing for lunch, and again later on.

In the heat of the afternoon, they made love right

out in the open on a patch of moss that felt like carpet. Their exertions made Lars hot, so he waded naked into the water. When he turned, Jayla was hurrying back from the campsite but soon followed suit. She came up behind him and wrapped her arms around him as he took in the scene, which never got any less spectacular.

"This was some day," he said.

"Yes it was. And guess what?"

"What?"

"I have something for you. For us, really."

"You just gave me something."

She smiled. "No, something else."

He turned and wrapped her up in his arms.

"Should I close my eyes?"

He did for a few playful seconds, but she said nothing and her arms left him. When he opened them and looked down, she was holding one of their folding knives.

"Um, wait," he said. "That's my present? It's already mine."

"I wanted this day to be perfect, and it was," she said. "If we lived our whole lives, we'd have a bunch more just like it. But we won't, and we can't. We had this day."

His arms fell from around her and he felt himself take a small step back.

"I'm not following you."

"I know why you took us here. And I want you to

know what a perfect thing it was to do. If you hadn't been there, I don't know what would've happened. But you were, and now we've had something that few people ever have. Stories don't need happy endings—just good ones. Proper ones. You gave us that."

She unfolded the knife and flicked its edge with her thumb. In that moment, he realized what was happening.

"Jayla, how about you give me the knife? It'll be dark soon, we'll make a fire, and tomorrow we can get up early, pack all this in the car and have a real breakfast. We can find a good hotel and clean up, and we'll figure things out from there."

"After we do it I think we should just sit in the shallow part over there where it's sandy and hold each other as the sun sets. We'll probably get super cold, but I don't think it'll be as bad if we're close."

"Wait. Just wait, okay? Let's talk this out. I don't want this and neither do you. Lemme—"

He lunged for her arm but she turned away, like it was all some kind of tease.

"Oh no you don't, mister!" she said, and swam quickly for the shallows. He followed as fast as he could, but she put 20 feet between them in just a few seconds and turned back toward him, now sitting with everything below her shoulders submerged.

"One of us has to be first," she said, trembling. "Just don't forget to hold me after, okay? I love you."

"Jayla, don't!"

With less than six feet between them, she drew the blade up one wrist to her elbow, then the other, as casually as opening an envelope. For a few seconds there was nothing, as though she'd pantomimed it, but then a dark red stripe appeared and her life started emptying out into the water. Lars drew in a sharp breath and stood there, aghast. She stared at her arms dumbly for a moment then smiled and let herself fall back into the water. She lifted the knife up out of the water, now stained deep red.

"Grab it," she said. "It's slippery."

Her voice shook him from his stupor. He slid toward her in the water and took the knife, carefully. He switched hands and tossed it toward shore so she wouldn't see, then collapsed in the water beside her and pulled her to him. The color was already going from her face, and she was trembling.

"Did you do it?" she said sleepily. "I couldn't see …"

"Yeah," he said, tears streaking his face. He plunged his arms in the water beside her. "It stings."

"It doesn't last long," she said, and reached across his chest with her left arm, her head on his shoulder. He could feel the long gash on her forearm and the warmth flowing from it. His body shook.

"It'll be okay," she said. "We'll be okay. I love you."

She groaned softly but said nothing. He knew the

darkness was coming fast for her, and he knew what she wanted to hear. No harm in saying it now.

"I love you, too."

He felt her fingertips move up and down his chest, just a little. Then, nothing.

49

The silver and blue GIG helicopter hummed over the mountains, its speed hampered by a building north wind. Bizarrely strong currents threw it around like a paper airplane, and had he skipped the motion sickness pill he would've coated the cabin with vomit. As it was, he was only mildly queasy.

He hadn't flown to this property. He'd only driven there before, maybe twice, and neither it nor the glorified puddle at the top were identifiable on a map. All he could do was help navigate to the nearest town and direct the pilot from there. It was hard to tell from his very brief, curt conversation with President Earle whether any of her people might converge on the same spot, but since he couldn't articulate exactly where it

was to them either, he figured he was on his own
for now.

He didn't know what he'd find when he got there.
During the 20 minutes they'd been in the air, it dawned
on him that his initial reaction to the situation might be
wrong. *Lars would never take his own life,* he'd thought,
but he didn't know that. Lars had been on his own the
past few years and he couldn't know his state of mind.

The sun was falling out of sight, bathing the land
beyond the Rockies' long shadow in orange. The tiny
town of Nederland appeared in the distance, which
helped him get his bearings. He directed the pilot to
turn around and follow the road that headed back west
from there. If he remembered correctly, that would lead
to the gate and the jeep trail up the mountain. They
dropped down to 400 feet and he saw a familiar rock
outcropping that preceded a sharp turn in the road. The
gate was down there, along with the faint outline of a
trail. They followed it up the slope. A few minutes later,
he saw the car.

"There's the car!" he shouted. "Follow the ridge
straight north from there."

In the gloaming, Teacup Lake was mostly black. He
could see a tent and maybe a table of some sort, but no
signs of life.

"How's the surface down there?" the pilot asked.

"Solid rock. That should work right there," Erik
said, pointing to a flat spot about 200 feet from the

campsite. The wash from the rotors would probably blow everything away, but that didn't matter.

Erik's feet were on the ground before the skids. He ran toward the tent, which had held up against the downdraft, though everything else was now in the water. The front flap was open, and 20 feet away he saw a foot. The girl. He slowed, looking around for Lars. Nothing. He ducked down low and peered inside. Jayla Earle was staring up lifelessly, her face almost white, inside her sleeping bag. Lars sat next to her with his legs pulled tightly to his chest, staring at her. Alive.

Erik dove in and threw his arms around Lars.

"My boy," he said. "Are you hurt?"

He pulled back and looked Lars up and down for some sign of injury. His arms were covered in drying blood and his skin was freezing, but he appeared to be okay.

"I couldn't stop her," he said, to no one in particular.

"I know. Her mother got her letter."

A realization visibly washed over Lars. He dropped his head down and nodded, as though silently acknowledging his role in this.

"I need to talk to her," Lars said. "She needs to understand what she was going through, and why I never ... why I never saw this coming."

"Okay, we'll talk about it. Right now we need to get

her in the chopper. Just sit tight outside and I'll have Tom come help me—"

"No, I've got her," Lars said firmly, meeting Erik's eyes for the first time. "I've got her."

Erik nodded and backed out of the tent. Lars slid his arms under Jayla and gently lifted her free of the tent. Tom, the pilot, was out of the helicopter and started toward them as if to help, but Erik waved him off. He stood and watched as Lars laid her carefully in the back of the helicopter, then he climbed in and cradled her head in his lap. Erik nodded toward Tom and twirled his finger in the air. The car could wait.

A few minutes later, the chopper lifted off. This time the wash from the rotors got the better of the tent, and it, along with just about everything else around the little campsite, was blown into the lake, like they'd never been there.

PRESIDENT EARLE and a small retinue of Secret Service arrived at GIG a few hours before dawn. Erik arranged for Jayla's body to come back to DC. Although he didn't think it wise for Lars to speak with her just then, he insisted. They sat across from each other in a small conference room, just talking behind a closed door, for more than an hour. When they were done, Lars began to weep uncontrollably and rose to embrace her when she did the same. Erik waited across the hall.

When they emerged, President Earle walked straight toward Erik, still wiping tears from her face, though she drew herself up to her full height and struck a practiced, measured tone.

"Thank you for finding them," she said. "Your son … he's a good kid. My daughter's had a lot of problems. This wasn't his fault. You both need to understand that."

"I'm deeply sorry for your loss, Madam President. If there's anything we can do …"

"You've done enough," she said, and walked away.

THAT NIGHT, back at the house, Lars slept for a long time. Erik couldn't. Lars' short, mile-a-minute life was the product of a lie. Every friend he'd made, every powerful experience, every ounce of meaning and gravity he derived from the simplest things was both real and false. He would have to tell him, of course, but not yet. Not now. There were questions to be answered and broader implications to discuss. There would be just him and Geller, in another room behind another door, and in that room there would be no hugs.

50

What Erik told her was unambiguous: Scientifically speaking, she had nothing left to offer. And yet it was ambiguous, because he wanted her to stay. For his own sake. Their time together was nice, and it had potential. Even though she'd thus far dodged the fate of her peers, it didn't change how Heidi thought about love. It never seemed like there was time for it. It still didn't.

The doorbell rang. Out of habit she checked her hair in the mirror en route to the foyer. She hoped it was Erik again, so they could talk.

It was Geller.

"We need to talk," he said, pushing in without waiting to be invited.

"Please come in."

He brushed past her and made a beeline for the

cupboard beside the fridge, which they kept stocked with booze. She wasn't much of a drinker, so most of it was untouched. Geller started pulling bottles out to get at something at the back, which he opened and poured into a rocks glass without ceremony. Scotch, probably. She watched it all happen from the half-wall that separated the kitchen from the sunken living room. He came around the side of the island and sat on one of the stools with a deep sigh, running his fingers through his silver hair.

"I'm good, thanks," she said, smirking. Geller was always Geller.

"I'm not here about Erik, if that's what you were wondering," he said. "I don't care about that."

"And to think I was so concerned about your approval," she said, drolly.

"I brought you here under a false pretense."

"What do you mean?"

Geller sighed heavily and shifted in his stool. He was agitated. This was harder than he expected.

"You're not an anomaly," he said. "You're proof."

"Proof of what?"

And so Geller told her a story.

AROUND THE TIME Baz and Lucia got married, development of the Cure had begun to stall. Each layer of protection Geller added multiplied the serum's complexity because of how everything interacted. One protein would make another unstable, or the vector for one gene replacement would overwhelm its host cells and prevent the next from taking hold. At each turn, Baz urged Geller to pump the brakes and save it for a future iteration. But Geller kept pressing. Baz wasn't spending as much time in the lab anymore on account of Lucia and Biermann stayed out of his way, so he toiled away on the big score until he had it. That work he did alone was what ultimately became the Cure.

But before any of that started, after an argument with Baz, Geller produced a batch of the earlier serum. It could take care of all but a handful of rare disorders, which to his way of thinking was a half measure. That wasn't his style, but Baz had made a compelling argument for sticking a flag in the ground. So he made two batches, put it in a cryo-tube, and tucked it away in the back of the lab's freezer, labeled as something innocuous.

Years passed, and Geller's more audacious formulation earned him and Baz the Merriweather Prize. He got his lab, his company, and investors by the boatload. They brought his treatment to scale, jumped through all the FDA's hoops and started injecting mothers-to-be with the second serum. Baz and Lucia adopted Perfecto, the first of the Perfect Generation. The first of millions. But then something unexpected happened: His mentor and friend, Jim Robb, came to him with a request to personally administer the Cure to his daughter's unborn child. Heidi.

A long time ago, Baz observed that Geller thought people were sheep. Merriweather said cattle. Some four decades later, he'd come to realize they were mostly right. The truth was that people were walking puzzles—problems to solve. That's why he did all this. It wasn't out of some high-minded desire to better humanity; it was to push his abilities to their absolute limits. The complexities of the human body were the only frontier that mattered to him. But when Jim Robb came and asked for Geller's personal involvement, it became personal. This wasn't just a person who'd been admitted to the trials—this was the flesh and blood of a man he genuinely cared about.

In truth, Geller didn't know until the last moment which serum he would use to treat Hannah, Heidi's mother. He recalled a lecture Jim gave once about the inherent rigors of the scientific method, and entropy, and realized that the serum he'd consigned to the freezer was the only one that would've passed Jim's test.

"THAT'S why I'm still alive," Heidi said.

"Yes."

"And you've known about this my whole life."

Geller nodded. Heidi slumped down against the wall, overcome.

"This was all about you," she said.

"For you to still be alive meant one of two things: Either the first serum was safe, or something about your genetic makeup kept you from getting sick from it. The only way to know for sure was to bring you here."

"You made people hope. You made *me* hope."

"I know."

There was a pregnant silence between them that hung there for a few minutes. He'd said all he needed to say. Finally, Heidi broke it.

"There are these parties," she began. "Some PG kids have a celebration right around their 23rd birthdays. That's, like, still a pretty safe age. The people who come to those parties are there to celebrate life, and to say goodbye. It's like attending your own funeral."

"So I've read," Geller said. His mouth was a little dry, and he suddenly remembered he had scotch. He took a drink before continuing. "I take it you had one."

"I did. It was … it was special. Cathartic, even. You know what's really fucked up? All I can think about right now is that my fucking farewell was all for nothing. That my parents spent a shitload of money they didn't have on a party that they didn't have to have. How dumb is that?"

"Let's say I knew you were going to be fine, which I couldn't have. What would that have changed?"

"Well, for starters I wouldn't be here right now."

"Okay, but what else?"

"I would've finished high school and gone to college. I probably wouldn't have drank and slept my way through Europe when I was 16. I would've lived like a normal person!"

"So what?" Geller said. "So you didn't live the same life your parents did, and their parents did. Cautiously. You lived like you didn't have a lifetime to do it in. What did you do that you genuinely regret?"

"I terminated a pregnancy!" she screamed through tears. "Because of your lies!"

He wasn't ready for that.

"I didn't know."

She stared back at him, seething. "You don't know anything."

"I've lived with what happened all these years, knowing there wasn't anything I could do about it. I always blamed the science. When I learned who you were and that you were still alive, I realized it wasn't ever the science—it was me. All this is my doing. But so are you. You're the only proof that the science was actually sound."

Geller poured himself more scotch. Heidi sat on the floor, her arms pulling her legs in tight against her chest.

"So what happens now?" she said.

Geller shrugged. "Another 14 million people will die. In four or five years, the oldest children of PG parents will turn 25. Until then, we won't know if the flaw gets passed on. In the meantime, you have a life to live."

"So nothing changes. All this …" she gestured upward, indicating the guest house. "… all this was for your ego. You killed the world."

"You won't have the specter of death hanging over you anymore," Geller said, taking a drink. "Also, I understand you and Dr. Heiser have gotten close."

Heidi's eyes narrowed at him. "How could you possibly—"

"Cameras," he said. "On the entryway, I mean. I get reports from security. I'm not judging."

She shook her head. "You disgust me."

Geller tossed back the rest of his scotch and reached in his pocket. He threw a set of keys onto the floor by her feet.

"Here. Take one of the cars in the garage. For your trouble. Good luck."

With that, he left.

51

Jeanine said Baz was in the cafeteria. Geller knew what strolling in during lunch hour would mean, but Baz was less likely to cause a scene that way. As he made his way downstairs and into the airy, domelike expanse of the central cafeteria, he realized he'd only ever taken lunch alone in his office, and that there were still many parts of GIG in which he'd never set foot. On a few occasions he showed up at someone's retirement or to present some kind of award, but toward the end he didn't even do that. It always seemed like such a waste of time. They weren't there to pat each other on the back; they were there to change the world. And they had. Oh yes, they certainly had.

Baz was at a small table near the window with a young, dark-skinned man Geller didn't recognize. His tray bore just a tuna salad sandwich and a hard-boiled egg pretty much the same thing he'd eaten for decades. When Geller sidled up to them, the young man stopped mid-chew and stared. He swallowed his bite and stood at attention.

"Dr. Geller! Wow. Hello. My name is Josh. From compliance."

"You've got a little …"

Geller gestured toward the corner of his own mouth to indicate that a scrap of food still clung there.

"Oh God," he said, wiping it away with a napkin he grabbed suddenly from the holder on the table. Baz continued to eat.

"How's the food?"

"Good. Great, really. I was just—"

"Leaving? As it happens I need to talk to my old pal Dr. Montes here."

"Of course. Yes. I was done anyway."

"Thank you …"

"Josh."

"Right. From compliance."

"Yes!"

"Thank you, Josh," Baz said.

Josh's face lit up and he smiled broadly as he left. Geller distastefully brushed crumbs off the chair where Josh had been sitting and eased himself into it. Baz barely glanced up.

"Seems like a good kid," Geller said.

"We were having a nice conversation."

"Listen, there's something you need to know."

"Make it fast. I have a staff meeting at 1."

"Remember when you were about to go on your honeymoon? You came to the lab and we had a bit of a row."

"That was a long time ago."

"You said we should pump the brakes and produce a sample of the Cure as it was. The simpler version."

"What's your point?" he checked his watch.

"You were right. I realized it as soon as you walked out, but I wouldn't give you the satisfaction."

Baz looked up from his sandwich and met Geller's eyes, really for the first time since he showed up. "What do you mean, 'You were right.'? I'm not familiar with that phrase."

"It made sense. Each new vector we added increased the complexity of the serum, so it made logical sense to set one aside. Really, we should've been doing it all along."

"So you did?" he asked, a little incredulous.

"I did."

"You said it would take weeks."

"It was done by the time you got back. I put it in the very back of the freezer. Enough for a few hundred doses."

"Is that it?"

"Not exactly."

Geller told Baz what he had told Heidi earlier that day. Baz' face went as ashen as he'd ever seen it.

"And that's why she's alive."

"Something after that caused the gene switch. Something you would've waited to add only after years —decades—of testing."

Baz sat back in his chair and went very quiet. All the air went out of him. He stared out the window.

"This is my fault, not yours," Geller said. "You shouldn't have to bear it."

"You needed to prove the first serum worked. That's what this was all about."

"And that we were right, once. More to the point, you were."

"And all the people who've been busting their asses to find something in her, something to hope for—what do we tell them?"

"Not the truth, obviously."

"Obviously. This is you we're talking about."

"That's fair."

"And where is the first serum now?"

"Gone. When we got FDA approval I incinerated it."

Baz nodded.

"Good."

He checked his watch again.

"I'm late," he said, and rose to leave. "Anything else?"

"No," Geller said.

Baz nodded, gave Geller a tired half smile, took his tray, and left. Geller turned his head back toward the inner part of the cafeteria in time to see several hundred employees pretend they weren't staring. It would be the last time they ever spoke.

PART III

2067 – 2076: TIME CAPSULE

52

On April 1, 2067, a young man named James Palicki walked into a bar in Austin, Texas. A small group of co-workers gathered around one of the tall tables loudly greeted him, giving him a hard time for being late to his own birthday party. He laughed it off in his usual good-humored way and poured himself a beer from one of the two fresh pitchers on the table. He chose the darker of them, probably a bock or a porter. Not that it mattered—it had been a long week. It was still a treat, though. The beer industry was coming back, but it was still expensive.

Seven or eight beers later, he raised one toward the ceiling.

"Mom and dad, this one's for you," he said, and his friends followed suit.

"To Mom and Dad!" they exclaimed.

His friends knew nothing of his parents. They didn't know that he was 10 when he watched his father die at 24, or 11 when his mother went one year later to the day. They were all younger than he—maybe 23 at the oldest, and he knew for a fact they weren't the children of PGs because their parents were all still alive.

Suddenly the lights in the bar dimmed, and before he could look to see what was happening, his friends joined in a clumsy version of Happy Birthday. Moments later, the rest of the bar followed suit. From the kitchen came their server, carrying a small chocolate cake filled with candles.

"Happy birrrthdayyy tooooo youuuuuu!" they sang, just as the girl put the cake down. She smiled at him, her eyes lingering on his for just an extra, rather communicative moment.

James made a wish and blew. He didn't count the candles, but it looked like all 26 were there.

The next morning, the waitress from the bar was in the shower when his phone rang.

"Hello," he said, his mouth dry and awful tasting.

"James Palicki?" said an official-sounding voice at the other end.

"Yeah."

"This is Dr. Stafford from the Geller Institute of Genetics. How are you feeling this morning?"

53

The mood at Funk Library, the third oldest but most decrepit of Laird College's main buildings, was upbeat save for Paul Schoeneman, archives director, who was especially grumpy. A longtime friend (and user) of the library, Mrs. Barbara Smart, left $25,000 in her will for the sake of "improving the comfort of the archives' reading room," by which she meant new chairs.

That would've been fine if not for the fact that its existing chairs were less than five years old and had been chosen by him. Everyone thought they were great except for the late Mrs. Smart, who came in every freaking Tuesday after bridge to research her book on Laird history (which now would never get finished). She'd make a show of how hard the chairs were on her back, making sure he was watching. When their planned-giving officer giddily informed him of the estate gift and its specific restriction, he almost told her nothing would improve everyone's comfort like Mrs. Smart's permanent absence. Almost.

Chairs aside, there was another reason for the shuffle in everyone else's step today: An anonymous donor gave $50 million to renovate and expand Melvin Hall, the science building, and rename it Robb Hall. Of all places! It was dedicated just 30 years ago—still a young building by most college standards—and had been well looked after. A gift that size represented almost half the college's entire endowment. It could've funded every deferred-maintenance project in the queue with enough to spare for a whole new library. No one doubted the building's importance to the college's relative success over the past few decades. Enrollments were steady now and it had become known for the sciences. But it needed another money injection like the football team needed new uniforms, which is to say, not at all. Two million was just to endow a chair in virology, which seemed frivolous.

Adding insult to injury for Paul was the fact that the building's time capsule, which was only the same 30 years old, was being opened as part of the ground-breaking ceremonies for the new expansion. It might not have been a consideration, but the monolith in the fountain where it was entombed was among the planned renovations. After the big reveal of the positively *ancient* and historically significant artifacts therein (all of which were thoroughly documented by the student news bureau), a *temporary* display was to be made in the archive room until they decided whether to put the old stuff into a new time capsule or start all over.

Guess who got stuck with that unhappy task.

This would be a strange year. Laird was one of just a handful of private colleges in the country that remained open, at least partially, since everything happened. They survived the way most others did: cutting costs and personnel to the bone, aggressively recruiting foreign students, and employing a small army of volunteers. But the first class of post-PG students was just about to graduate from regular high school and a modest number of them would matriculate in the fall. It wasn't that he minded the mostly Chinese and Korean students who were there now—not at all—but he was very much looking forward to a more, say, Midwestern demographic being back on campus. It seemed right somehow.

He'd spent most of the previous afternoon emptying old junk from a glass display against the east wall of the archives and making it look good for the new junk. The dean of students opened and removed the contents of the capsule that morning, then a student walked them across the quad to Paul. His goal was to get everything labeled and displayed by early afternoon—maybe by lunch if no one bothered him

But no sooner had he started playing music on his computer and taken the lid off the box than the door opened and an older man stepped through. He had his collar up and a baseball cap on, and he spent a moment getting his bearings. Paul watched him silently, then greeted him when he finally noticed he was there.

"Morning," Paul said.

"Good morning," said the man, who started purposefully across the room toward him. As he came closer and Paul got a good look at him, his jaw dropped.

It was Brent Geller.

"Holy shit," Paul said, almost reflexively, though he rarely swore. Geller was a political touchstone at Laird, for obvious reasons, and no one really had claimed him as an alumnus for a very long time, but he was still one of the most famous people in the world. He was a little star struck.

Geller relished the opportunity to trot out one of his favorite lines. "I believe my reputation for arrogant presumption precedes me."

Paul forgot to reply for a few moments. "Welcome back, Dr. Geller. No one's seen you on campus for quite a while."

"Yeah, well, I'm here under the radar. I'd prefer it stay that way ..."

"Paul."

"Paul."

"Of course. So, what brings you to the archives?"

Geller's eyes moved down to the open box.

"That."

"The time capsule stuff?"

Geller nodded.

"I was just going to put it in a display."

"I know. I was hoping to have a look at it before you did though."

"Oh. Well, I guess that'd be fine." His voiced was tinged with suspicion. He slid the box a couple inches toward Geller, who regarded it briefly.

"Alone, I mean."

Paul glanced around. No one was outside.

"Why? If I may ask."

"You know, the first thing I thought was when I came in was that this building looks almost exactly the same as when I was a student—and it seemed old then. I actually wrote a paper once in this very room. It looks *exactly* the same. New chairs maybe."

"The chairs are less than five years old," Paul noted.

Geller shrugged. "Seems like this place could use a facelift. In fact, I'd say you're due for a whole new building."

Paul's eyes narrowed like an amateur detective trying to piece together clues. In his mind, a narrative was starting to form about Melvin Hall's anonymous donor.

"Are you saying that all I'd have to do to get a new

library is leave you alone with this box for a few minutes?"

Geller leaned forward conspiratorially.

"You're on the ball, Paul. And you can't let anyone know I was here. Ever."

Paul cast his eyes down at the box, then back at Geller. His mind swirled with questions about what in hell could be so important. He didn't like the idea of being bought, but he also didn't like the idea of spending the next 15 years putting buckets down on the floor every time it rained.

"I'm walking over to the union for coffee," Paul said. "It takes a long time to cool down, if you know what I mean."

He winked. This was as much subversion as he'd ever engaged in, and he wanted to savor it. Geller put a finger aside his nose and winked.

Paul slipped on his jacket, checked for his keys and wallet, then paused while Geller stood there and looked at him. Maybe he expected some final exchange. None came and he nodded to Geller on his way out.

When Geller was satisfied that the archivist was gone and no one was looking in on him, he took the lid off the box.

54

It was raining when they buried Baz. Though he'd spent half his life in and around the eastern slope of the Rockies, his heart was always back in Chicago where he grew up. It also turned out there was a Montes family mausoleum and an immense extended family, facts which underscored how little Geller really knew about his oldest, if not dearest, colleague. If they'd ever truly been friends, they didn't part as such.

The way Geller heard it, he was helping himself to a piece of cake at a farewell party for a retiring colleague —Baz having retired himself just a year prior—and suffered a massive stroke that killed him on the spot. Lucia, of all people, had gotten word to him about what happened and convinced him to attend the funeral.

It was lovely as far as funerals went, but it made Geller consider his own mortality and he tended to avoid such thoughts. No one asked him to say anything at the service, and even if they had, he wouldn't have known what to say. Either Lucia knew that or she didn't want to risk having him speak, either of which was a strong possibility.

Baz' second wife, Kalpana, was being consoled by Lucia, who'd had a new family and life for decades. Baz was the second husband she'd seen lowered into the ground, and her face suggested it was one too many. The deep furrows around her eyes told the tale of a woman who had known both deep sorrows and profound joys, though not in equal measure. Whatever strength she possessed had left her body, and it wouldn't have surprised him if she joined Baz within the year.

He and Baz never regarded each other as intellectual peers. It was Baz who recognized the comparatively simple perfection of serum one and advised that Geller go no further—advice that would have saved 18 million lives to date. It was also Baz who said once that people were sheep to Geller, an observation he took some umbrage with at the time but one which he could now admit reflected Baz' unique understanding of his nature.

For what he lacked in charisma, however, he more than made up for as a businessman and manager. That GIG weathered the storm was a credit to his work ethic and leadership. Geller got out of his way and everyone else's. Those who stayed did so because they believed they could still accomplish great things. In the end, it was more Baz's house than his.

All this went a long way toward explaining how many people came out to pay their respects. He figured the church alone had about 800 people in it—shocking, when you consider how long it had been since Baz had lived in Schaumburg.

Erik was there with Heidi. They had it out after the incident with Lars and Connie's daughter was settled, and it got ugly. Erik was right to hate him. Geller stood by his reasons for doing *what* he did, if not *how*.

After the ceremony concluded, Geller spotted Erik and Heidi walking hand-in-hand toward the long line of cars at the cemetery. He caught up with them just before they got to their vehicle.

"Erik," he said. They both stopped and slowly turned toward him. Geller forced a smile, indicating he meant well, but it wasn't returned by either of them.

"It's good to see you both. Heidi, you look well."

Erik looked him up and down for a moment before speaking.

"Nice service," he said.

"Yes, I was impressed by the turnout. I wasn't sure if you saw me—"

"I was terrified you might speak."

"Lucia made it clear that wouldn't happen."

"Listen, we've got plans in the city tonight. What do you want?" Erik said.

"Two minutes of your time. That's it."

Erik sighed heavily and ran his hand through his hair.

"I'm not interested in anything you have to say."

"Please. You'll never hear from me again."

"What is it?"

"Confidential," Geller replied, glancing apologetically toward Heidi. She subtly shook her head at him and mouthed, *don't*. Geller's eyes returned to Erik.

"Come on. Let's go," Heidi interjected, and started pulling him away.

"No, no, it's okay," Erik said. "Brad and Jenna are staying at our hotel. Why don't you catch a ride back to the hotel with them. I'll be right behind you."

Heidi glanced again at Geller. "Are you sure?"

"Yeah, I'm sure."

She kissed him on the cheek and gave Geller another warning look before joining her friends. Geller lingered on her a bit, though not so long that Erik would notice. If anything, she was even prettier now.

"Let's walk," Erik said. "I've been standing still for too long."

They crossed the line of cars and continued on through the enormous cemetery grounds, eventually finding a gravel path between the tombstones. They exchanged some tense pleasantries about how things were going at GIG and how Geller was enjoying his second retirement. Geller learned that Heidi was pregnant with their first child and that Lars was teaching in Malaysia.

"That's tremendous—congratulations," Geller offered.

"Yeah. So how about you say what you need to say so I can have the pleasure of telling you to fuck off once and for all?"

"It has to do with Baz and me. And Heidi."

Erik looked into Geller's eyes for several seconds, squinting. Then:

"She's no mystery to you, is she? I'll bet she never was."

Geller raised an eyebrow. "No."

Erik nodded, his eyes darting all around the cemetery as though his brain was too busy assembling puzzle pieces to control them. After a moment, they found Geller's again.

"She had the markers like everyone else, but not quite all of them. That's what we couldn't quite figure. You gave her something different. I knew it, man. Deep down, I fucking knew."

He meant the isotopes. Heidi didn't seem to have as many markers, which had mystified Erik and his team.

Geller explained everything about serum one, up through his very expensive clandestine trip to Laird to retrieve the cryotube sewn into the pocket of his time-capsule jeans. Erik's walking cadence slowed until he finally stopped, staring down at his feet until Geller was finished. After a moment he spoke, but didn't raise his eyes.

"That day at Laird, when we hung out and talked shop? That was the greatest day of my life. From that point on, I was going to do whatever it took to be in your company. To learn from you. I spent my whole life trying to get out from under your shadow, only to realize that you don't cast one. You're not even here."

Erik trailed off and stared across the cemetery, shaking his head. Geller let him. After a time he turned to face him again.

"And where is this serum one right now?"

Geller reached in his pocket and withdrew a small metal tube the size of a cigar.

Erik looked at it, then incredulously back up at Geller, shaking his head.

"Oh, you've gotta be shittin' me."

"I thought a treasure map would be pretentious," Geller offered. Erik didn't laugh.

"What am I supposed to do with this?"

"I don't care," Geller said. "I had half a mind to throw it in with Baz."

"Yeah, well, that would've been better than giving the fucking thing to me. Did he know?"

"It was the last time we spoke. I told him I destroyed it."

"Why didn't you?"

"It was my life's work."

"What am I supposed to do with it?"

"Throw it away. Hide it. It doesn't matter anymore."

"You know, it's just *such* a coincidence that you show up with this when Heidi is two months pregnant."

"What? I couldn't have known about that. Congratulations."

"Fuck you."

Geller continued to hold the little tube out toward him.

"If you don't care what happens to it, why go to such lengths to get it?" Erik said.

"If someone else found it, there's no telling what would happen to it. Where it would end up, and with who. This way at least I know. You're a good man. Whatever the right thing is, that's what you'll do."

Erik stared at him, incredulous, as though wondering how Baz ever held Geller in such high esteem.

"You diminished him. Every bad thing he ever went through was because he believed in you."

"I know."

Geller, expressionless, continued to hold the tube out. After several moments, Erik took it.

"No one will ever know this existed," Erik hissed, shaking it in Geller's face. Tears formed in his red eyes, but he blinked them away. "I'm going to see to it. Your only legacy will be how you played God."

"Nothing you do or don't do will change that," Geller said.

Erik tucked the tube in his coat pocket and walked away without another word. Geller never saw him again.

55

Colorado had its share of great fishing, but for Geller it never quite measured up to Montana. The water seemed cleaner and colder, the trout more eager and large. Of course, it didn't hurt that the stretch through Geller's vast property was basically inaccessible from above or below, on account of a strong current that made upstream travel virtually impossible. During the nearly 20 years he'd spent alone there, Geller had only seen two kayakers come through, and only one while he was actually in the water. The point was that he'd sought privacy and gotten it.

Three years had passed since serum one went to Erik, and he still didn't know what happened to it. It wasn't entirely true that he didn't care, but it was true that it didn't matter. Maybe serum one would've been the right thing, and maybe neither serum was. Maybe people were supposed to acquire horrible afflictions and die.

His indicator stopped abruptly at the end of a riffle, and he tugged quickly on the line. A strike! He pulled quickly on the line with his left hand while raising the rod and moments later landed a fat, surprised-looking rainbow. He admired it for a moment and slipped it into his creel, and that was it. He only took fish when he planned on one for dinner. He could've stayed longer, but he was getting tired. There was no more dawn-to-dusk fishing in him, as much as he would've liked to. He carefully crossed back to his low spot on the opposite bank, climbed up onto the well-worn path back up to the house and started walking.

He removed his waders and boots on a rug inside the garage, which he left open so his gear could dry. Then he picked up his creel and went to the back door of the house. When he entered the kitchen, the last thing he expected to see was a man sitting on one of the barstools around the island, yet there he was.

"I see you had some luck," he said. He was dark-skinned, perhaps of Pacific Islander descent, barrel-chested, and roughly Geller's age. There was a touch of an accent.

"Who're you?" Geller asked calmly, setting the creel down in the sink. He made a mental note to install a more secure property fence.

"My name is Rubin Beecher," he said, and paused to see if the name meant anything to Geller. Seeing no recognition, he continued. "Marius Beecher was my son."

This name Geller knew.

"The singer."

"That's right."

"Connie's— er, President Earle's daughter—she never quite came to terms with what happened to him. I'm sure you read all the stories."

"He was a special young man."

Geller moved far enough to the side of the island that he could see Beecher's hands. He was carrying a silver semiautomatic pistol, though it wasn't pointed at him just then.

"Can I get you a drink, Mr. Beecher?" he said. "I'm having one."

"I don't drink anymore."

"Suit yourself."

Geller opened a bottle of 22-year-old Scotch and poured some into a rocks glass. It was smoky and smooth.

"I take it you're here to kill me," Geller said.

"That's right," Beecher said.

"Mind if I enjoy my drink for a bit?"

"I'm not going anywhere."

Geller walked straight into the living room. "Those stools are terrible. Come in here. These are covered in Italian leather. Like sitting on your momma's lap."

Beecher obliged, choosing the couch across from Geller's enormous lounge chair. He remained on the edge, leaning forward. His right hand, which held the pistol, rested across his leg.

"Most people would've just offered me something non-alcoholic. Like water. When I said I quit drinking, I mean."

"You showed up in my house with a gun. I hardly think I'm the impolite one here."

"You really think now's the time to be an asshole?"

"I've always been an asshole," Geller said matter-of-factly, and leaned back in his chair. "So you blame me for what happened to your son and you've come after all these years to settle the score. Is that about the size of it?"

"Have you watched a PG die, Dr. Geller?"

Geller remembered the conversation he'd once had with Heidi, and how vividly she described it. Still, he hadn't ever seen it with his own eyes.

"I'm sorry to say I haven't."

"Oh. Well, then let me show you."

Beecher turned on Geller's living-room display and navigated to an amateur video taken six years ago at the Clockwatchers show called "Marius Beecher dies at Red Rocks 6/3/63." Geller heard about this, of course, and read about it but he never had the nerve or desire to watch one of the videos. He shifted in his seat. Beecher's eyes never left him.

The amateur video was taken by someone in the crowd, maybe 50 feet from the stage. Everyone was standing and remarkably quiet because the band had gathered downstage to sing their quiet, sweetly harmonized version of "I'll Fly Away." Many were gently swaying back and forth. You could barely hear the music it was so soft. And then it happened. Marius, crumbling to the stage and convulsing. And blood. Everywhere blood. It was violent and ugly, made all the more so by the context. After a few minutes of the stunned crowd watching it all happen close-up on the screens to the side of the stage, people started crying and hugging each other. What happened to Marius was going to happen to every single one of them and they all knew it.

Geller didn't truly understand the significance of the event until that moment, nor had he ever understood why it robbed Jayla Earle of all hope. Between what he'd just watched and the resigned look on Beecher's face, it was starting to sink in.

Beecher turned off the display and turned to look at him.

"My wife died 10 years ago," he said, running his fingers along the barrel of the pistol. "Huntington's. She believed in your Cure. Ot at least she wanted to, for our baby. But she wouldn't have done it if I hadn't gone along. Thirteen years I watched her suffer. Thank God she didn't live long enough to see Marius ... I'm only here now because she wouldn't have approved. Woman didn't have a vindictive bone in her body. But I do. And I've got nothing left to lose."

"I'm sorry about your boy," Geller said. "And your wife."

Beecher continued staring at Geller as though expecting him to continue, but he only sipped from his glass and returned Beecher's gaze.

"All the pain you've caused me—my family—and you're *sorry*?"

"What more is there?"

"That's just one man!" he shouted, pointing at the blank screen. "One of *millions*. What do you have to say to their mothers and fathers, who trusted you? Who trusted your so-called science when playing God was closer to the truth? What do you say to them?!"

"They aren't here. If they were, I'd say the same thing. What else can I offer? You didn't want a drink."

Beecher raised the pistol suddenly and pointed it at Geller, who only flinched a little. "There's a lot more you can give me, you goddamned sociopath. A *lot* more."

Geller set his glass down on a small, glass-topped end table crafted from some exotic-looking tree stump, then shifted in his seat to face Beecher directly.

"Then do it. If it'll make you feel better, then go

ahead. I'm ready. But you did say you'd let me finish this, so …"

Beecher's hand shook. Tears streamed down his face as he grimaced, wrestling with the choice before him. Geller was still trying to place the subtle accent and his features. A wide nose. Close-set eyes. Prominent jaw. Fiji, maybe? Samoa? He closed his eyes, fully expecting to hear a shot and then find out what came next—the greatest mystery of all. The only one he was still interested in.

"He was barely *25 years old*," Beecher said, his voice cracking. "He meant so much to so many people. Brought so much joy and life into the world. That hole that runs through the middle of every PG—he tried to fill that with music. Marius was hope. Do you understand? Never mind that he was all we had in the world. He was all a lot of people had. You didn't just take him away—you took people's hope away. There's no reason to live without hope."

"I don't disagree. Do what you have to do."

Geller closed his eyes and waited for the muffled explosion—the last sound he would ever hear. What came instead was a soft rustle of clothing. He opened one eye to see that Beecher had lowered his arm and was sobbing uncontrollably. He half expected Beecher's arm to come back up to level the gun at his own head, but that never happened either. There was only him and a man with nothing left to feel. This wasn't his bailiwick.

He thought about saying something else, but reasoned it might be tragically counterproductive. He felt as much empathy for Beecher as he had for anyone, which wasn't saying much.

"Maybe I will take that drink," Beecher said.

56

E rik was getting tired, not to mention dizzy.

"Faster!" said Otto, clinging to the outside of the aptly named merry-go-round, his toes on the very edge.

And so he obliged, again, now more concerned with breaking what surely was a state record for dad-powered RPMs on a playground implement. It briefly crossed his mind that his son's grip might not be strong enough for the centrifugal force he was creating, but by then his equilibrium had passed a crucial point and it was he, not Otto, who lost out to physics. He slipped and went headlong in the sand, then rolled out of the way to make sure Otto's feet wouldn't slam into him.

He rolled onto his back, the world still spinning, as Otto's wide-eyed face went by him again and again, laughing merrily. He stared at a tree limb overhead, eager to reacquaint himself with a fixed point. He was in excellent shape for 58, but this seriously messed with his equilibrium. It was a bit too late; he lolled onto his side and retched about half his breakfast onto the grass. Then he was okay.

He looked around to see if anyone witnessed this, and immediately saw they had. Young mothers were lined up shoulder to shoulder on long benches around the playground, seemingly amused by his exertions and their aftermath. He was accustomed to gawkers, though less so now. The community of Emerald Creek was overwhelmingly GIG employees, and even though he knew many of them personally it was still a novelty to see the CEO out and about, let alone rolling around in the sand with his son.

The New Generation Project, or NGP, was a $200 billion nationwide program undertaken by GIG to get the next generation of kids off to a fast start, giving kids a normal, happy childhood while helping prepare them to be little economic, entrepreneurial engines. Most of the money went toward education, renovating under-used or vacated schools (and colleges) and building new ones. Dozens of foundations had stepped forward to match GIG's contributions, seeding endowments that would eventually provide millions of college scholarships. There were massive investments in early childhood education, ensuring that all kids got the help they needed to succeed. And of course, there were the new playgrounds that replaced thousands of old ones in virtually every decent-sized town in the country. You could tell an NGP playground by its hexagonal layout, meant to evoke a benzene ring—a major building block of organic molecules. Denver alone got 27 new playgrounds.

All of this was a form of damage control. Most people now viewed GIG in a favorable light but it was hard to say whether that was a function of time or its enduring contributions to global society. In any event, it had the cash and access to cheap debt that it needed to fund such an ambitious undertaking without taking on much risk. The way Erik saw it, no restitution could ever be enough.

Heidi remained an artist at heart, and had started a children's theatre in town that had trouble accommodating all the kids who wanted to take part. Otto had proven himself to be quite the talent, with a sweet voice that made Erik cry the first time he heard it on stage and a fair sense of rhythm (for a five year old, anyway). Plus, he was drop-dead funny without trying. Sometimes he made Erik laugh until it hurt.

Lars' revelation that he was going to live a normal, full life affected him in ways that Erik couldn't understand. For a while he traveled, ostensibly to surf some of the world's most famous breaks again, but he had no way of knowing if that was his real objective. He'd been back stateside for weeks before he heard from him, at which time he said he was helping the last remaining PG bands on the East Coast organize a big music festival. He was working on this until Otto was almost three, but after the festival wound down—which brought nearly 100,000 PGs together on a former golf course in Eastern Tennessee for five days—Lars returned to Colorado for what Erik hoped would be a long time. Though they began as strangers, the two half-brothers took to each other quickly, and so Lars experienced a normal childhood vicariously through Otto. He would watch him play for hours, winnowing time away like he didn't have a care in the world, endlessly fascinated.

Erik hadn't seen Geller since Baz' funeral. Though he still carried a lot of resentment toward his former mentor, and always would, he'd come to understand why the truth about Lars had been kept from them. In the process, he also saw how expertly Geller had concealed his fallibility and self-doubt over the many years of their association. The most brilliant scientific mind in generations had been willing to roll the dice on a generation of strangers, but not on someone close to him.

As angry as he was with the old man, he always tried to remind himself that Lars was alive and would be until long after Erik and Heidi were gone. His old life was rich and full, and he would likely continue to live this way because that was who he was. Heidi wouldn't have come forward were it not for her grandfather's association with Geller, and so they might never have met. His family owed a somewhat perverse debt to the man, which very few families could have said.

The last members of the Perfect Generation numbered about 5 million—the youngest of them now 23. By 2068, satisfied by the science showing that the children of PG parents didn't inherit the genetic defect, there was a new baby boom. Birth rates in the US had returned to levels not seen since the 1960s, and little kids returned to doing the things little kids were supposed to do. The oldest of the post-Cure generation were just graduating from college, and finding that the job market was very, very ready for them. GIG, naturally, was arranging to fund the graduate educations of hundreds of these students, and many more from outside the US. Things were slowly getting back to normal, but they weren't the same—they were better. The Cure had taught America a painful lesson, and though Erik doubted that lesson would be retained forever, he held out hope that it would. He absorbed a lot from Geller, but not his cynicism.

Otto stood over him, a puzzled expression on his face.

"Are you okay, Daddy?"

Erik smiled. "Yeah, buddy. I just got really dizzy. Did you get enough spinning for one day?"

He nodded, though Erik suspected this wasn't true. The kid liked to spin.

"So now what?"

"Snow cone!" Otto exclaimed.

"That sounds good," Erik said. "Are you buying?"

Otto suddenly looked worried, so he let him off the hook.

"I'm just teasing, pal. Snow cones are on me today."

With that, he brushed himself clean, doing his best to ignore the stares of other park goers. Otto held his hand as they crossed to the other side of the park, where a lonely snack bar attendant sat playing a game on his phone. He was maybe 19, an ordinary American slacker with all the time in the world. There wasn't much acknowledgement when he first glanced up at Erik, but then he did a double take and sprang into action. Erik was nowhere near the household name that Geller became, but he was still well known. The young man looked down and saw Otto in tow and shifted his focus immediately.

"Hey, little man. You hot, hungry, or both?"

Otto merely nodded, either out of shyness or puzzlement at the question.

"Two rainbow snow cones, please," Erik said.

"You got it, Dr. Heiser," he said. Erik was rarely seen wearing shorts and sandals, with a three-day beard and a generally disheveled look.

A few minutes later, he handed them two enormous snow cones, which appeared all the larger in Otto's tiny hand. Erik paid the attendant and led Otto to a small table nearby. They sat and ate their treats, which melted quickly in the June sun. By the time Otto tipped the cone back and drained the slurry of syrupy water into his mouth, half his face was a sticky, splotchy rainbow. Erik fetched a wad of napkins, dampened them in the fountain, then set about cleaning Otto's face. He grimaced as Erik wiped, but after a few moments his small face was clean and framed a bright smile.

Erik stared at him for several seconds, admiring the unadulterated newness of him. His skin was clear and elastic, his eyes a sharply delineated white and blue. His mop of light blond hair fell partly over his eyes, as it had (and still did) with Lars.

In the healthy symmetry of his boy was an unsubtle perfection, the kind that could never be wrought by man and all his flaws. His hubris. His foolish determination to improve and bring order to nature's chaos. The best any man could hope for was that this chaos would never intrude in the lives of his children, though Erik had more hope than most.

A NOTE TO READERS

Thank you for reading *The Perfect Generation*. Making it to the end is the second-best compliment you can give a writer. The best is to take one small action that helps me continue to pursue a lifelong dream. Here are some great ideas I just pulled out of thin air:

• LEAVE A REVIEW ON AMAZON OR GOODREADS. Even if you hated it, even if you're ambivalent. But especially if you dug it.

• Sign up for my email list (if you haven't already). As a thank-you, you'll get a digital copy of my novella, *The Technician*, a prequel to my upcoming series, *The Cytocorp Saga*. I'll only email once or twice per month and won't ever share your info with anyone. Also, I won't come to your home or office and ask if you saw my email. I know that pain. That's the C.P. James Platinum Promise™.

• Share your read with friends on social media along with the link for the free book: signup.cpjames.com.

• Email me at cp@cpjames.com with your comments, questions, expressions of concern for my mental welfare, favorite jokes, or unabashed adoration.

- Follow me on Facebook (facebook.com/authorcpjames) or Twitter (twitter.com/authorcpjames).

- Peer into my soul at cpjames.com/words

ABOUT THE PERFECT GENERATION

It took about 2 1/2 years to finish a first, coherent draft of *The Perfect Generation*. I put it in a virtual drawer for a few months and read the whole thing when we were on vacation near Barra de Navidad, Mexico.

I wasn't happy with it. When we got back to Oregon, I started new Scrivener documents with titles like, "Part 2 Threads" (which would spawn "Part 2 Threads v2", v3, etc.). There's another one called "What's wrong with this." I made the mistake of sitting down to write with a pretty clear idea of the beginning, a pretty clear idea of the end, and almost no idea how the middle part—a.k.a. about 70 percent of the book—should unfold.

That's basically like deciding to build a house when the only thing you know how to do is pound nails and cut wood. Not a great idea.

In the end, it took about six complete drafts (not counting the passes at the end for polish) to get it to this point. That was all while working full-time and sneaking in maybe 3 hours a week of actual writing. The fact that I stayed with it that long speaks to how interesting I personally found the story and characters, but I learned many painful lessons about storytelling in the process. I leave it to you to decide whether I did enough.

If you want to get into the weeds about the real-life science behind aspects of the book, then check out *The Perfect Generation* Reading Companion at cpjames.com/tpg-companion.

I love science. Always have. Its entire purpose is to establish objective truths about our world, which is extremely difficult. People you've never heard of spend entire careers moving their field forward just a tiny bit. The reason you seldom read about major breakthroughs is that science doesn't work that way. It's slow by design. It's exhaustive. It generates reams of data. It does NOT move at the pace it moves in this story, no matter how smart anyone is. But since it already spans a large chunk of time, there was no reason to get bogged down in how long things actually take. (See: any movie ever.)

I don't know what would really happen if 22 million young people wouldn't make it past age 25. I know I've only scratched the surface of how devastating that would be to our society and what steps we might take to accommodate that reality. Given how our government regards youth in general, I think something like the Exception Act of 2051 is pretty unlikely. But you never know. At one point I had a whole gigantic subplot cooked up where we sold a few hundred millions of acres of South Dakota farmland to the Chinese in order to raise revenue, but then I realized that was a whole other book. I'll be curious to know what readers think of as unexplored avenues.

I also don't know what I would do if I learned as a little kid that I only had 17 or 18 years to live. I really don't think I'd trouble with college or finding any sort of job if I could help it, and I don't think most of us would. But I don't know if I'd just wander around the globe either, or how I'd pay for stuff if I did. I think you'd have a bifurcation between kids who just wanted to party and those who wanted to leave a mark somehow and do good. I'd like to think they would follow their hearts and do whatever the hell they wanted (within reason), and that we'd have little choice but to let them.

In any event, I think they would live very fearlessly, and that is something to envy. In one of my favorite films, *Big Fish*, the reason Albert Finney's character lives such an amazing life is because he knows exactly when and how he'll die. I always responded to that notion. It's an interesting question to ask yourself.

Heidi and Lars, to me, are interesting characters to try and empathize with.

Heidi made her peace with her fate at a young age and lived her life as though it would end like all her friends. But it doesn't, and I think she'd feel this weird mix of survivor's guilt and something like disappointment. The question, "Why am I not dead right now?" would consume her, and she'd have no idea what to do besides try and find the answer. When she learns she'll most likely live a very long life, she tries to understand whether her life to that point was wasted (because it wasn't directed "toward" anything) or if it's just the opposite because she's lived life purely on her own terms.

Lars has a similar problem, but for different reasons. His life also won't end anytime soon (at least not from natural causes), and he would also go through a period of feeling lost and betrayed, though perhaps not regretful about his choices.

Many years from now after I've written a few dozen books, I hope I still like Geller as much as I do now. He doesn't have a filter, lacks humility, and has a self-confidence bordering on delusional. He's a terrible collaborator. That the Cure has a flaw bothers him more than what it cost the country. He's loathsome in almost every way. And yet, I think he's the only kind of person who would even attempt something so audacious. He's the only one who could possibly win the

Merriweather Prize. The story doesn't work without him.

I still wonder about his self-imposed exile. I'd like to think he would have his own lab in the basement where he'd work in secret to try and fix the Cure, but I think it's more interesting if he knows he'd never top the work he did on the Cure and that it simply can't be fixed. Would it have been more satisfying if he somehow found a way to save several million PGs, or even just one? I don't know. All I know is that not everything can be fixed.

In all likelihood, the Cure would become a global thing, not just a US thing, but again, it would've become too complex. Would an in-vitro genetic treatment that only a relative handful of facilities was equipped to deliver really become as commonplace as the DTP vaccine? Not likely. But if it was free and people believed it was safe, who knows?

Genetic engineering is going to come a long way in the next few decades. I think we'll be able to stop terrible diseases before they start and correct genetic errors before they propagate. I think we'll effectively cure a number of diseases, including many cancers. But I also think there will be costs to this progress, and we can't possibly know how our actions echo into the future. That uncertainty was behind this narrative and will inform many that follow, and I look forward to exploring it further.

THE CYTOCORP SAGA
(COMING FALL 2019)

Nearly a century has passed since Cytocorp began the Dome Project, yet Dome Six remains completely cut off — a self-sustaining city under glass. AI determines everything from job placement to population control, enforced by the privileged bureaucracy known as the Authority. As far as anyone knows, they're the last vestige of society, perhaps of humanity itself.

But the protection it has long provided has never been weaker. The Dome's core systems are starting to fail and a nameless saboteur may be responsible. The Authority schemes to maintain order and control over a fearful and weary citizenry desperate for hope. If they don't act soon, Dome Six will be their tomb.

When unanswered questions from the Dome's past expose some of its many secrets, a group of determined citizens will risk everything to learn how deep the rabbit hole goes. What's become of the outside world? What remains of Cytocorp? And if history is constantly rewritten and even the dead tell lies, how can you ever know the truth?

Find out in *Dome Six*, Book 1 of the Cytocorp Saga, coming fall 2019. For release updates, special deals, uninformed opinions, drunken rants, and other mildly amusing feats of magibloggery and wordstidigitation, visit cpjames.com.

ACKNOWLEDGMENTS

Books aren't written in a vacuum. There are scores of people who, in ways big and small, nudge you forward. Others carry you over the finish line. No one does anything alone.

My parents, Doug and Judy Pinkston, deserve some kind of award for not dropping me off at a facility after reading my weird stories as a kid and later indulging my fondness for Stephen King, Clive Barker, Brian Lumley, and all that twisted stuff. You couldn't have been more loving and supportive.

Thank you to Doug Robertson and Jim Elliott, the high-school English teachers who believed I had something under the hood, and to Rachel Dolezalek, Glenn Bildsten, and Joyce Woletz, who may have believed it first.

My dad said the best friends I'd ever make were in

college, but it turned out a lot of them were from friggin' high school. Thanks to Mike Shiffler, Tom Kinlen, Troy Pugesek, Jeff Ashbeck, Jamie Molitor, and everyone in the old gang who nurtured my love of story, particularly the nerdy and obscure. I'd watch a shitty horror movie with any of you, anywhere. *Alien Syndrome* is now 19 years behind schedule.

Thank you Robert Boswell, author and New Mexico State professor who wrote, "The quality of the prose is top-notch. Stick with it and you could make a real career as a writer," on the first short story I turned in. For reasons I'll never understand, I ignored that advice for 20 years.

A small army at Dell helped me become a better writer in general, but special thanks to Anne Camden and David Frink for showing me the difference between puking out pretty words and communicating.

To my beta readers, thank you for taking the time to give me feedback. You came from different perspectives and attitudes, and though I hadn't seen many of you in years, I think you took the time because I finally listened to the universe and started writing like I meant it. My deep gratitude to Ruthann Bartman, Melissa Bemus, Justin Duellman, Lisa Fortin, Shannon Hansen, John Jensen, and Mike Shiffler. If I missed you here, it's because I no longer have access to the reader survey results and didn't have the foresight to print off a report before leaving U of O, but you know who you are.

More people nominated the book for Kindle Scout or helped solicit nominations through Facebook than I can list here, but know that every share and positive comment was noticed by me. I know Cary Camden worked extra hard on my behalf. Thank you all.

Which brings us to the present. The big constant through this journey has been my wife, Amy, whose belief in me has more than made up for my self-doubt. It means so much to me that we're doing this together and that you're starting to find your own voice as a writer. Whether it takes two books or 50, we're going to get everything we want and more because nothing else will do. Not anymore. We're not just on a journey, we're on a mission. I love you.

ABOUT THE AUTHOR

C.P. James writes smart, cinematic sci-fi and dystopian novels. He lives in Bend, Oregon with the lovely and talented romance novelist, Amy Pinkston. His first novel, *The Perfect Generation*, was published in February 2018. His upcoming trilogy, the Cytocorp Saga, is slated for a fall 2019 release.

When he's not writing speculative fiction, you can find him on the fairways, where he carries a 0 handicap. A lover of the outdoors, he also enjoys alpine skiing, hiking, camping, and fly fishing.

Learn more at cpjames.com or facebook.com/authorcpjames/

Made in the USA
Monee, IL
03 June 2021